DARK DESIRES AT DAWN

DIVINE DESIRES
BOOK 1

STEPHANIE JULIAN

MOONLIT NIGHT PUBLISHING

The Barbarian and the Goddess...

Tessa is the Etruscan Goddess of the Dawn, worshipped by an entire civilization. At least, she used to be. Now her powers are weakening, and she's been targeted by a malicious god who wants to consume her remaining magic. She needs a hero and fast...preferably one who's good in bed because sexual energy boosts her magic. She seeks out Caligo, a barbarian whose sexual prowess is legendary...

Caligo is a fabled Cimmerian warrior determined to stay out of the affairs of the deities. He thought he'd learned his lesson after his last affair with a goddess left him barely breathing. But there's something irresistible about Tessa, something that draws him in.

Now they're on the run from the God of the Underworld, and Caligo is Tessa's only chance to escape the encroaching darkness...

Formerly titled HOW TO WORSHIP A GODDESS

*For my love, David, without whom it just wouldn't be worth it.
And for my guys, Taylor and Joshua, who make me laugh, cry,
scream, and smile, usually at the same time.*

PROLOGUE

The third blow from the iron hammer sent Caligo to the ground.

His face hit first, of course, and he spit blood until it pooled on the blacktop beside him. He thought about getting up, but really, why bother? He'd just end up back there again.

Three blows from the pissed-off Roman God of Volcanoes and Blacksmiths were two more than enough to convince Cal that no woman was worth the beating.

Not even Venus.

"Not so pretty now, is he, babe?" Vulcan shook his head, the girly black curls he was so proud of quivering around his ruddy face. "I don't know why you continue to bed these inferior humans. They're weak. And you know they can't satisfy your needs."

Cal couldn't help himself. "Maybe because she knows your dick is no bigger than my thu—"

Vulcan stepped on Cal's neck, effectively cutting off his air supply and his voice with one dainty Italian loafer. "Let's go home, babe. I'm sick of this crap."

"Oh, fine," Venus sighed. "I'm bored now anyway."

The Roman Goddess of Love and Beauty flung flame-red

hair over her shoulder and barely glanced down at Cal as she stepped over him to take Vulcan's arm.

Her heel landed mere centimeters from Cal's nose.

He remembered those shoes. She'd worn them the last time they'd fucked. He probably still had the indentations in his thighs from where she'd dug them in, screaming his name as she came.

As Cal watched the deities walk away, Venus turned, her little black dress swinging around her ass, to give him a wink and a little wave.

To which he replied with a time-honored, one-fingered salute. *Bitch*.

As the couple disappeared down the deserted alley off South Street in Philadelphia, Cal dragged himself to the nearest wall and leaned against it, wiping blood from his chin and his left ear. The ringing in his head sounded like the extended buzz of a heavy-metal guitar, and his face throbbed, though he felt no pain. Probably gonna have a few new scars to add to the collection.

He shook his head, which just made him dizzy, and began assessing the damage. "When are you going to learn, asshole?"

He'd asked himself the question before. But here he was again, wounded and pissed off because he'd gone out of his way to help a pretty woman who obviously hadn't needed his help.

Fucking goddesses. Never a good idea.

As he cataloged the various bruises, cuts, and broken bones, he considered making the trek back to his car on Bainbridge but he figured someone would call the cops at the first sight of him.

Here seemed as good as any place to die. And if, by some miracle, he didn't die, this was the last fucking time he ever took a job for a deity.

They screwed you over every damn time.

ONE

Dying was so beneath her.

Of course, she hadn't done much living lately, so if he caught her now... Well, that would just suck. Because she'd recently decided it was time to change her ways. Get out more. Live a little. Get laid.

How pitiful was it that she couldn't remember the last time she'd had sex? Or if it had even been any good.

Pretty freaking pitiful.

Thesan, Etruscan Goddess of the Dawn, Lady of the Golden Light, was sick of being a pretty, useless deity. Much less a pretty useless one usually just called Tessa.

For centuries... millennia... she'd brought light and beauty to the world. She'd guided the sun into the morning sky. She'd seen the rise and fall of empires. Gods had lusted after her. She'd worn out her share of mortal men in her bed.

She'd been worshipped by millions. Okay, maybe millions was stretching it just a bit. Still, she'd had a following, people who'd adored her and who'd worshipped her.

Now she was being chased by a crazed god intent on

consuming her powers and leaving what was left of her soul to rot for all eternity in the dreary Etruscan Underworld of Aitás.

That totally sucked.

So did this. Her lungs heaved as she ran through a dark forest, the night sky black. No moon shone above. No stars twinkled. No reflected sunlight gave her even a hint of power.

Her legs shook like wet noodles, threatening to collapse at any moment. The underbrush swiped at her calves, and tree limbs caught at her hair, yanking and pulling.

Peering over her shoulder, she saw a dark shape weaving through the trees behind her. Her heart hurt as it pounded in her chest. Her bare feet bled and ached as she stumbled along.

Oh, she knew she really wasn't running. She was actually asleep in her lonely bed in her home in the quiet hills of eastern Pennsylvania. She knew that because she'd had the same dream for the past three weeks.

Charun, that black-hearted bastard, was taunting her like a high-school bully picking on a weaker kid. But Charun's intent wasn't to merely frighten her, though the bastard did get a kick out of it.

No, he was wearing her down, waiting for her to make a mistake so he could pinpoint her location. So far, she'd been able to keep her whereabouts a secret. But when he broke through her defenses, he'd send one of his demons to drag her down to Aitás. To him.

The bastard couldn't come himself. He was tied to Aitás by bindings even he couldn't break. At least, not now.

But if he found her, if he managed to accomplish what she thought he had planned, then soon, maybe, he would be able to break those bonds. And this world would suffer as the demons and the damned escaped with him.

And she'd never get laid again. Damn it, she'd much rather go out with a literal bang than a figurative one.

With a gasp, she broke free of the dream and sat straight up in her bed, blinking at the bright light even though it was... three o'clock in the morning, according to the clock on the bedside table.

She'd left all the lamps blazing in her bedroom. An infomercial blared from the television, and the stereo on the nightstand blasted Puccini. None of it had been able to keep her awake. Probably because she could count on both hands the number of hours she'd slept in the past three weeks.

Damn it, she needed help.

Her nose wrinkled at the thought. She, a goddess, needed help. Wasn't that a real kick in a perfectly fine ass?

"Which won't mean a damn thing if Charun gets hold of it," she muttered to absolutely no one.

Hell, if she survived Charun, she needed to get out of the house so someone could see her fine ass again. Playing the hermit didn't suit her. She'd been one of the original party girls in her day, playing all night before hurrying off to meet the lovely sun each morning.

But now she was a forgotten goddess, her main reason for being usurped by that bitch of a Roman goddess named Aurora—

She took a deep breath. No, she couldn't think about that. Those thoughts led to teeth gnashing and sore jaws.

Still, she'd become a goddess without a true calling. What should she do with her never-ending life?

Oh, she delivered a baby or ten or twenty every year. In addition to being a sun goddess, she also helped bring new life into the world, one of the more pleasurable aspects of her life.

But that left her with a whole hell of a lot of time to fill. A girl could only do so much shopping and have so much sex before it all became so very... mundane.

She wanted to be useful again. She wanted the remaining

Etruscans, those who still followed the old ways, to remember that she even existed. And she most certainly did not want to be eaten by Charun.

She needed help. And she knew just the person to help her find it.

"HANG TIGHT... I'm coming. Just give me a minute."

The voice came from the second floor as Tessa stood in the entry hall of the small townhouse in Reading, Pennsylvania.

In front of her, a stairway led along the right side of the house to the upper floors. To the left of the stairway, a hall led straight down the center of the house. To the far left, a doorway led into the front sitting room.

Every inch of the place looked like it belonged to an inner-city Brady Bunch, from the '80s-era paisley wallpaper to the colonial blue paint on the trim. Cream carpet covered every inch of the floor, and an umbrella stood next to the small half-round table in the entry.

It all looked so normal, Tessa thought. So middle class.

Until Salvatorus began to stomp down the stairs. Then what would have seemed completely normal to any *eteri*, any non-magical human, made a complete left turn into mythology land.

At four-foot nothing, Sal had the fully developed upper body of a grown man. Wide shoulders, strong arms, nice pecs.

His face was a true marvel of his Etruscan heritage, handsome and strong. And those brown eyes, so dark they looked almost black, held a knowing warmth that always made Tessa smile.

As did the two shiny black horns sprouting from just above his forehead to peek through his glossy, black, curly hair. On any other man, those horns would have been enough to make a grown man choke on his own breath.

On Sal, well, the goat legs stole the show.

Beginning just below his belly button, those legs were covered with hide, a silky chestnut brown fur that was not a pair of pants. No, Sal had the actual legs of a goat.

"Hey, sweetheart," he said as he clomped down the stairs. "Haven't seen you for a while. What's up?"

His deep Noo Yawk accent made her smile grow. But her fear must have shown in her eyes because Salvatorus's gaze narrowed.

"Are you hurt, Tessa?" He descended the rest of the steps on those small hooves, so fast she worried for his safety. But he made it safely to the bottom, took her hand, and began to lead her through the house.

"No." *Not yet, anyway.* "I'm fine."

"Well, you let me be the judge of that."

Salvatorus led her to the kitchen at the very back of the house and pointed her toward a seat at the small table there. He didn't speak, not right away, but set about making her hot chocolate, the rich scent of it making her stomach rumble.

Tessa had been here many times before, mainly for parties. She did love a good party, and Salvatorus threw some of the best. But his home also served as a safe house for anyone of Etruscan descent, including those deities who needed his aid.

She'd never sought aid from Salvatorus before. Really, a goddess who needed help? It sounded ridiculous.

And yet, not so much now.

Sliding into a straight-backed wooden chair, she let her gaze wander out the window over the sink and into the courtyard in the back. The August garden burst with color and fragrance that wafted in through the open window, enticing her to draw a deep breath. Roses, herbs, perennials, bushes, and trees bloomed and thrived in Sal's garden, no bigger than twenty feet by twenty feet.

It was beautiful, a testament to the sun's nurturing power and Salvatorus's skill.

Tears bit at the corners of her eyes. She tried to blink them away before they fell, but one escaped and plopped right into the mug of hot chocolate that appeared in front of her.

"All right, babe." Salvatorus slid into the chair opposite her. "Spill. And I don't mean tears."

She lifted her gaze to his. "Did you know Mlukukh has been missing? For more than a month."

If she'd surprised Salvatorus with her statement about another forgotten Etruscan goddess, he showed no sign of it. "No, I hadn't heard. But then Mel has dropped off the face of the earth for years, sometimes decades. She's always returned."

Tessa shook her head. "I don't think she will this time. In fact, I'm pretty sure I know what happened to her."

Salvatorus's eyelids lifted. "And that is...?"

She took a deep breath before leaving it out on a sigh. "I think Charun had her snatched and taken to Aitás where he consumed her powers and left her shell to rot in the underworld."

Now Salvatorus's eyes narrowed. "And you know this how?"

"Because he told me. He told me that's what he's going to do to me, as well."

TWO

Okay, maybe she should have gotten a second opinion.

Looking around her, she saw nothing but trees. Huge old pines and oaks that looked ominous in the fast-falling dusk.

Behind her, she barely saw the deer trail that passed for a lane. She'd had to leave her car almost a half a mile back on that lane, afraid her little Mini Cooper would get stuck in a rut, especially when the rain began to pour from the sky in sheets.

Her soaking wet clothes clung to her skin, chilling her to the bone.

Just freaking perfect.

Tessa *really* didn't want to be here. But she had few choices left to her.

It royally pissed her off that she'd been reduced to begging for help of any kind, but especially from a man. She'd taken care of herself for as long as she could remember.

And she'd done a damn good job of it so far, if she did say so herself. Still, death was such an unappealing option.

Sal said she needed this man, Caligo, to protect her.

Grimacing, she wondered what parent would saddle their

child with a name that meant "darkness" in Latin. Probably more of an affectation than a calling, if you asked her—

"Oh, Uni's ass," she muttered to herself. "Yes, I'm stalling. So who cares?"

Nobody, really. Except Charun. He'd be very happy if she stalled long enough for him to catch her.

So just do it.

Taking a deep breath, she lifted her hand and knocked on the door, which was surprisingly sturdy beneath her knuckles. She placed her hand flat on the surface and let her senses sink into the metal—and felt steel laced with iron bars and a healthy coating of magic.

Since she was in the middle of nowhere northern Berks County at an abandoned-looking shack, that combination of strength and protective magic proved she was in the right place. As did the runes worked into the graffiti covering the walls of the structure.

To anyone not of Etruscan descent—and really, what good was anyone who wasn't—the runes would look like random lines and curves. But Tessa recognized an intricate Etruscan spell of protection alongside an ancient Egyptian curse and a Norse hex.

She was fairly sure she saw a few spells of Sumerian and Celtic origin as well, but it'd been a while since... well, better just leave it at it'd been a while.

"Suck it up, Tessa." She straightened her back. "You need him."

After another deep breath, she knocked again, this time loud enough to echo in the surrounding woods. This part of Pennsylvania still had a few dark corners, and this man had found one of the darkest.

Damn it all, was he ignoring her? Dead drunk? Or just

dead? Salvatorus had told her all three were distinct possibilities.

She sighed and glanced up at the sky, gray and nearly black. It would be dark soon, and she really didn't want to be alone and unprotected out here after the sun went down. She'd be practically powerless. A shiver ran up her spine.

Where the hell was this guy?

Pressing her ear against the door, she listened. Nothing. Not a sound except for the ping of rain off the metal roof.

Great. She'd finally decided to get help, and the man had the audacity not to be home.

A steady stream of water dripped down her back, and when she shook her head, water flew from her hair. Well, damn it, she wasn't going to stand in the rain and wait for him.

Putting her hand on the doorknob, she felt the pulse of magic guarding the house through carefully set wards. They were such an odd mix of spells, none of which had the power to keep her out.

She was a goddess, after all.

Turning the iron knob, she pushed open the heavy door and tentatively stuck her head into the building.

Forcing a smile, she called out, "Hello. Anyone home?"

She couldn't decide if she was relieved no one responded. Or frustrated. Maybe a little of both.

With a sigh, she slipped through the door, feeling the tingle of Caligo's wards as they slid off her without effect, and closed it tightly behind her.

Surely this protector to whom Salvatorus had sent her wouldn't be upset that she'd taken refuge in his home. She presented no threat to him. And not many men could resist her when she turned on the charm.

Moving further into the room, she noted that this future protector of hers wasn't much of a decorator. He had a couch, a coffee table, and a cabinet holding a flat-screen TV in the front part of the house.

A kitchenette with apartment-sized appliances ran along the side of the house. The two open doors at the rear led to a bathroom and a bedroom.

She yawned, catching herself off guard, and shivered as her wet hair dripped water down her front and onto the floor. In the bathroom, she found a clean towel and dried her hair as much as she could, sighing at her reflection.

"Gods, I look like a drowned cat. I'll probably scare the guy away."

Although, as she looked down at herself, she knew she'd be a shoo-in to win a wet T-shirt contest. Her purple silk top conformed to each and every curve. So did her denim shorts, but they were a bit more uncomfortable at the moment.

Another yawn had her shaking her head as she moved back into the front room. Damn, she was tired.

Sinking onto the surprisingly comfortable couch, she laid her head back on the cushion. Just for a second. She couldn't let herself fall asleep. Charun—

Her eyes closed and darkness descended.

CAL REALIZED someone had gotten through his wards the second he put his hand on the doorknob of his home. He felt the disturbance in the wards like a shiver running up his spine.

Well, fuck. He didn't need this shit.

Closing his eyes, he put his ear to the door and could just make out the rhythmic sound of breathing. Someone was sleeping in his house.

Cal shook his head. Who the fuck would be stupid enough

to break through his wards and then fall asleep waiting for him to get home?

Obviously someone who didn't know him.

Well, they were about to get up close and personal. Pulling the knife from his pants pocket, he got ready to fight.

Turning the knob a quarter inch at a time so it wouldn't squeak, he pushed open the door. When no one started shooting at him or screaming, he stuck his head through the opening.

And spotted his very own Goldilocks passed out on his couch.

Didn't she know the real ending of Goldilocks and the three bears? Goldi became dinner. But what a meal she'd make.

Easing through the door, he closed it behind him without a sound.

The female continued to sleep, her long, wavy strawberry-gold hair spread along the ugly-ass plaid cushions and framing a too-pretty face.

Too pretty to be completely human.

Sharp cheekbones, small round nose, and uptilted eyes in a heart-shaped face. Hair the color of the sun and full lips begging to be licked and sucked and...

Maybe that last one was just him projecting. It'd been a while since he'd gotten laid. He'd had to lie low after that last job, which hadn't been a job at all. Venus, that bitch—

Hell. He needed to get over that one.

Rubbing the back of his neck, he contemplated his unexpected guest. Had to be an immortal of some sort, which would make sense of how she'd gotten through his wards.

Not one of the Greeks; she was too fair. Maybe one of the Romans, but he knew most of those by sight. Etruscan? Yeah, he'd have to go with Etruscan.

She should know better than to let her guard down and fall asleep in a strange man's house.

What the hell was she doing here?

Stalking to the couch on silent feet, he watched for any sign that she was waking up, but she was out cold. Or, she was a damn good actress.

He reached out and nudged her shoulder. No movement, nothing.

Was she injured?

Come to think of it, she looked... wet. Soaking wet, actually. Must have gotten caught in the rain.

That still didn't explain what she was doing here making a mess of his couch. Whatever it was, it probably wasn't good. Damn deities always brought trouble with them. And he was sick and fucking tired of trouble.

Well, this little Goldilocks was about to find out what happened when the bear got home.

Bending, he picked her up and turned toward the bed in the back corner of the one-room shack. She didn't wake, and he barely registered the load. Hell, she couldn't weigh more than one-hundred-ten pounds, soaking wet, which she was.

Wonder what she looks like naked and standing in the shower?

Well, what do you know? His libido still worked.

At the bed, he dropped her on the mattress. She didn't move, didn't groan.

Shit. What the hell was wrong with her? And how the hell long was he going to have to wait to talk to her?

Standing over her in the perpetual twilight of his cabin, he studied her, trying not to notice how damn pretty she was, but he couldn't deny it. Her pale skin gleamed, and her hair shone almost copper against the dark sheets on his bed. She was too bright, too beautiful for his place.

What the hell could this little bauble be on the run from that would force her to come to him?

Oh, he knew there were ugly things out there, monsters in the shadows, in the dark. Hell, he was one of them, though he could be bought for a price.

Had she come to pay for his services? What was she willing to pay? Maybe a little sex to go along with the gold?

She wasn't his usual type. Of course, the last one had been, and look how that had ended up. But something about Goldilocks made his libido, among other things, sit up and take notice.

She was small, only five-two, maybe five-three. And skinny, all tiny bones and features. He liked women with more meat on their bones. More like Amazons. He was six-two and two-ten, his body honed by constant training, constant vigilance, and constant violence. He liked his women to be able to keep up with him, not look like they'd faint from his weight on top of them.

He'd never been attracted to fey little blondes.

Still, since he wasn't exactly sure *what* she was, he wasn't going to take any chances 'cause he was that kind of guy. Careful. Meticulous. And a prick, if you listened to a few of the women he'd been involved with.

Yeah, yeah, tell it to the choir. He'd learned not to make promises to women. He almost always ended up breaking them.

And he certainly never trusted women. You never knew what secrets they were hiding. To that end, he stripped her naked—just to make sure she didn't have any weapons stashed on her, of course. Besides, her clothes were wet, and he didn't want her to ruin his mattress.

Uh-huh.

The scrap of denim she wore as shorts fell in a tiny pile on the floor. Her bright purple T-shirt followed, but not before he'd rubbed the material between his fingers. It had the texture of silk and caught on the rough skin of his hands.

She wasn't wearing a bra, and her underwear consisted of little more than two strings and a triangle of satin.

His heart wanted to race but he refused to allow it. This wasn't a seduction. Maybe she'd come to hurt him. Mercenaries couldn't be too careful.

He grabbed the ropes he kept under the bed. A few slipknots later, he'd tied her arms and legs to the four corners of the bed frame.

Spread-eagle on his mattress, pretty little Goldilocks gave him a raging hard-on. Small but lush, her body curved in all the right places. Her breasts sat high and firm; her arms and legs were long and sleek; and her sex—

Hell, he didn't know where to look first.

After last month's fiasco in Philadelphia and—more to the point—the cause of it, he'd figured a naked woman would leave him as frigid as a few hours in a deep freeze.

He still couldn't believe he'd been duped by that Roman bitch, Venus. Goddess of Love and Beauty, his ass. She'd been smart enough not to use tears on him when she'd begged him to protect her from the big, bad blacksmith god. No, she'd played the strong but wronged heroine to Vulcan's evil rapist.

What Venus had failed to mention was the fact that she'd slept with Vulcan to steal his magic hammer. She wanted to use that hammer to off Mercury, who'd told her to take a flying leap when she'd tried to seduce him.

Vulcan had gone easy on Cal. The coma had only lasted two days. And Cal was back to full strength now. But the fact that this little piece stirred his desire made him uneasy.

Getting a clean towel, he pulled the only chair in the house to the side of the bed and watched her chest rise and fall at a steady pace, her breasts quivering slightly with the movement.

Shaking his head, he lifted his gaze to her face before he did something really stupid. Like touch her. That would be really stupid.

He noted color returning to her cheeks. Good. She should come around soon.

He pressed the towel against her forehead then her cheeks. Her skin glistened as if she was warm. He glanced at the thermometer on the wall by the door. Nearly eighty-five in here. Not that he could feel it, but she definitely could.

Folding the towel over his fingers, he swiped at her throat then between her breasts. As his gaze continued down to the pale gold hair trimmed tight to her mound, his brain short-circuited.

Shit, that's not good.

With an effort, he dragged his gaze back up to her face. Minutes ticked by as he stroked her cheek with the soft terrycloth, careful not to let his skin touch hers, and watched for any sign of her regaining consciousness. But her eyelids didn't flutter; her breathing pattern didn't change; and her lips didn't move.

She barely made a sound, and he found himself watching her chest for each slight rise. That, of course, meant he was back to staring at her breasts. Full, round, beautiful.

When he lifted his hand to cup her, they felt great, too. Soft and female and... everything he'd been missing all his life.

Shit. When had he become such a sap?

His grip tightened for a second, and she arched into his touch, as if encouraging him. He was probably just reading too much into an involuntary movement, but damn, he really wanted to believe she liked his touch.

Her breast fit in his palm perfectly, and when he rubbed his thumb over the dusky pink nipple, it tightened into a firm point. His cock gave a hard throb against the confines of his pants, and he lifted his free hand to her other breast.

It'd been way too long since he'd gotten laid if just her breasts in his hands brought him this close to coming. There was a warning in there, but he ignored it and continued to knead her, treating her more gently than anything he'd ever held in his life.

Why? Hell if he knew.

He released her breasts and brushed his fingers against the pale skin just below her chin. Her pulse beat strong, and her skin felt... warm.

He pulled his hands back as if she'd burned him. That couldn't be right. He hadn't felt heat or cold since he'd been a teenager. Couldn't remember the warmth of hot water or the brush of a cool breeze on a fall night.

But he swore he felt the heat of her skin against his.

How was that possible?

He was Cimmerian, one of the legendary warriors immortalized by that bastard Homer in *The Odyssey*. Their existence had been a closely guarded secret until that fucking Greek had outed them. Good old Homer. Between Atlantis and the Cimmerians, the ancient Greek historian really knew how to fuck up history.

Yeah, they were born in the mist and shadow between the planes of existence, in the land they called Cimer. The Cimmerians' strength and resistance to pain were legendary. Their bravery was unquestioned and their ability to fight until they died a useful skill for those who bought their aid.

What no one knew was that Cimmerians felt no pain, no heat, no cold. The lack of sensation made them fierce warriors, the kind of men most humans or immortals wanted at their backs if they were in serious trouble.

The only problem? After years of battle, the lack of physical sensation bled any and all humanity from the Cimmerians. Conversations usually ended in fights to proclaim dominance.

Sex became nothing more than a release. Mates were for procreation, not affection.

Emotion of any kind made you weak, according to Cimmerian thought.

Still... if he and his visitor were both naked and he spread his body over hers, would he feel that warmth all over? Would he want to?

He took a deep breath... and put his hands on her cheeks.

Holy shit.

He drew in a sharp breath at the pure bliss that lit up his nerve endings and zipped through his body like a lightning strike.

He ripped his hands away. This changed everything.

No. Hell, no.

He was crazy. He had to be. What he was feeling was some aberration or a trick. An illusion. But, as he stared at her body, he couldn't quite seem to care.

Her skin was completely free of tan lines or imperfections, sun-kissed peach except for her nipples. Those were a ruddy raspberry, puckered and erect. He wanted to bend down and take them in his mouth. Lick them, nip them, suckle until she arched into him.

But first, he had to know if what he'd felt had been real or imagined. He lifted one hand... and stopped centimeters above the indentation of her navel.

Idiot. Just touch her.

Slowly, he laid his hand flat on her stomach to find her skin as soft as... Well, hell, he didn't know what to compare it to. Or the heat of her body as it soaked into his skin.

He sucked in a deep, almost painful breath. God... damn, that felt incredible. Even though it shouldn't be possible.

Well, fuck that. Possible, impossible, who the hell cared? Every nerve ending in his body had suddenly fired to life.

He'd never realized how much he didn't feel until this very moment. And now he wanted to revel in it.

He put his other hand next to the first and closed his eyes, blocking out every other distraction except the feel of her. His body tensed, his balls tightening to the point of pain, and his cock hardened with a fierce throb.

Who the hell was she?

Fuck it, he didn't care.

Sliding his hands up and over her ribs, he felt each bone covered by warm satin skin. So delicate, so easily harmed. Sliding further, he let his hands touch the underside of her breasts. Soft and smooth, her skin warmed even more as he brushed his thumbs back and forth.

Had he ever taken the time to caress a woman there? Why would he have bothered?

Why are you bothering now?

He stuffed his internal censor back into its box and took the full weight of her breasts in his hands. They weren't huge, but they filled his palms, her nipples pebbling even more as he ran his thumbs over them. So warm, so tight.

He had to taste her.

THREE

Tessa struggled out of a much-needed sleep because she felt someone close.

Someone desired her. Ached for her so badly that his need brushed against her senses like a cat rubbing against her leg and begging for a caress.

How long had it been since someone had truly needed her?

She took a deep breath, her eyes still closed, and caught the scent of a male. Oh my, he smelled good. No, he smelled wonderful—a little sweat, a little spice, a whole lot turned on.

He wanted her. She felt his desire like a blanket of heat on her skin.

Forcing her lids to open, she found herself staring into moonlight-gray eyes, half hidden beneath midnight-black bangs.

Those bangs nearly reached the tip of a slightly crooked nose that'd been broken at least once in his life. Possibly more than once, if the scar on his left cheekbone and the one under the cleft in his chin were any indication of the life he'd led.

She followed the line of his jaw back up to his ear, noting that the rest of his hair wasn't as long but clipped tight to his head. She lifted her hands to brush the bangs out of his eyes—and realized he'd tied her to the bed.

She glanced down.

Naked.

Hmm.

Closing her eyes for a second, she took stock. She wasn't injured. But, sweet Mother Goddess, she was horny as hell.

She ached. For him.

At the second she realized what she was feeling, her lungs constricted and her lips parted to try and draw in more air. Her nipples tightened into unbearable points of heat and her sex moistened, making her ready.

The man watched her through slitted eyes, his expression unreadable. But his labored breathing told her he was just as aroused.

Then he bent and took her nipple in his mouth.

Her gasp echoed in the room as his warm mouth closed over her, and she strained against the ropes as her back arched. His tongue flicked the sensitive tip, slicked around it. Then he pulled back so he could nip at the tip with his teeth.

Not hard, but a moan broke from her throat at the exquisite pleasure that coursed through her.

Closer, he needed to be closer.

She needed him to suck her into his mouth and draw on her, maybe bite her harder. Just a little harder. But he only licked at her, the warm air and his rough tongue making her nipple harden almost to the point of pain.

Then he did bite her, and she arched her back off the bed with a short cry.

"More. More."

The sharp shock of his teeth made her muscles clench and ache, but his hands squeezed her breasts gently. Almost tenderly, his fingers stroked and caressed. Teased. But it wasn't enough to give her any ease.

Damn him, she wanted him closer. Needed him closer. She wanted to pull his head down to her and force him to take her breast further into his mouth, but the ropes held her back.

And he knew exactly how to torment her.

He lapped at one and then the other nipple. Back and forth, he licked and nipped until she thought she might actually cry from frustration.

"Gods, please…"

He lifted his head and stared down at her, a question in those stormy eyes. "Please what?"

"Please don't stop."

He continued to stare, his expression showing no emotion, his hands idle. And her sanity began to return.

What the hell was going on? And why did he kiss her body with such care?

Then he dipped his head and sucked her nipple into his mouth again, pulling the flesh into the warm, wet cavern and rolling the tip with his tongue, and all questions evaporated into thin air.

Oh, Blessed Mother Goddess, that felt absolutely divine. Who would have guessed that a man who looked as hard, as rough as he did would have such soft lips? And really, at the moment, who cared? As long as he kept using them on her body, which he did.

His large hands kneaded as he suckled her and then pressed her breasts together until they touched. With his tongue, he licked at the seam where flesh met flesh and then released her breasts to press kisses to her sternum and below.

He dragged his hands down her sides as his lips laid a trail straight to the hair on her mound. But before she gathered the breath to gasp, he pulled away and stood.

She moaned. She couldn't help it. The bastard was teasing her.

Had she fallen so far that she couldn't entice a man into bed with her?

Then again, maybe she wasn't as far gone as she'd thought when she saw him rip his T-shirt over his head and unbutton and unzip his black pants.

He was commando under there, his erection a thick, ruddy shaft jutting straight out from his groin. Her mouth dried at the sight.

The man was absolutely beautiful.

She let her gaze make a leisurely path up his body, lingering on the washboard abs and the flexing pecs before meeting his gaze.

A smile curved her lips, and his gaze narrowed.

Good, she wanted him to wonder. And to want.

Because she wanted him with a ferocity she'd worry about later. Right now, she just wanted him to take her.

He must have read her mind—or maybe the scent of her arousal was enough—because he crawled onto the bed beside her. He loomed over her for several seconds, his eyes traveling the length of her body before he moved first one knee then the other between her legs.

Her lungs struggled to draw in enough air, and her hands lifted again before being caught by the ropes.

Sitting back on his heels between her spread legs, he stared into her eyes as he lifted his right hand and set it on her left thigh. Then he did the same with his left hand on her right thigh. Heat shot up her spine and his hands clenched as if he'd had the same reaction.

Good. She wanted to know that the man she desired lusted after her as well. It would definitely make him easier to manage. But she'd worry about that later.

Right now, she wanted to enjoy the anticipation and the promise of lust in his eyes.

After a few seconds, his fingers began to knead her thighs as they had her breasts. The feeling was so luxurious that she let her head fall back onto the pillow.

How long had it been since someone had caressed her?

Way too damn long.

As his hands stroked down to her knees and back up, he moved closer to her sex each time. She was soaking wet for him. She wanted him to know it, to touch her. She arched her hips... and he pulled his hands down to her knees.

Damn him. She bit back a groan and settled back onto the bed. He rewarded her by smoothing his hands back up to her hips, his thumbs finally grazing through her curls and brushing against the lips of her sex, sending tingles shooting into her womb.

She bit her tongue on a moan, not wanting to give him any cause to pull away. And felt his thumbs begin to part her.

"You're wet." His voice vibrated through her skin and into her soul as he placed one hand fully over her mound. "I can smell your desire. Is this why you're here?"

She shook her head, straining against the ropes, wanting to force him to touch her as she needed.

He removed his hands, and she nearly screamed in frustration. She opened her eyes and found herself staring into his as he planted his fists next to her head and bent over her. His knees brushed high on the inside of her thighs, crowding her and forcing her to try to open her legs even further, over the protest of the ropes.

"Did you come for sex?" he asked. "You must need it bad if you trekked all the way out here. But I can't believe you couldn't crook your little finger and have any man you wanted. So, I gotta wonder what the hell you're doing here."

His eyes were such a pure gray, more silver than blue. Mesmerizing.

"I need you," she panted. "I need you... to protect me."

He smiled, but it was not kind. "Yeah, well, who's gonna protect you from me?"

Hell, she didn't want anyone to protect her from him. She wanted him to ravage her. For hours. She hadn't had a man in her bed for ages. She felt like she'd been on the run for years, not weeks. Ages had passed since she'd been able to sleep or had known whom to trust.

She trusted Salvatorus, and he'd sent her here.

To this man.

"I don't need protection from you," she said. "Right now, I just need you to take me."

His eyebrows lifted but he didn't move. "Take you where, babe? Where're we going?"

She looked him straight in the eyes to be sure he did not misunderstand her. "Do me. Right now. Fuck me. Please."

CAL SHUDDERED, and the bed shook with him.

He'd never expected her to be so blunt. She was too damn preciously beautiful to have a mouth like that. But that word, that one word coming from those lips made his cock throb and his muscles ache with the need to shove inside her, to get so far inside her that she'd forget she'd ever had anyone else.

He wanted her to wrap her legs around his waist and her arms around his shoulders, to sink her nails into his back as he rode her hard and satisfied this raging lust. And to make her come, hot and wet around him, until she screamed and passed out.

He must be fucking nuts.

He must have knocked his head sometime in the past few hours. That would explain his insane need to have her and mark her in some way as his. Because that's exactly what he wanted.

Well, he could have her, but he wouldn't be keeping her.

With his eyes trained on hers, he lowered his hips until he could brush the tip of his cock against the soft hair on her mound then further down, against the satin-soft lips of her sex.

Her eyelids fluttered closed and her soft moan made his arms shake as he held his body above hers. He did it again, this time letting his cock slip between her lips and rubbing her moisture all over the head.

God, he could feel the warmth of it, so fucking beautiful it nearly made him cry out. But that would be showing emotion, and this had nothing to do with emotion.

So he reared back and thrust into her. Not brutally hard. Just with enough force to sink deep, almost to his balls. Slick heat enfolded him, milked him.

She cried out, though not in pain. No, she ground against him, wrapping her hands around what little slack there was in the ropes and using them to angle herself to him.

On his arms above her, he forced himself to watch her face, to watch every expression. The relief, the ecstasy, the frustration.

He figured if she looked up, she'd see the same expression on his face. And that was probably not a good thing. With his cock lodged inside her sex, he lowered onto his elbows and shoved his face at her neck. Nipping at the soft flesh beneath her ear, he flexed his hips and pulled out, one centimeter at a time, letting the drag of flesh on flesh tighten his balls.

God, she was hot and he could feel that heat. No other woman he'd fucked had ever made him feel like this.

But this didn't feel like fucking. This felt more... reverential. That was a dangerous path.

But, it was going to be fun while it lasted.

At the point where he'd nearly slipped free of her body, he shoved back in, making sure to catch her clit at a good angle. He must have done okay, because she gasped, her warm breath brushing his ear and raising the hair all over his body.

Damn, being this close to her was a revelation of all the sensations he thought he'd lost forever. And he was determined to enjoy the full extent of every one.

Removing his teeth from her neck, where he could see the beginning of a bruise, he rubbed his nose against the skin under her ear on his next retreat, breathing in her scent, fresh and clean, like clear air at the first touch of the sun. Something he hadn't experienced in almost a century but remembered for its purity.

Obviously this woman wasn't untouched, but there was something about her, something pure. Something he wanted. Something he needed.

And that was so totally bad.

This time, he shoved in a little harder and immediately cursed himself for it, though she seemed to enjoy it, if her breathy moan was any indication. Lifting his head, he finally let himself kiss her full on the mouth. He wanted to taste her and needed to penetrate her again. To conquer her.

Her tongue slid along his, his hips hammering faster now, his tongue halfway down her throat. Her mouth was just as warm as the rest of her, even more so, and his cock twitched, warning him he was about to come. He froze, not wanting to, but she broke away and pressed her lips to his ear.

"Do it," she whispered. "Come on, harder. I need to come and so do you."

Her rough-edged words flicked a switch in his brain, allowing his body to take over the rest of the ride. His hips pulled back before he slammed into her again and again. Her moans fueled his lust, and he made a small adjustment to the angle of his thrust until she cried out and clenched around him.

Her orgasm cut the last thread of control he had on his sanity, and he released into her with a cry and a sense that he'd finally found home.

Now that really scared the shit out of him.

THE MAN FELL all over Tessa like he'd passed out.

Breathing heavily in her ear, he lay on top of her, his heavy body providing a curious sense of safety. Which was great, considering why she was here.

The problem was going to be the sex. It had been good. Maybe too damn good. How was she going to keep her hands off him?

Then again... she tugged on the ropes. That might be the easy part.

Convincing him to be her savior was going to be more difficult. According to Salvatorus, Caligo wouldn't want to help her.

Something about a deal gone wrong. Though Salvatorus hadn't elaborated, the probability that Cal had been screwed, possibly by someone she knew, was a very real possibility.

Still, he was a mercenary, a man who could be bought for a price. Hopefully, he'd want more of what she could give him. She didn't mean only the sex, but that definitely wouldn't be a hardship. She hadn't felt this level of lust in centuries.

Lying silently, she felt his cock still twitching inside her, pulsing his seed into her.

After that great orgasm, she felt more rested than she had in... Well, she couldn't remember how long. She wanted to close her eyes and sleep, at least for a little while, but they needed to talk.

As if he'd read her mind, he sighed, his chest moving against hers, the dark hair on his pecs teasing her nipples. As he eased his hips back, his cock pulled free, and he sat back on his haunches.

He stared into her eyes for several seconds before his gaze shifted to her left arm and then her right. Leaning forward, he released her arms from the ropes, which had begun to chafe. Then he got off the bed and released her legs.

She lay there for a minute, rubbing her wrists and flexing her ankles. He watched her, his jaw clenching as he stood by the bed and then turned and tossed his shirt on the sheet next to her.

"Put this on," he said. "Then we'll talk."

His tone brooked no dissension but at least he wasn't kicking her out. Yet. "Can I use your bathroom?"

He pointed to the wall to her right.

Okay, not much of a talker. Sliding off the bed, she headed for the bathroom next door, feeling his gaze on her the whole way. The slickness of his essence between her thighs made her hips sway just a little more than usual.

Closing the door behind her, she noticed there was no mirror in the utilitarian room, only a toilet, a sink, and a tiny shower stall. Guess there'd be no shower sex. And thinking about sex was not going to get her head together, which was part of the reason she'd stepped in here. She needed just a little distance to think.

After she cleaned up a bit and washed her hands, she pulled the shirt on, shaking her head as it fell almost to her knees. She'd have to ask what he'd done with her clothes. Then she took a deep breath.

She had to go back out there and convince him to help her. But fear rooted her feet to the floor. If he turned her away, she was dead.

"Oh, just get out there and talk to him. It's not like you haven't just had sex with the guy."

And it wasn't like she hadn't had sex with lots of guys. Of course, she hadn't needed any of them to save her, which was the real kick in the pants.

How low she had fallen.

Stepping out of the bathroom, she found him standing before the open front door. In this brutal August heat, he was wearing long pants but wasn't sweating. She was used to the heat, but even her skin was slightly damp.

He turned and she knew from his expression that the real interrogation was about to begin. And the Great Mother Goddess help her if she didn't give him what he wanted.

"Who are you?" His voice brooked no resistance. At any other time, she probably would have turned up her nose at him and told him to stuff his question. "And don't give me any bullshit. I'm not in the mood."

Now, she couldn't help but smile. She did so love men who didn't screw around. Well, not with business, anyway.

"My name's Tessa."

"What the fuck do you want, Tessa? And if it's anything other than sex, you're outta luck."

Well, the sex *had* been amazing but she did have more pressing issues.

"It's about a job."

He continued to stare at her. "What kind of job?"

"One for which I would pay you a lot of money." There, that was sure to get a response.

But the man paused again. "To do what?"

Okay, maybe this one was smarter than the average bear. "Keep me alive."

He made a sound that could have been a snort or a laugh.

"Yeah, well, that's easier said than done most times, ain't it? What's so special about you, babe?"

Not much. That was both true and very misleading. "You *are* Caligo, correct? I need to know I'm talking to the right person."

Again the snort. "Probably not."

That was complete bullshit. This was definitely the man Salvatorus had told her she needed. And if Salvatorus said she needed him, then this was the man she wanted.

"My name is Tessa. Salvatorus sent me here to seek protection. He told me you'd provide."

"Huh." The man's mouth twisted in a smirk. "Now, I know that's not right because Salvatorus should know better than to send your kind to me."

"Special circumstances. Please, I need you."

Some emotion crossed his hard face, something she didn't understand, so she pushed on.

"My name is Thesan, but I go by Tessa now." She paused, waiting to see if her name struck any chord at all with him, but his expression never changed.

She sighed. So much for being a formerly beloved goddess. That and five bucks would get her a Starbucks mocha latte these days.

"Your name's supposed to ring a bell?" He crossed his arms over that deliciously perfect chest.

She shook her head. "It's okay. It's been several thousand years since anyone worshipped me on a regular basis. Of course you wouldn't know my name."

His gaze narrowed. "Worshipped you?"

She stood a little taller and pointed her nose into the air. "Thesan, Goddess of the Dawn, at your service."

"Yeah, right," he grunted. "Goddess, my ass. The deities don't live down here with the common people, babe. And the only Goddess of the Dawn I know is Aurora, and you ain't her."

She held her smile though she had to grit her teeth to do it. "No, I am *not* Aurora, for which you should be grateful. She's..." *a worthless, ugly cow...* "not worth talking about. And most of the Etruscan pantheon still lives in this time and place."

His gaze never faltered. "And that's what you are? Etruscan?"

She nodded, unsure if her affiliation would help or hinder her cause.

He grunted again, but in response to what she couldn't tell. "That still doesn't explain why you need me for protection. Aren't you deities supposed to be all powerful and shit like that?"

Absently, she rubbed at a raw spot on her wrist from the ropes and saw his gaze arrow in on it. "Not really. I was never all powerful, but I very much enjoyed what I did."

And then that bubble-headed, Barbie-doll bitch Aurora took my job and—

Okay, deep breath. No need to hash all that out again. It'd been centuries. She should be over it. Really.

"When the Roman pantheon usurped our roles, some of us became... obsolete." She truly hated that word. "There's only one sun, after all, and, well..." She forced a smile. "Anyway, I retained my midwifery duties, but over the years, some of us have become mostly... forgotten." And that really sucked. "Some of us still serve the magical races of the Etruscans, the *Enu* and the *Fata*. But mostly," she shrugged, hating the hollow feeling her chest, "we merely exist."

Was that pity she saw in his eyes? Damn him, that's not what she wanted. Her back straightened, but he spoke before she could say anything else.

"That still doesn't explain why you need me."

No, it didn't, and she could only hope that when she told him, he didn't kick her out on her butt.

"Charun has—"

He held up one hand. "God of the Underworld, right?"

She nodded. "We call it Aitás, but yes. He's one of the gods who has retained his position through the millennia, and he's not very happy about it. He's been stuck in Aitás, trapped there, really, and he's decided he wants to be released from his service."

"And what does that have to do with you? And me?"

"He plans to consume deities and absorb their powers, which will make him more powerful." She shuddered just thinking about it. "I believe he's trying to break free of Aitás and is tracking Etruscan goddesses through their dreams. I believe he's already taken one and has decided I'm next."

His expression remained unchanged. "I can see why you might have a problem with this, but why should I care?"

"If Charun is released from Aitás, the dead will follow him out, and then everyone on earth will have a problem."

His eyebrows lifted. "So? I'm not the police, lady. I'm not a god. I don't have an infinite lifespan, and I don't like to do dirty work for deities. They tend to fuck you over. I'm just a guy—"

"No, I know that's not true. I know what you are, Caligo of the Cimmerians."

Well, shit.

Amazing how that one word—Cimmerian—was guaranteed to throw Cal's life in the toilet.

At one time, it would have been murmured with respect and fear. Men wanted to be Cimmerian, and women just wanted them.

Then fucking Robert E. Howard had screwed Cal's people six ways to Sunday with his books about the Cimmerians. Hollywood had compounded the problem by casting Arnold

Schwarzenegger in the film version, *Conan the Barbarian*, making the true remaining Cimmerians cringe at the horrifying spectacle.

Yeah, Cal was Cimmerian, one of the legendary warriors born in the mist and shadow of the land between the planes of existence. They were a race an evolutionary step above mortal humans, though fewer than five hundred remained of a once-thriving civilization now reduced to little more than a tribe.

And this pretty little goddess with the willing body and intelligent blue eyes had given him a taste of a heat he shouldn't be able to feel.

That made her dangerous.

He really should kick her out, whether Salvatorus had sent her or not. That little horned bastard had a lot to answer for.

Thesan continued to stare at him, waiting for an answer, though she hadn't asked a question.

And since she wasn't going to win this battle, he gave her a blank stare. That might have told her more than he'd wanted because she smiled as if he'd blurted out, "Yes, I'm a Cimmerian, and I'll do whatever you want."

No matter how good the sex was, it didn't entitle her to his life story.

"So," she said, "do I have your attention now?"

Yeah, she did. Especially when she kept rubbing her wrists.

He shrugged in response to her question. And changed the subject. "I've got some salve for your wrists."

He walked to the small kitchen area and removed a tin from the tiny refrigerator. He let his hand linger in the interior for a few seconds, but he didn't feel the cold at all.

Good, that was good. It meant something about her made him feel heat. Not some deficiency in him.

Walking back, he flipped the tin to her.

"You can take that with you when you leave. It's not my

turn to be a hero today, babe, and definitely not for a spoiled little goddess. And you can't buy my services with a little sex."

But maybe for a little more...

No. He had to stand strong here.

"I can pay. However much you—"

"I don't want your money, either."

She drew in a sharp breath as if he'd hit her, and his heart gave a wrench. Damn it, he was not going to cave on this. Not even when he saw dainty little tears pool at the corners of her eyes.

Cimmerians were warriors, and these days they were forced to be mercenaries to live. They didn't cave to feminine wiles. They were strong and brave... and, oh, for fuck's sake, this wasn't fair. For some stupid-ass reason, he wanted to wrap his arms around her and tell her he'd never let anything hurt her.

But he knew better than to get involved with the deities. Everyone did. They screwed you over royally. And he didn't mean in bed. Although that fuck definitely had been fit for the gods.

Blinking back the tears, she turned and headed for the door.

"Then I guess I'll just say thanks for the sex." She turned the knob and stepped outside. "It was good."

Closing the door, she disappeared.

TESSA HAD WONDERED if the tears would work. Not that they weren't real. She really was screwed well and good now. Especially since Caligo didn't seem to be following her.

Stepping off the rickety wooden porch, she headed in the direction of her car, her thoughts reeling.

Now what? Did she return to her little house and wait for Charun to catch her in her sleep when she could no longer keep her eyes open? Return to Salvatorus's home in the city and risk Charun discovering possibly the only Etruscan safe house in the States?

Was there anywhere she could go that Charun would not find her?

Sighing, she headed for her little, blue convertible Mini Cooper, parked just beyond the bend in the road. When she arrived, she'd had to park the car and walk because of the deeply rutted path. But that meant she now had to walk back with the soreness between her legs a constant reminder of her failure.

Damn Caligo.

Salvatorus had warned her that the Cimmerian might be hard to convince. Sal had mentioned something about Cal having been screwed over by another goddess recently.

It had never really occurred to Tessa that Cal would refuse to help her because she was a deity. She had enough gold to pay him anything he wanted. And she would have gladly given him her body again. The sex had been... amazing.

But really, what had she expected from a mercenary?

Sure, he'd taken the payment but hadn't rendered a service. Okay, that wasn't technically true. That wonderful orgasm could be considered a service, but still...

All she had to show for her day were sore wrists and ankles, a headache, and the remaining tingle of sex in her body.

Now what?

She stopped and took a deep breath, inhaling clean, country air. At least it was no longer raining. All around her, the forest soothed. She felt the hum of living energy in the beat of her heart, felt the earth's power beneath her feet. Just because she was—had been—a sun goddess, that didn't mean she wasn't in tune with the earth.

And this was an old forest, unusual for this part of southeastern Pennsylvania, where the Europeans had harvested most of the trees several centuries earlier.

No wonder Caligo chose to live here. It was secluded. Peaceful.

But where did she go now?

She couldn't risk contacting any of the other deities she'd been friendly with in times past for fear of leading Charun to them. Besides, Usil, the Sun God, had disappeared many centuries ago, and Nethuns, the Sea God, probably wouldn't talk to her anyway because of that whole Kev affair.

Sue her, she had a thing for young men. Neth had known that from the start and—

She sighed. That wasn't going to save her ass. Or the world's.

Lifting her hand, she rubbed at her burning eyes. That nap at Caligo's had only made her more tired.

She didn't know how much longer she could go without a full night's sleep. She wouldn't be able to keep herself awake through sheer force of will much longer. And when she dreamed, Charun would find her.

Dreams existed in a state other than reality, one that Charun, who lived in the plane of existence where dreams originated, could access with little effort.

When she fell asleep and her unconscious brain took over, her dreams would stand out like a beacon for the God of Aitás, especially since he was specifically looking for her. Once he'd located her, he'd send his minions to bring her to him for a little dinner party where she would be the main course.

Opening the door to her car, she slid into the driver's seat and dropped her head on the steering wheel.

Think, Tessa, think. Just because you're blonde and haven't used more than a tenth of your natural skills for almost two millennia doesn't mean you can't come up with a—

A hand slid around her arm and she screamed.

CAL WAS CONGRATULATING himself for getting rid of Tessa with a minimum of hysterics when her scream rang clear into the house. Adrenaline dropped into his system and he raced for the door, wrenching it open before he even realized he'd moved.

Then the sound cut off as abruptly as it'd started, and he tore off down the rutted dirt path that led to his house.

Fuck, this was his fault. He shouldn't have let her go.

Before he got to the blind bend about a quarter mile from the house, he slid into the trees, heading in the direction he'd heard her scream. Through the breaks between trunks, he caught glimpses of a small blue car.

He slowed to a stop behind a huge old oak then peered around the side. What he saw inside the car made him freeze.

A blue-skinned demon with long black hair held Tessa's pure strawberry-gold waves in one hand and a knife at her throat with the other. Tessa's hands gripped the steering wheel, her knuckles white with strain. Her face was just as pale, and those same damn tears he'd cursed her for earlier ran down her cheeks.

Shit. Shit, shit, and double shit.

If he rushed the car, the demon, probably one of Charun's minions that Tessa had mentioned, would have enough time to hurt her, even though Tessa had said Charun wanted to consume her. That meant the demented god probably wanted her alive and the demon couldn't kill her.

But it could injure her. And that would seriously piss him off, which was fucking stupid logic, considering he'd just kicked her out.

Pushing those thoughts out of his head, he dropped to the ground and crawled through the underbrush toward the car. Since Cal was really good at what he did, the demon never made any indication that it heard or saw him.

Cal would have been awfully fucking offended if it had. Still, he wasn't inside the car yet.

Ignoring the scratching of fallen branches against his bare chest and stomach, he reached the back end of the car then carefully dragged himself around to the passenger's side. Luckily, Tessa had parked close to the side of the road so he didn't have to crawl into the open.

Getting to the door only took seconds but it felt like forever because he could hear snatches of conversation from the open car window. The demon wanted Tessa to drive, but she was arguing that she couldn't drive with a knife at her throat.

Her voice sounded slow and sure, but it held a tremor of fear that infuriated him. He wanted to reach inside the car and pound the demon into oblivion for putting that tone in Tessa's voice. But that wasn't the best course of action. So he waited.

And, after a few more seconds, he got the opening he needed.

The demon must have moved the knife because the car started. Before Tessa could drive away, Cal reached up, opened the door, and grabbed the demon's arm.

In that split second of surprise, he managed to drag the demon out of the car and onto the ground before it started to fight. Dirty. And like a girl. It pulled his hair and grabbed his ears. It used long black fingernails to scratch at his face and brought its feet up to gouge its toenails into his legs.

Cal fought back, punching the demon in the head and kneeing it in the side. Ignoring the blood running down his face and legs, he heard Tessa gasp but couldn't take the time to see if she was okay. The demon was stronger than it had any right to be for its size, but Cal knew that wasn't unusual for lower-plane creatures.

To subdue it, he tried to roll and trap it under his body, but the demon rolled the other way and punched its fist toward his face. Cal dodged at the last second, but the demon brought its knee up and caught him in the balls. Good thing Cal didn't feel pain because that one might have really hurt. He'd have to check later to make sure the kick hadn't done any lasting damage.

Right now, he was losing his grip on the thing. Its skin grew slippery with sweat. At least, he hoped it was sweat. The damn thing could be poisoning him, and he wouldn't know until it was too late. Still, he couldn't let it get away.

With a burst of strength, Cal wrapped his hands around the demon's thin, wattled throat and tried to cut off its air supply. It just smiled, showing off four rows of razor-sharp teeth, and rolled him like he was a kid.

Cal found himself on his back, staring up at the demon.

Shit, this was bad news. He'd underestimated the thing's strength.

But Cal still had a few tricks up his sleeve. He began to throw deadly hard punches, aiming for the thing's head. Only a few of them connected because the demon was fast and limber. And each time it moved, its teeth got closer. Cal lifted his arm, hoping the demon would bite that before taking a chunk out of his face.

The demon opened its mouth and hissed—

And suddenly it wasn't there.

Tessa stood over him with a tree limb shaking in her trembling hands, panting, eyes wide. Then they both turned to look at the demon, which Tessa had managed to smack a good ten feet away. On all fours, it shook its body like a dog after a bath. Then it stood, a wiry mass of naked flesh with no sex organs to indicate male or female. It hissed again, showing off those pointed teeth, and smiled before loping into the forest away from the house.

Cal pushed himself off the ground, watching the tree limb bob and weave in Tessa's hands.

"Tessa."

Actually, Tessa's whole body trembled, making that limb extremely dangerous to Cal. Eyes wide, she stared in the direction the demon had run. Her breath rasped hard and rough out of her body, and her knuckles had turned white.

"Tessa, it's okay. It's gone. Put that down before you hurt me with it."

There, that got her attention. Her gaze swung around to his, and he was almost startled to see real fear in her eyes. Apparently deities were afraid of some things, which meant the demon was probably not something he wanted to run into again.

"Are you okay?" Tessa asked as she stepped closer, dropping the limb at the last moment before it batted him in the side. "It didn't bite you, did it?"

He shook his head. "I'm fine. What about you? You okay?"

She took a deep breath and then another. With a visible effort, she forced her body to stop trembling. Then she nodded. "Yes, I'm fine. It didn't hurt me."

"You wanna tell me what the fuck that was?"

She shivered, her entire body getting in on the action. "Tukhulkha demon. Charun's bringing out the big guns."

And that scared the shit out of her. He saw it in her wide eyes and the paleness of her skin.

"Come on," he said. "Let's get back to the house. Then we'll figure out what to do next."

She blinked. "We?"

He sighed. "Yeah, we." Although he was probably going to

regret this. "I don't like to be attacked on my own ground. Pisses me off."

Her eyes widened even more. "So you'll help me?"

Putting his hand on her arm, he let the warmth he shouldn't be able to feel seep into his skin. Obviously, something about this woman, this goddess, brought out a part of him he'd thought lost.

"Yeah, I will. Let's go."

FOUR

"I tell you to do something, you do it. No questions asked."

Tessa kept her eyes trained on Cal as he drove his Jeep Wrangler down a dirt road in the woods. Actually, "road" was too kind to describe what was little more than a deer trail. The Wrangler barely fit between the trees, and branches whipped by at terrorizing speed. Her fingers had cramped from holding the roll bar so tightly.

She was watching him because she couldn't bear to look out the front window. She didn't want to see the tree they were surely going to hit if he didn't slow down.

So she focused on her savior. She was so grateful to him for saving her life back there that she was willing to put up with anything he told her. But if he didn't slow down, she might just have to curl up in a ball on the floor and cry like a baby.

"Tess, hey. You listening to me?"

"Yes. Yes, I am." She had to yell over the whistle of the wind. "I do whatever you tell me to."

Cal must have heard something in her voice he didn't like because he turned, for a brief and terrifying second, to look at her.

Great Goddess Uni, please don't let us die.

"You look a little green around the gills, babe. You sure you're okay?"

"Yes, I'm fine. Please, just keep your eyes on the... path."

He laughed, his expression transforming with the accompanying smile, and her breath caught.

Damn, the man was quite gorgeous. And that was saying something coming from a goddess who'd had her pick of beautiful men and gods over the millennia.

But Caligo wasn't her typical pretty boy. He was young, yes, but he was rougher around the edges than any other man she'd ever wanted.

His broken nose only added to his charm. Same for his mouth. His bottom lip was a straight slash, yet his upper curved into a bow. And his eyes... that gray should be cold, but she went hot all over when he slid his gaze her way.

Which it did again, making her heart pound—and not in fear.

"Babe, I've got this path memorized like the back of my hand. I know every rut, every turn, every tree along the way. We're not gonna crash."

Surprisingly, his words eased her fear. A bit. "How can you be so sure?"

"Because I haven't yet."

"There's always a first time," she muttered under her breath.

Obviously, he heard her because he laughed again, shook his head, and pressed a little harder on the gas pedal.

They drove in silence for a few minutes while she continued to study him. His hair was military short on the sides and longer on the top, where it hung down into bangs, the color a deep black but shot through with strands of pure silver. He couldn't be more than twenty-five so she had to wonder why he was going gray already. Probably the high-stress life he led—

They bumped over something, the tires leaving the road for a few terrifying moments, and Tessa closed her eyes. But not before watching Caligo wrench the steering wheel to the right. She froze, certain they were about to head over a cliff.

Then relief allowed her to draw in a deep breath as she realized they'd turned onto a paved road.

Thank you, Great Mother Goddess.

"So where are we going?" She finally dared to open her eyes and look at her surroundings. The road didn't look familiar, but she wasn't overly familiar with this part of Berks County.

"To see Salvatorus, find out if he's learned anything else. He must've had a reason for sending you to me specifically. I want to know what it is."

"Other than the fact that you're Cimmerian?"

"Yeah, other than that."

"What else could it be?"

He slid a glance her way. "Haven't gotten that far."

He must have seen fear surge though her. "Relax, Goddess. I've done this a few times. I'm good at thinking on my feet."

"Please, call me Tessa."

"What's with the name, anyway? I thought you said it was Thesan."

She snorted. "Says the man named Darkness."

Cal shrugged, though he'd always wondered if his dad had been trying too hard when he'd slapped that name on him. "I never got a choice, Your Highness. Cimmerian males are named by their fathers when they come of age, usually around thirteen or so."

"What do they call you before then?"

Half-blood. Inferior. Unworthy. "'Son of' whatever your father's name is."

"And you were 'Son of...'"

"Diritas."

In his peripheral vision, he saw her mouth drop open. "Your dad's name is Cruelty?"

"Yeah."

She shook her head. "Wow, you're a happy people, aren't you?"

"This coming from the goddess of a pantheon that demanded ritual sacrifice."

Her cute little nose wrinkled. "We did not demand it. I personally preferred my offerings alive, twenty years old and very male, thank you *very* much. Besides, that was a long time ago. We've evolved since then."

And that should have been a reminder that he was much lower on the cosmic scale than she was. He was mortal. Stronger, faster, longer lived, and with a few more features than regular humans, sure. But he would eventually die, and he could be killed if he was stupid enough to let that happen. And deities tended to change the rules mid-job.

Still, there was something about this one... something he liked, even though he didn't want to. "Liked 'em young, huh?"

Her lips turned up slightly at the corners. "I still do."

Lust shot straight into his bloodstream like an adrenaline dump.

Damn, he really liked his—this, this little blonde goddess. "Then you're outta luck with me, babe. I'm nearly a hundred."

"Really?" She turned to study him again, the heat in her eyes making his lust boil. "Well, compared to me, *babe*, you're still in diapers."

Yeah, when you looked at it that way...

"So," he steered back to safer waters, "what else can you tell me about Charun and his plans?"

She shrugged. "Honestly, not that much. A month ago, Mlakukh, another member of the FoGEs, called me to say she'd been having dark, violent nightmares that depressed her so much, she began to feel suicidal. She said she thought she knew what they were, that Charun was searching for her. She disappeared two weeks ago, and my dreams have gotten worse since then."

"Wait, what the hell are the Fogies?"

"The Forgotten Goddesses of Etruria."

His eyebrows lifted in amusement. "You got a clubhouse to go with the name or what?"

He glanced her way, and there was that smile again, the one that screwed with his brain. "Actually, we do, but we have a strict no-men-allowed policy. There are about ten of us who no longer serve our people in the way we once did. We've become... somewhat obsolete yet we remain. Anyway, Mel went missing a week ago."

"Can deities off themselves?"

She nodded. "Especially those of us who... no longer have much function. But it is forbidden, specifically because Charun can absorb our spirit when we arrive in Aitás and become more powerful from it."

"And the deities are afraid of Charun."

"Of course. Who wouldn't be? If he consumes you, you cease to exist. Mel knew this and was rightly terrified. She couldn't sleep for fear of dreaming. She grew tired and listless, moody and angry. Nothing she did was right. Nothing I did could soothe her. Then she disappeared."

"How do you know she didn't just go into hiding?"

Tessa shook her head. "Because there is nowhere on this earth where she could hide. And Invol, the plane of existence where we were born, is no long open to us."

Cal knew that, probably better than she did. He knew about the other planes of existence beyond this one, the underworlds and the otherworlds, which some called heaven and hell.

"The only place I could not check was Aitás," Tessa continued. "None of the goddesses are strong enough to resist Charun's power. Not anymore.

She sighed. "And then my dreams began to worsen."

Her face had turned almost green, and he reached for her hand without thinking. She flipped her palm up so she could lace her fingers with his, and her warmth struck him again.

He really needed to find out what was happening with that. Was he reverting? His father had always feared the possibility that Cal and his brother would regain their feelings and be less than full Cimmerian.

Cal hadn't felt any pain at all while fighting the demon. And he couldn't be upset that he felt Tessa's warmth. He wanted to feel more. All over his body.

Okay, time to get his head together. "Tell me about the dreams."

Her shiver shook her entire body. "They're awful. Just... so awful. Dark and bloody. Horrible."

Considering that this Etruscan goddess had lived through the Dark Ages, the Inquisition, and the Holocaust, these dreams must be excruciating.

Cal wanted to smash Charun into bits for daring to bring that fear to Tessa's expression. Then he thought of something.

"When was the last time you slept?"

"Your house."

That must have been when Charun discovered her location.

"When did you sleep before then?"

Her gaze narrowed and she bit at her bottom lip. "I'm not sure. Two weeks, maybe."

Shit, that wasn't good. "So, you're basically running on fumes."

And running out of time. How long could anyone, even a goddess, go without sleep?

"I'll be fine. For a while."

He glanced over at her again, noticing her frown. "Don't bullshit me. How do you feel?"

"I'm tired, but I have to admit the short rest helped. And the sex."

Her smile said maybe she wanted a repeat of what'd happened when she woke.

The sex had been the best of his life.

They fell silent as the road whipped by, the rolling green hills of southeastern Berks County giving way to fields and farms and then later to suburban sprawl.

After crossing the Schuylkill River on the Penn Street Bridge, they hit the city just before dawn, passing the Reading Area Community College campus before turning left into the heart of the city's south side. The center-city streets were still fairly deserted this early in the morning, but after they crossed Fifth Street, the activity level increased.

A few souls loitered on the street corners, prostitutes looking for one more john or drug dealers hoping for one more sale. A few people hung in the doorways of all-night groceries.

After turning east on Spruce, Cal wound his way through a half street and two alleys before stopping in front of Salvatorus's home.

From the outside, it looked like any other house on the block, a three-story, red-brick building surrounded by more of the same. The house was well maintained but not too much so. It didn't stick out in any way, and only someone familiar with Etruscan runes would realize what the decoration around the door frame was.

No one walked the streets here, but Cal hustled Tessa out of the car and up the walk to the front door. Already, he could see the weak morning rays of the sun. If he stayed out much longer, he'd burn. Not that he'd feel it, but he couldn't afford to be injured right now and he'd packed his shielded hoodie in his bag, not thinking he'd need it.

Once on the covered porch, he released Tessa to ring the bell.

"Come on, you little goat-legged bastard," he muttered. "Where the hell are you?"

He turned to make sure Tessa hadn't gone far and found her standing at the edge of the porch, facing east with her eyes closed and a smile on her face.

The sun broke over the horizon as the door opened.

"Hey, Cal. Didn't expect to see you yet." Salvatorus stepped to the side of the door and waved a hand, dropping the protection wards so Cal could enter.

Cal turned back to Tessa. "Come on, babe. Inside. Now."

She didn't answer, her expression one of reverence. And she didn't move.

"Fuck, Tessa. Now."

She sighed and took a few steps backward, close enough for him to grab her arm and pull her into the house.

"Sorry." Her lips turned up in a bittersweet smile. "It's dawn."

As if that said everything.

Cal took a deep breath, biting his tongue on his suddenly raging fear that this—their situation—was one giant clusterfuck about to happen.

"And the sun can't touch my skin or I burn, Tessa. Don't do that again."

"Match made in heaven, if you ask me." Salvatorus's rough New York accent broke through the silence that fell as Tessa stared at Cal with her mouth hanging open. "Well, you're both still in one piece. Come on in, and I'll get some coffee going. Lady, welcome back."

Tessa forced herself to look away from Cal and acknowledge Salvatorus's sweeping bow. How the *salbinelli* pulled that off so gracefully with those legs was a mystery even to her.

"Hello, Salvatorus. Thank you for inviting us into your home." And now that the formalities were over, she turned back to Cal. "What did you mean, the sun will burn you?"

As Salvatorus walked toward the back of the house, Cal started to pace the small entry hall. "Gods damn it, Tessa, when I tell you to move, you move."

His fierce growl didn't scare her. But what he'd said had. "Explain what you meant."

Cal ran a hand through his hair. "This isn't going to work. I knew this wouldn't work."

Oh, shit. He was having second thoughts, and that was all her fault. She'd assured him she would listen to his every command, and already she'd screwed up.

Fear sank low in her gut like a hot lead pellet, burning through her body. Damn it. She didn't want to lose him already.

"I'm sorry. Caligo, please." She reached for him, and her hand on his bare forearm stopped his restless movements. "It won't happen again. Now, tell me what you meant about the sun."

He lifted his head, and the anger she saw in his eyes wasn't directed at her. "Exactly what I said. If the sun touches my skin, it blisters and burns. The Cimmerians are born in the mist and shadows between the planes. We're comfortable in those shadows. We see more clearly in the dark than in the light. We blend into the dark.

"I have more resistance to the sun than most because my mother wasn't Cimmerian. But I still can't be exposed to the sun's rays for more than a few minutes before my skin starts to burn.

"And *you* are a sun goddess."

He stared at her, his expression hard, but his eyes... oh, they told a different story.

She squeezed his arm. "Then I'll stay out of the sun. I'm sorry, Caligo. Please—"

He bent his head and kissed her. Hard. With his hands on her shoulders, he pushed her backward until she hit the wall and trapped her there with his body.

The heat of his body seeped into hers, his scent so enticing. She let him plunder her mouth without protest, opening wider to take more of him.

He took the hint and thrust his tongue into her mouth, forcing her tongue to duel with his. When his hands slid down to land on her hips so he could tilt her pelvis into his, she ground herself against his rock-hard erection.

His groan lit her up like a firecracker exploding in her belly, and she wrapped her arms around his waist, smoothing her hands over his butt. He had such a great butt, firm and strong. When he thrust against her, as he did now, she felt the muscles tighten and release, even through his pants.

From his butt, her hands moved up to his slim waist and muscular back. His fingers tightened on her hips, and she felt his muscles ripple with the motion. So much strength. So much warmth.

Her hands lifted higher, stopping to knead his broad shoulders before moving down his arms and latching onto his bulging biceps as if they were her last chance for survival.

He kissed her like he wanted to get inside her body and stay there for hours. Which she didn't have a problem with. Not at all. Only...

"Hey," Salvatorus called from the kitchen. "Get your tongue out of her throat and come get some coffee. We need to talk."

Cal froze, said tongue retreating, but he kept his mouth on

hers for several more seconds. When he finally pulled away, he took a deep breath and opened his eyes.

"Cal—"

"Don't." His gaze burned into hers. "Just don't say anything right now. Sal's right. We gotta talk. And if you open your mouth now, I'm gonna take you upstairs and lock a door behind us. And then I'm gonna make you use that mouth on my body."

"SO YOU THINK JUST the fact that Tessa's with me will be enough to keep Charun from sending another demon after her?"

Sal nodded as he tapped a finger against his coffee mug. "Yeah. That's why I sent her to you. The Cimmerian reputation should be enough to keep him at bay. At least for now. But you have to stay close."

"But what about the others?" Tessa's soft voice held sadness. "He'll just go after Lusna or Alpan or Thalna or one of the others. We need to find a way to stop him."

"Tessa honey, I told you," Salvatorus said, "the only way I can think of to do that is to get the other Etruscan deities to accept that Charun is enough of a problem to pool their power and strengthen the wards holding him in Aitás."

And that, Cal knew, was the problem. He turned to look at Tessa. "You don't think you can talk enough of them into attempting it, do you?"

She shook her head, her expression grim. "There are a few who would. Selvans, Nortia, Tivr, and Lusna, for sure. Possibly Turan. Maybe Fufluns and Laran. But there are others who haven't been seen in centuries. Nethuns, Usil, Veive, Lucifer. We have no idea where they are or how to find them. And even if we could, I don't know that there would be enough to create the kind of power needed to strengthen the ward. It took Uni, Tinia, and Menrva to do it before they disappeared."

Cal heard the bitterness in Tessa's voice as she mentioned the three main deities of the Etruscans, the equivalent of Juno, Jupiter, and Minerva in the Roman pantheon. He heard the despair, too, over the desertion of those deities centuries earlier.

"The other goddesses like me," Tessa continued, "the members of the FoGEs, we no longer control that much power. Not even all together."

That bothered her. He saw it in the slump of her shoulders. He wanted to put his arm around her and pull her against him.

Damn it, that was just one big hole waiting to suck him in. Emotions made you weak. He knew that. And he and Tess had met less than half a day ago. Still...

"But if he consumes seven," Tessa shook her head, "maybe eight of us, combined with his own powers, Charun would have enough to escape Aitás."

Cal forced his gaze away from Tessa and turned back to the goat man. "And you don't think you can get some of the others to listen to you?"

Salvatorus shook his head. "Not a chance, at least not enough of them to make a difference. They're a damn stubborn bunch."

Much like all the rest of the deities he'd ever met. Stubborn, selfish. Stupid.

His gaze slid to Tessa. Maybe not all.

Shit.

"So... what?" Cal threw his hands in the air, wondering what the hell Salvatorus wanted him to do. "How are you supposed to stop a god intent on breaking out of his prison?"

Good question.

Tessa watched the men fall silent as she sipped hot chocolate. She could've used the caffeine in the coffee but she'd craved chocolate. Luckily for her, Salvatorus knew his goddesses and stocked four kinds of hot cocoa mix as well as dark and milk chocolate syrup.

She wished she could really enjoy the chocolate. The sweet had magical properties that allowed it work on the biochemistry of the deities. Unaffected by all diseases, man-made drugs, and most poisons, the deities had discovered many millennia earlier that chocolate acted as a sedative.

And she definitely needed one. Between the attempted kidnapping by the demon and Cal's kiss just now, she needed to calm down. She couldn't think clearly, and that would not help them.

"Have you told the other goddesses what's going on, Tessa?" Cal asked, drawing her back into the conversation. She took a few moments to think before answering.

"Not yet, no. I've been a little preoccupied." Trying to stay alive. "I can try to contact them, but it will be tough to get them all in one place at the same time. Deities can be notoriously difficult, and several have had, ah, disagreements over the years."

Cal snorted, his expression clearly showing he thought she'd understated the matter. Then he sighed, long and deep, as his expression became dead serious. "And you haven't tried to reach Uni or Tinia? To see if they'd help?"

She shook her head. "No. We've tried for centuries with no luck. Some believe they've deserted us for good."

Cal's gaze sharpened. "What do you believe?"

Another good question.

Did she, like some of her fellow deities, believe that Uni, the Great Mother Goddess, along with her consort, Tinia; sister goddess, Menrva; Ani, God of the Sky; and Voltumna, God of the Seasons, had deliberately abandoned their children, the Etruscan pantheon, and cut them off from Invol, the ancestral home of the Etruscan gods? That they'd hidden the entrance to

Invol and forced their children to live forever on this plane of existence?

Some days...

Then she shook her head. "I honestly don't know. I would like to believe they're unable to answer us. That something is keeping them from us. But I don't know what that could be."

Something flickered in Cal's gaze, something she couldn't identify. "Could it be related to the problem you're having now?"

She frowned. "Do you mean, do I think Charun has gotten to them? No. If he had their power," she had to stop to yawn, putting her hand over her mouth before shaking her head and continuing, "nothing would stop him from leaving Aitás. The world would be overrun with the dead, and Charun would spread death and destruction in this world."

Cal's eyes narrowed as he thought about that, still holding her gaze. "You need to rest."

Her mouth tried to quirk into a smile. "You know I can't do that."

"Then at least lie down. If you don't, you'll get pissy and not listen to me and then we'll both be in deep shit."

Now, she couldn't stop her grin. "Oh my, Cal. You have such a way with words. Do you talk to all the girls like that or only ones you have sex with?"

The man didn't flush, didn't look away, didn't show any sign of discomfort at her teasing.

And she *was* teasing. Salvatorus started to laugh, and finally Cal broke their gaze to give the *salbinelli* a glare.

"Sounds like you've been on your best behavior, Cal."

"Yeah, well, fuck you, Goat-Legs. If you'd given me a heads-up—"

"You would've been long gone when she showed up." Salvatorus gave Cal the finger. "Don't piss me off, boy, or I'll give you a tail."

Cal shut up. Salvatorus had the power to do it.

"Lady, the kid's right, though. You look beat." Salvatorus stood, his hooves clopping against the tile floor as he walked to the sink. "Why don't you take the bedroom at the top of the stairs? I gotta go out for a while, see a few people. You'll be safe here for now. We'll talk when I get back."

THE ROOM WAS DARK, spare, and comfortably cool, with a double bed, a wooden chair, and a television sitting on top of a low chest.

Cal immediately grabbed the remote, sat in the chair, and began to press buttons. Tessa had to stifle a laugh. No matter what race, religion, creed... hell, no matter the species, some things were universal.

Sitting on the bed, her back against the pillows, she let him flip around the channels for a few minutes.

"How old are you?" she asked when he stopped at the Syfy Channel for an *X-Files* rerun.

"Ninety-eight."

"Really? I didn't realize Cimmerians were so long-lived. But you're still a child, comparatively."

He flashed her a quick look. "Well, you did say you like 'em young."

Yes, she did. And she really liked him. "Please, anyone is young compared to me." She shifted into a more comfortable position on the bed. "So, how did you come to live in the States, Cal? You said you were born in Cimer. When did you leave?"

He didn't bother to look at her, just continued to stare at the television. "A few years after my naming. I traveled for a while, did a few jobs. Discovered I liked this part of the world so this is where I decided to stay."

Now, why did she think there was more to that story? "Are there many Cimmerians living here, like you do, instead of in Cimer?"

He nodded. "Some."

Ooh-kay. This was worse than pulling teeth. Tessa decided. But she wasn't going to give up just yet. "So, tell me about your culture. I only know that your people are carefully bred to produce great warriors."

His face contorted into a grimace that he quickly wiped away. "Yeah, well, don't believe everything you hear."

She frowned. "What do you mean?"

"It means some of us aren't as carefully bred as others."

She heard something in his tone that made her consider his words carefully. "You're not purebred Cimmerian, are you?"

Now he did look at her, lifting one eyebrow. "Wanna trade me in for a better model?"

Not on her life. And it very well might be her life. She rolled her eyes at him. "Don't be foolish. You're stuck with me. I'd just like to get to know you a little better since we're going to be spending some time in close proximity. I'm going to assume your father is Cimmerian. So who's your mother?"

He leaned back in the chair, the wry smile on his face hiding the uneasiness she could sense in him. "Pretty sure of yourself, huh? But you're right, my mother's *aguane*, which is probably why Sal sent you to me specifically."

Tessa's mouth dropped open for a brief second before she recovered. *Aguane* were elusive, elemental Etruscan water spirits. Unlike many Etruscan descendants, most *aguane* had remained in their homes in Etruria, while the other *Fata* had moved to the United States two centuries earlier.

Aguane were solitary beings for the most part, but obviously some of them had found Cimmerian men irresistible. And, she had to admit, who could blame them, if Cimmerians looked like Cal? "How long have they been living there?" she asked.

"My mom's been living in Cimer for more than a century. And she's not the only one."

"But... why? Why would they choose to leave their forests and hills for the constant gloom of Cimer?"

His expression hardened, and he turned to stare straight into her eyes. She felt the force of that stare like a physical weight. "You've never been to Cimer, have you, Goddess? It's not all gloom and doom. We might not have sunlight, but it's not always pitch black. There are many levels of darkness, from the pale blue of morning to the silver gray of day, light purple in twilight, and velvet black at high midnight.

"Those colors soothe the soul. They camouflage and hide and conceal. The dark holds a freedom you can't find in the light, where your every move, your every fault is revealed. Cimer is forest and wood, mountains and valleys. And a lot of beautiful water."

Tessa found his deep, raspy voice completely mesmerizing, her gaze riveted to his beautiful mouth as he painted a picture of his world.

"At one time, our people had settlements all over Cimer, but now we live mostly in communal homes in the valley near the river. The boys and girls sleep in separate barracks, away from our parents' homes. Easier to train that way."

"Are you trained from birth?"

He nodded. "Pretty much so."

"Are there many children of mixed blood, like you?"

He held her gaze steadily. "No. When I left, there were three. I don't know how many there might be now."

"So you had to be doubly tough, didn't you?"

He didn't answer right away, seeming to think about his

response as his gaze slid back to the TV for a few seconds. "We all had it tough."

"But they were harder on you because you were part *Fata*."

Cal knew Tessa wasn't asking him a question. He heard it in her soft tone and saw it in the rueful tilt of her lips. "I'm a better warrior for it."

"But who do you fight for now?"

He shrugged. "Whoever pays."

"No matter what they want that help for?"

Ah, he knew what she wanted to know. "We don't wage war against the undeserving, no matter who that might be. We might be considered mercenaries, but we have to believe in the cause."

"Do many of your people leave Cimer for this plane?"

"No."

"So what do your people do?"

He couldn't answer that question truthfully. He had sworn an oath he would never break. "We exist. Like you."

"Exist." Her mouth twisted in a sad little curve. "That's a good word. Don't you ever want to go back?"

His answer was immediate and didn't require any thought. "Not if you paid me. I love it here. There's always something to do, always someone to do." There was that wicked smile again. "What about you, Lady? Would you leave this world? If you could?"

She blinked, as if processing his question. Then she frowned as her gaze turned inward. "I don't know. After the gates to Invol were lost to us, it wasn't an option. I... I guess I'd have to give it a lot of thought. I still have duties that I perform for the Etruscan races. Ones I enjoy."

Good. He needed to get her onto another subject so he sank back, trying to get as comfortable as he could on the hard chair. "Like what?"

"Well, I'm a damn good midwife." Her back straightened

and her little chin pointed higher. "I've yet to lose a baby or a mother."

"Good track record."

"I think so."

He shifted on the chair again. Wouldn't have to worry about falling asleep on this thing. His ass hurt too much.

"Cal, why don't you come sit over here?" She patted the bed beside her. "You'll be more comfortable."

Yeah, he would be. But he'd be way too close to her. Because even though they weren't talking about sex, the time they'd spent on his bed played on an endless loop in the back of his mind. He thought about the softness of her skin. Of the warmth he'd felt and shouldn't have.

Neither of them could afford for him to be distracted.

"I'm fine here."

Her lips kicked up into a smile. "No, you're not. What are you worried about? It's not like we haven't had sex. And since we're stuck here all day and I can't sleep…"

She let her implied suggestion hang there, tempting him closer. Her soft grin shouldn't have lit a fire in his gut, but it did. His cock stiffened in his pants, pulsing with blood and heat. He wanted her. Hell, all she needed to do was be in the same room and he wanted to tear her clothes off.

And why the hell shouldn't he have her? She was right. She couldn't sleep, so neither could he. They were safe here, at least for the time being.

Why couldn't they relieve a little stress? That first time had damn near blown his mind. He could only imagine how good it would be if he let her use her hands…

But if something happened to her on his watch…

He tried to tear his gaze away from hers but couldn't manage it. "Why don't we just watch a little—"

"Are you afraid of me?"

He heard the indignation, but that twinkle in her eyes made him grin. Afraid? "No. But you're paying me to protect you, and I can't do that if I'm fucking your brains out."

"Well," her smile turned wicked, "we didn't exactly discuss payment for your... protection services."

His cock throbbed.

Holy hell, if she smiled at him like that, with that heated look in her eyes, he'd take whatever payment she offered.

Lust tightened his balls and his cock hardened even more. His body urged him to crawl onto the bed, strip her naked, and fuck her, hard and for the rest of the day, until the sun sank and they could safely head out.

But where the hell were they going to go? Was there anywhere he could take her that she'd be safe from Charun?

His place was warded out the ass but not against someone like Charun. The most Cal had been able to manage had been to rig an early warning system where deities were concerned.

That's what had tipped him off about Tessa.

But was there anything he could do about Charun personally? Anything he could do to stop the god from breaking out of Aitás?

He'd had an idea earlier tonight, one he'd let sit in the back of his brain to simmer. It was risky and might actually put her closer to the bastard who was searching for her. And it would require a major sacrifice on his part but—

"You're thinking again."

He caught her gaze, those bright blue eyes giving him a glimpse of the sky as he'd never see it. She'd already given him a taste of a warmth he'd never thought he'd feel again, and his addiction to it grew every time he touched her.

He shouldn't touch her. Hadn't meant to, but his body had acted without checking with his brain. He rose to his feet and walked to the bed, staring down at her as she smiled up at him.

And when she reached for him, that was all it took to break his control.

He fell on her as if he'd been starved without her, his mouth slanting over hers and grinding down to force her to open to him. She did so without hesitation, and he shoved his tongue into her mouth. He was rough with her, but instinct had taken over and he couldn't stop.

His tongue wound around hers while his hands stripped her clothes from her body. Sun-kissed flesh, sleek and soft under his hands.

Her arms wrapped around him, and her fingers dug into his back through his shirt. He felt her moan, felt her hot breath seep into his mouth. It acted like a shot of adrenaline straight into his heart. Lust exploded in his gut, potent and powerful.

He needed to feel her hands on his skin.

Sitting back on his haunches long enough to rip his shirt over his head, he dropped back onto her, her breasts smashed to his chest, nipples digging into his skin like tiny branding irons. He wanted to crawl inside all that heat and let it burn him to ash.

He dropped his mouth on hers again and took that heat into him as her hands splayed on his back and began to explore his skin. They moved from his neck to his shoulders, smoothing along the muscle and then down his spine to his pants. She traced the waistband, raising goose bumps on his flesh and making his already hard cock throb.

She grazed along his waist twice before she slipped her hand under the fabric and scraped at his skin with her nails. His groan made her entire body quiver under his, and her hands shot around to the front for the button.

She squirmed and wiggled, but she couldn't release the button because he was pressed too tightly against her.

The next thing he knew, he was flat on his back with Tessa

sitting on his thighs and one hand slipping the button through the hole.

She'd flipped him as if he didn't weigh a hundred pounds more than she did.

Gods damn, that really shouldn't turn him on as hard as it did. He shouldn't want her to smile at him like that, so sweet and hot that his lungs had to fight to suck in air.

Dangerous. Too damn dangerous to his peace of mind.

He shouldn't want to touch her so badly that his hands shook as he cupped her breasts, kneading the firm flesh and playing with the nipples until they pebbled and turned rock hard. And oh so fucking warm.

God, her heat...

She reached for his zipper and began to release it tooth by tooth, her eyes glued to the sight.

With each audible snick, he gritted his teeth in brutal frustration. He felt every small release of metal against the sensitive skin of his shaft. It was torture, more punishing than having his nails torn from his fingers because the promise of the pleasure to come was killing him.

When she'd finally lowered the zipper all the way, she leaned forward. His mouth dried as he expected her kiss, but she bypassed his lips and whispered into his ear. "Grab the headboard and don't let go, Cal." Her voice became a husky growl. "It's your turn to squirm."

Oh, fuck. He was ready to come just from the sound of her voice.

He did exactly as she told him without thought, so completely caught up by the desire in her eyes and the heat of her hands as they gripped his pants and boxers and started to pull them off his legs.

They didn't go easily. They fit like a glove, and his cock was so hard and thick that she had to work at it. But once she'd gotten them over his hips and down below his knees, she stopped, trapping his legs.

"That's to ensure you don't go far if you try to get away." Her smile let him know she didn't think he was going anywhere. "I don't have any ropes on me."

"I'll do whatever you tell me, babe. Just don't stop."

Lifting her hand, she stuck her index finger between her lips, sucked on it, and then slid it out slowly. It left her lips with an audible pop, and his cock jerked against his stomach.

Straddling his thighs, she pressed that finger to the taut head of his shaft and circled the slit, combining his moisture with hers. He nearly jumped out of his skin when she used her nail to lead her finger down to his balls, drawn up tight between his legs.

She flicked at the puckered skin then pressed her finger between the balls and slid back to rub the perineum. Combined with her warmth and the sensitive skin there, her teasing made the slats of the headboard creak in his hands as he forced himself to hold tight.

"Such a good listener," she crooned. "You should be rewarded for that."

Fisting his shaft and pulling it straight up, she bent and took just the head into her mouth.

Fucking hell, he'd never felt anything so damn good. He growled out his pleasure, thumping his head hard into the pillow and thrusting up to get more of his cock into that wet heat.

"Ah, ah, ah." She drew back, her smile wicked. "I'll let you know when you can move."

She sank over him again, holding his hips steady so he couldn't thrust, and played her tongue over the head of his cock, bathing it with delicate flicks.

After she'd tormented the head, she licked down his shaft

and tongued his balls, sucking each one into her mouth before licking her way back to the tip. Then she opened her mouth over him again and encased the head. As she sucked on him hard, he nearly came right then.

He wanted to come, wanted to shoot in her mouth, but he also wanted more. He wanted her to scrape her teeth on the shaft as she took him deeper. As if she'd read his mind, she did exactly that, letting her lips sink lower until he swore he couldn't go any further. Then she swallowed and took him deeper.

The sensation forced another groan from him and an involuntary thrust, which he curbed before he choked her. He felt her lips curve into a smile around him. She began to pull away until she reached the tip and sucked him back in.

She did this several times, and each time he had to control the ever-increasing urge to shoot into her mouth. That's not where he wanted to end this.

"Tessa." That's all he could say, no matter what he wanted. "Tessa."

With one last suck and a kiss on the tip of his cock, she shifted forward, angled his cock up with one hand, and lowered herself onto his shaft in one smooth movement.

Fuck. She was wet, so fucking wet. He slid in without effort, like satin on smooth skin. But then her sheath clenched around him like a fist and nearly did him in.

As her head fell back, her spine arched and her hands reached behind her for his thighs.

Then she started to ride him.

Her hair spilled down her back, the tips brushing against his thighs and sending a bolt of erotic sensation through his body. Releasing the headboard, he reached for her hips. He needed to have his hands on her. The heat of her scorched him. He felt like he was touching the sun. So hot.

Closer. He needed to get closer, needed to hold her against him. Sitting upright, he pulled her legs around his waist and seated his shaft even more deeply inside her. Then he swung his legs over the side of the bed and planted his feet on the floor.

"Come on, babe. Now you can ride me."

Her smile was pure bliss, her eyes slits of electric blue as she wrapped her arms around his shoulders and stopped, damn her. "I thought I was."

She tightened her sheath around him until he gasped.

"Better this way," he managed to say. "Tess, please..."

Finally, she started to move, but she took her damn time about it. She went slow, moving only in tiny increments up and down his shaft. As if he'd last forever. Jesus, he wanted to, but the angle of penetration hit that sweet spot right on the underside of his cock, making him pant.

He was going to come, could feel it building in his balls with each slow glide of her sheath. But he wasn't going without her. Moving his hands until his thumbs were positioned on either side of her clit, he pressed in, squeezing that little organ with each downward slide and rubbing it against his cock.

She gasped, her eyes opening wide, and... holy shit, her eyes glowed, hypnotic, stunning, and so fucking warm. He exploded just as she came with a gasp.

FIVE

Tessa clung to Cal's broad shoulders, feeling his cock pulsing his seed into her, warm and full. He held her just as tightly, his chest rising and falling so fast she worried she might have injured him inadvertently.

Because something else had just happened. Something she hadn't experienced in centuries. Power. True power. Goddess power. Only a flash, a quick burn in her blood, and then gone. But she had felt it.

What the hell had happened?

"Tess?" His voice sounded muffled. "You okay?"

Okay? Great Mother Goddess, she was more than okay.

"Yes. I'm fine."

He turned his face into her neck, nuzzling his nose under her ear, his warm breath tickling the sensitive skin there. His cock twitched inside her and she tightened around him, eliciting another male groan.

"Babe, you do that again and I'm not going to be responsible for my actions."

She ran her hands through his hair before cradling his head

in her palms, wanting to keep him right there. "Then I guess I'll just have to take my chances. So far, things are looking up."

Still, until she figured out what had just happened with her powers, he was probably right. They should take a break. With a sigh, she loosened her arms so he could lift her off his lap and set her on the bed.

He looked straight into her eyes, his so dark the pinpricks of white gleamed like diamonds. "Are you gonna tell me what just happened? Your eyes glowed, babe. Like they were lit from the inside."

She drew in a sharp breath. "You're sure that's what you saw?"

He nodded. "You may have blown my mind, but I know what I saw. What the hell was that?"

Shaking her head, she sat back on the bed, drawing her knees up to her chest as he pulled up his pants then lay across the foot of the bed on his side, head propped on his hand.

Sweet Blessed Mother Goddess, the man was beautiful. A true throwback to the men of ancient Etruria. Broad, muscled, implacable, and unswerving. He'd pushed every one of her buttons and found a few more she hadn't realized she had.

She'd never really fallen for the strong, silent type before. In her heyday as a beloved goddess, she'd liked young men who made her laugh and had the stamina to keep up with her, in bed and out. Artists and musicians, rakes and hellions. Men with that glint in their eyes and a devil-may-care attitude.

Gods didn't usually do it for her, though she'd had her share of them. They were too sure of themselves by half and much too bossy, used to getting their own way and having everyone bow down to them.

Okay, maybe she'd been just a little guilty of that herself, but becoming obsolete certainly took some of the wind out of your sails.

Now, though, here she sat, with a man who was both supremely confident and too damn used to having his own way and yet...

"Why do I think you're trying to avoid my question?" the object of her obsession asked in a droll voice. "And why are you looking at me like I'm chocolate cake and you're PMSing?"

See? That's why he was so fascinating to her. He was too sure of himself, too cocky, but he made her smile with his dry humor.

When was the last time a man had made her smile?

She raised an imperious eyebrow at him. "I'll have you know, I don't do PMS. Although chocolate cake would taste mighty fine eaten off your body."

His cheeks flushed the slightest shade of pink, barely visible against his skin tone but there nonetheless. And her smile became a full-out grin... that died the second he shackled her ankle with his hand. The touch of his skin against hers made her want to melt into the sheets.

"I might be able to arrange that," he said. "But first—"

"Tessa, Cal," Salvatorus yelled from the first floor. "I'm back."

The *salbinelli's* voice startled Tessa out of her daydreams of spreading chocolate frosting around Cal's nipples and licking it off.

With a shake of his head, Cal broke their gaze and slid off the bed before holding out his hand to her. "Let's go, Lady. Let's see if the Goat-Man's got any great ideas."

SALVATORUS DIDN'T HAVE any great ideas. He had one fucking awful idea. He wanted to have a party. With goddesses.

Okay, Salvatorus hadn't called it a party. He'd called it a

strategy session, and before Cal had been able to open his mouth to protest, Nortia had appeared in Salvatorus's living room. And that didn't mean she walked through the door. One second she wasn't there, and the next, she was holding court with Salvatorus fawning all over her.

The Etruscan Goddess of Fate wore bright red, stiletto-heeled pumps and a fuck-me black leather dress that molded to each of her generous curves like a second skin. Like Tessa, she was a blonde, but Nortia's hair was silver and gold and she looked like a goddamn Barbie doll.

Tessa left Cal's side to hug the woman who could have been her sister. Hell, she probably was her sister.

And his brain really was not going to go there. No way. No how.

"Ooh, Tess honey, where'd you get the eye candy? Are you willing to share, or can you get me one of my own?"

Nortia had let her bright blue gaze travel all the hell over him like he was a piece of meat, and like a geek at his first school dance, he'd made a beeline for the kitchen where he'd been holed up with a beer ever since.

"Jesus Christ, Goat-Legs. This is my worst fucking nightmare. And you know it, don't you, you sick bastard?"

Salvatorus's laugh had a maniacal sound to it. "Suck it up, Conan. This isn't about you."

Cal bared his teeth and actually growled at the *salbinelli*. The bastard knew just how to needle him... and how he felt about deities. That was probably why Salvatorus hadn't told him the house was going to be infested with goddesses.

So what are you doing with Tessa?

Not going there, either. "Yeah, well, you think this is a smart idea, having them all in one place at one time? If Charun finds them, it'll be like an all-you-can-eat buffet, for fuck's sake."

"*Vaffanculo*, son. He's not going to know they're here. This place is untouchable and they're all awake. You need to chill the fuck out. Nervousness does not become you."

Salvatorus put the lid on the blender and hit the button, ruining perfectly good tequila by making it pink and prissy.

Cal picked up his glass of whiskey and took a healthy swallow. "I don't know what the hell you're talking about."

Salvatorus snorted and stomped one hoof on the floor. "Yeah, you're full of shit, Caligo. How long have we known each other? Forty years? Fifty, since I brought you up here?"

More like sixty, and Cal owed the guy his life, but he wasn't going to give the *salbinelli* any more ammunition than he already had. In all that time, Salvatorus had never mentioned the circumstances that had brought them together. It still shamed Cal to even think about it.

To be chained, shackled like an animal, and forced to beat weaker men into bloody masses of broken flesh for rich men's entertainment. His own stupidity had led to his imprisonment. And he owed a huge debt of gratitude to Salvatorus for getting him out.

To his credit, the *salbinelli* had never played that card to get Cal to help him. He didn't need to.

Cal knew all too well what he owed Salvatorus. So he kept his mouth shut, knowing the guy would get around to saying what he had to say on his own schedule.

"Look, kid. I sent her to you for a reason. You know that, right?"

"Because you like to bust my balls."

Salvatorus snorted. "Yeah, that was a benefit. But you're a sucker for the damsel in distress. You can't help yourself. I knew you'd protect her."

"What about the others? Who's going to protect them?"

Salvatorus began to pour the margaritas into glasses. "Don't need to worry about them. At least, not yet. Charun's focused on Tessa at the moment. Haven't been able to figure out why. She's one of the goddesses with the least amount of power left to her. Doesn't make any damn sense."

The *salbinelli* paused, his head cocked to the side as if listening. "Looks like they're all here. Hey, do me a favor and grab the other tray, will ya?"

"Christ, now I'm a goddamn waiter," Cal muttered under his breath but he followed Salvatorus's lead. After a deep breath, he headed back into a situation that would put a healthy sense of fear in any man.

A room full of honest-to—Huh, guess "honest-to-god" didn't really fit in this situation, considering the room was full of real-life goddesses.

Though his father had frowned on anything resembling religion, his mother had insisted Cal be versed in the Etruscan pantheon since he was half Etruscan. At night, his mother would sit on his bed and tell him ancient stories about the exploits of the deities. About their petty jealousies and epic battles. She'd mostly concentrated on the gods, but he knew enough to know each of the six women by sight.

Nortia and Tessa sat on a loveseat by the front window, which was draped in two layers of heavy cotton so no one from the outside could see in.

Lusna, Goddess of the Moon, sat cross-legged on an oversized chair facing the couch. Her midnight-black hair, shot through with streaks of pure moonlight, trailed down her back, and her gray eyes followed his every move as he entered.

The two redheads sitting on the couch had to be Turan, Goddess of Beauty, and Artume, Goddess of Nature.

He didn't see the last woman until he'd entered the room. She sat in what looked like a haze of shadow in a dark corner, close to the other women but obviously apart. Her dark hair was neither black nor brown but somewhere in between, her eyes a curious pale blue and her features soft and lovely.

As Sal walked straight to her, the woman's face lit up, a smile curving her lips. Just as quickly, she covered her reaction and her expression turned pleasant as she took the glass Salvatorus handed to her.

No one else seemed to notice the exchange as the other goddesses continued their quiet conversations. But Cal got the impression they were deliberately ignoring the goddess and the *salbinelli*.

Who the hell was she? What—

Fuck it. Not his business. None of this should be his business.

And yet, here he was in a roomful of Etruscan deities of the female persuasion, wondering how the hell he'd gotten dragged into saving them from the God of the Underworld.

No, not all of them.

Just one in particular.

His gaze shifted, caught, and tangled with Tessa's sky-blue eyes. She stared back at him, her mouth turned up at the corners.

Desire began to burn through his blood, hot and thick, and the urge to toss her over his shoulder like a caveman and take her back upstairs beat in his chest. As if she could read his mind, her smile got just a little bit wicked and the glasses on the tray he was carrying did a little shimmy.

"I think I'll take my drink before I'm wearing it," Nortia drawled, snapping Cal's attention back to what he was doing. "Do we tip with dollar bills down your pants, or is that only when you start to strip?"

"Nortia." Tessa's voice held a very soft edge. "Don't."

"Oh, don't worry, Tess." Artume sighed. "You know her bark's worse than her bite."

"But I do like to bite." Nortia's smile softened as Cal stiffened. "Don't worry. I don't poach. Well, not anymore." Then she sighed. "Okay, I guess we should get this little meeting started."

"Yes, we should. I don't have much time," the Shadow Goddess spoke, her voice a husky mix of smoke and honey. "I'll be missed."

"I know, Tilly," Tessa turned to her. "But I'm very glad you could come. Because we need to talk about Charun."

Ten minutes later, Tessa had finished filling in the goddesses on what was happening and Cal's stomach had twisted into a tight knot.

"That bastard. I had no idea he was up to anything like this."

Tilly, who Salvatorus had finally told Cal was Hinthial, Lady of the Shadows, started to pace the room like an expectant father.

"Of course you didn't know." Nortia waved one hand in the air as if batting away a fly. "Sit down, Tilly, you're going to make me tired. Besides, you know what he's like. He doesn't tell anyone anything. Hell, no one's spoken to him in centuries."

"I have, though it has been a while." Hinthial continued to pace. "Come to think of it, I don't know where he's staying in Aitás , . Has he given any indication of why he's targeting you?"

Tessa shook her head. "My impression is that he wants out. I don't have any idea why."

"So can't we just ask him?" Artumes looked at Hinthial. "Maybe if we held a rational dialogue—"

"Oh, please." Turan's snort of laughter cut off her sister goddess. "When have you ever known Charun to be rational? He's been down in the dark too long. And if we try to speak to him, he may be able to target us and send a demon for us. No, we need to find a way to strengthen the wards on the gate."

"We could try to do it ourselves," Nortia said.

"And if we fail, we could accidentally loosen the wards." Turan shook her head. "I don't think that's an option as of yet."

"But the only ones strong enough to do that are gone," Nortia said.

"Not gone." Lusna finally spoke, her tone coated in bitterness. "Just uninterested."

Like a wet blanket on a cold night, Lusna's comment brought the mood down and the goddesses all fell silent.

Cal knew what they thought. That the Etruscan founding deities had abandoned them, retreated to Invol, and barred the gate behind them, leaving the rest to fend for themselves. He watched Tessa's expression fall and felt an almost undeniable urge to comfort her. So he crossed his arms over his chest and planted his feet.

"Has anyone even tried to contact them recently?" Turan finally broke the silence. "Maybe we should start there."

Tessa's sharpened gaze landed on Turan. "Every other attempt to contact them has failed. Why would you think now would be any different?"

"Well," Turan glanced at Cal, her little smile immediately putting him on guard, "I don't think it can hurt to try. Especially if you offer up a sacrifice."

"YOU REALLY THINK this has any chance in hell of working?"

Cal stared down at her as she sat on the couch. His hands rested on his lean hips, and a scowl marked his handsome face.

Tessa had said good-bye to her sister goddesses a few minutes earlier and Salvatorus had headed for the kitchen, where she heard pots and pans clanking in the sink.

Already she felt whatever confidence she'd had in Turan's suggestion begin to seep away like air from a pricked balloon. But at least the suggestion was something to go on. Tessa was so tired, literally exhausted from lack of rest and sick of being someone's prey.

She was willing to try anything at this point, but Cal, didn't seem willing to get with the program. And that pricked at her pride. "I think if we don't try, we'll never know. Besides, it's not like we haven't had sex before."

"Yeah, well, before I wasn't being offered up on an altar as a sex sacrifice."

She cringed a bit at the wording, although he wasn't far off the mark. "You're not a sacrifice, Cal. There will be no blood spilled. I just need a little sex magic to fuel my request."

"And I'm just supposed to spread myself on the altar and let you do me?"

Her eyebrows lifted. "Would that be such a bad thing?"

His eyes rolled. "Christ, Tessa, I'm not a fucking sex toy."

Fine. He didn't want to have sex with her. She could accept that. But damn him for making her feel like her heart was being squeezed in a vise.

"You know what? You're absolutely right. You're not my sex toy. So I guess I just need to go out and find someone who won't mind giving me a hand. Or a cock, as the case may be."

She stood and began to stalk away but two strong arms wrapped around her from behind, lifting her off her feet. "Oh, no you don't. Don't even think about it, Lady. You will not go out trolling the streets for meat for your little party."

Struggling in his arms, she kicked at his shins but that didn't seem to bother him at all. He just continued to hold on. "You think this is a party? This is my life. It may not be much of a life lately, but it's all I have and I'm not ready to give it up."

She wasn't aware she was crying until she felt moisture drip onto her chest and slip down between her breasts.

"Hey, babe. Shh," Cal whispered in her ear. "I'm sorry. I didn't mean... Damn it, just calm down. There's no need for tears."

Yes, there was, actually. Other than this one suggestion, her sisters hadn't come up with anything to help her. Not that she'd thought they would, but she'd been hoping maybe they'd see something she hadn't, something she'd missed. Some way to avoid Charun's ever-tightening noose.

She didn't know why he'd targeted her, why he'd want the tiny amount of power she retained. She only knew she didn't want to live her life in constant fear of being consumed. She already lived with the fact that she was obsolete.

And thinking about that made the tears fall faster.

Against her back, she felt Cal groan. "Come on, Tessa. Don't cry."

That, of course, made the tears flow even harder.

With a muttered curse, Cal easily maneuvered her until he held her in his arms and against his chest. Her arms wrapped around his shoulders, and she rested her cheek against his broad chest.

How was she supposed to fight off a god intent on destroying her when she was so weak? When the man who'd brought her more pleasure than she'd had in centuries refused to help her?

She caught back a sob.

"Damn it, that's enough." Cal finally growled. "I'll do it. Okay? We'll go to Uni's Temple tonight, and we'll try your sex sacrifice. Just give me a break and don't cry anymore."

It took her a few more minutes before she could shut off the tears. They hadn't been for show. She was tired... of running, of hiding, of being unable to save herself.

She hated needing anyone. She was a goddess.

And yet... Hadn't she felt power pulse through her the last time she and Cal had had sex? He'd even commented on it.

Maybe this crazy plan did actually have some merit.

After a deep breath, she lifted her head from his chest to stare up at him. He'd carried her to the couch and eased down onto the cushion with her, his arms still wrapped tight around her.

It felt good. Comforting. Right. That made her smile, and some of the tension she'd seen on his face eased.

"So... what?" Cal said. "We go to Uni's Temple, have sex on the altar, and ask the Involuti to help you contain Charun?"

"That's the general idea, yes." She sighed, lifting her hand to cup his strong jaw and feeling the play of muscle and bone beneath. "Does that sound so repulsive?"

Cal shook his head. "Sex with you is not repulsive. But this is a Hail Mary pass, Tess. It's not really a plan."

"Then what can it hurt to try until you come up with something better?"

His sigh sounded long suffering. "You're safe here. Maybe you shouldn't leave until I have a better idea—"

"No." She shook her head for added emphasis. "I'm not going to continue to cower like I have been the past few weeks. It might only have one chance in a million of working, but even that's more than we have right—"

Before she realized what he intended, Cal dropped his mouth on hers for a breath-stealing kiss. He caught her off guard, the passion behind the kiss hot and fiery. She let it wash over her like the warmth of the sun. Bright, burning heat flooded over her skin and sank into her body.

She opened her mouth to him, letting his tongue sweep inside and tangle with hers. Her body went boneless as she responded to his passion. To the need in his kiss.

She'd never felt so worshipped in her very long life.

When he would have drawn back, she clung, keeping him tied to her, his mouth against hers, his body hard and ready. She tasted heat on his lips and strength in her arms and let both sink into her.

When she finally opened her eyes to stare up into his, she saw a hint of confusion there. And maybe resignation. But about what?

Going with her to Uni's Temple?

Was he really that reluctant for her to leave Sal's? Charun's demons would not dare abduct a goddess from Uni's Temple. She should be safe there. But she couldn't live there.

With a sigh, Cal set her on her feet and stood as well. She had to look up to see his face. She liked that he was big and broad and strong. She liked pretty much everything about this man.

"Come on." He took her hand and tugged her along with him toward the kitchen. "Let's go see if Goat-Legs has anything to eat. I want the sun to be long gone before we head out."

CAL HAD NEVER BEEN to Uni's Temple. He'd never had a reason.

He didn't worship the Etruscan gods. He didn't worship any gods. They always managed to screw you over somehow.

Pretty much the same reason he'd never taken a woman as a bed partner for more than a few months: because they could be almost as fickle as goddesses.

Now he was heading willingly into a temple to let a goddess fuck him on an altar. When the hell had his life become part of *The Twilight Zone*?

"Pull in there." Tessa pointed at a narrow, one-way alley

that cut off from Chestnut Street and ran parallel with Fifth Street. "There's a parking lot behind the building."

From the alley, he turned into the parking lot marked by a sign that read, "Parking for Marelli's Trattoria."

A city institution for more than a hundred years, Marelli's Trattoria served the best traditional Italian food in the state, maybe in the entire country. No, Cal had never been in the temple, but Marelli's was the only place he could get food that came close to being as good as his mom's.

The building was nearly two hundred years old and had been built specifically as camouflage for the temple. Originally, it had been all apartments, renting only to Etruscans, of course. The restaurant had been a later addition.

No cars sat in the lot at close to 1 a.m., and the only light came from the street lamp halfway down the block.

Beside him, Tessa reached for the door handle, but he stopped her before she could open it. "Sit tight a minute. Let me take a look around first."

Tessa opened her mouth but closed it right away. Good. She was learning.

As he cut the engine on the Jeep, he let his gaze roam over their surroundings. From this lot, all they could see were the back sides of buildings. The buildings on this side of the alley fronted Fifth Street. Those on the other fronted Pearl Street.

He saw no one at all. Curtains covered most of the windows, and those that weren't covered were dark.

"Where's the entrance to the temple?"

Tessa pointed at a barely visible breezeway between the Trattoria and the next building. "It's just a few feet in there. The door's locked, unless you have a key." She smiled at him, though he could barely see her in the dark. "Or you have your very own goddess."

The words tripped around his brain for a few seconds. His very own goddess.

Yeah, right.

"Stick close, Tessa. I don't want any surprises."

Getting out of the Jeep, he walked around to open her door and grabbed her hand to help her out.

The heat of her skin against his nearly made him drop her hand. He still had no explanation for that, but now wasn't the time to examine it.

She didn't say anything when he kept hold of her hand. Instead, she pressed closer to him, so close he could smell the faint, floral scent of her skin. Which he should not be thinking about right now. No way.

As they entered the pitch-black breezeway, he expected Tessa to let him lead. His eyesight was exceptional in the dark, but she didn't hesitate as she headed straight for the door he saw ahead on the left.

It looked like any other service entrance to any other building, a big slab of metal with a handle. However, this door was made of iron, not steel, and you didn't necessarily need a key to open it. Tessa only had to touch it, and it swung wide for them to pass through.

As the door closed behind them and the lock clicked into place, faint light began to glow around them. Not enough to blind him, as bright fluorescents could. Just enough to lead the way down the short, plain hall.

"If you have any weapons, you'll need to leave them out here, Cal. You can't take them into the temple."

He thought about arguing, but her expression made it clear that wouldn't matter.

Not a problem. He didn't need weapons. He was one.

Pulling the iron blades from his boots, he set them in a small alcove by the arched wooden door in front of them and took the thin wire garrote from his pocket and put it there, too.

Tessa looked at the garrote and the blades then back to him and lifted one eyebrow.

"That's all I got, babe. Let's do this."

That sweet-hot smile she gave him made his cock twitch and start to harden. "I plan to."

As she pushed open the door, the mellow glow of candlelight surrounded him when he walked into the temple. For a brief second, Cal had the sense he was stepping back in time. Back to when there were no such things as electric lights or cars or computers. Back to when a belief in deities, plural, didn't make you politically incorrect. Or just plain crazy.

But this place would make a believer out of anyone.

The white marble walls shone with the red-tinged light of the torches on the walls. Real, oil-burning torches. Enough of them to light every nook and cranny of the temple.

The large room was open to the top of the three-story building. Three columns on each side of a center aisle led to a wooden altar decorated with gold leaf at the front of the room.

Cal let his gaze deliberately pass over that altar while he checked out the rest of the space.

Wooden benches lined the sides of the temple, leaving the floor mosaic bare for everyone to see.

It must have taken months to create the beautifully intricate piece of art featuring various members of the *Fata* and *Enu*, the two main races of the Etruscans, in a forest of huge trees.

A half-hidden *salbinelli* chased after a winged *folletta*, the *folletta*'s smile teasing, sexy. A mass of tiny human-shaped *candelas*, glowing like fireflies, danced around a tree stump as a *linchetti* couple, their pointed ears prominently displayed, lay entwined on a moonlit patch of grass.

Several *lucani* howled at the bright moon, the wolves a sleek gray or midnight black, while a *strega* bent over a moon bowl set on a tree stump and her male companion held an athame in his hands.

In his peripheral vision, Cal saw Tessa take a seat on one of the benches closest to the altar. He felt her gaze follow him as he circled the room, checking for any other access points. He found only the entrance they'd used, and he walked back to that door to flip down the solid iron bar that acted as a lock. Probably wouldn't do a damn bit of good if someone really wanted in, but still...

Finally, he walked back to the altar. The top slab was as wide as a twin bed and as slick and shiny as glass. He'd probably slide off the damn thing.

Christ, was he really going to go through with this?

He reached up to scratch the nagging itch at the back of his skull.

"So... what? You want me to just strip down and spread myself out here?"

Her laughter sent a wave of lust so fucking hot through his blood, he thought he'd come right then.

He turned to find Tessa standing only inches from him, smiling up at him. "I think we have time for a little foreplay, unless you're really that eager to get down to business."

He crossed his arms across his chest so he didn't grab her, strip her, and spread her on the altar so he could worship her with his mouth. "So why don't you tell me how this is supposed to work, Tess."

"Well..." She walked over to run her hand along the top of the altar and circled until she was on the opposite side from Cal. "The idea of a sacrifice is to offer something to the gods in order for them to hear your plea. In this case, I'm hoping the energy we create by having sex will give my plea the necessary power to reach the Involuti. Uni, in particular, since this is her temple, and theoretically at least, she should be monitoring what goes on here."

"The Involuti have been gone for centuries. You can't tell me someone hasn't tried this before."

Her brows lifted as she faced him across the altar. "Are you trying to find out if you'll be the first sex sacrifice on this altar?"

He shook his head. "I wasn't born yesterday. I'm sure this table's seen more action than a by-the-hour hotel. But that's my point. No one's heard from the Involuti. Not since they left. What makes you think you will?"

Doubt crept like ice through Tessa's veins, making her shiver.

And that's the problem, isn't it?

She had no faith that she'd be able to reach Uni, much less convince the Great Mother Goddess to listen to her.

Why would Uni hear Tessa's plea when she'd not answered anyone else's in all the centuries since Uni and the rest of the founding gods of the Etruscans had returned to Invol and hidden the gate?

"Shit, Tessa." Cal sighed, his expression one of self-disgust. "Look, forget I said that."

Shaking her head, she gave him a brief smile. "No, you've got a valid point. I just don't know what else to do."

"Then we've got nothing to lose."

So true. She'd already lost so much that she was obsolete. And really sick of feeling sorry for herself.

Maybe, just maybe, she could find a way to make this work. Especially with Cal by her side. Or on top. Or beneath.

Yes, sex with Cal was much more pleasant to contemplate than failure.

She let her gaze eat him up from head to toe. The man truly was a prime specimen of masculinity. Definitely not one of the pretty boys she typically found to amuse herself.

No, Cal wouldn't bow to her every whim or fawn over her beauty. Not that she needed to be fawned over. Well, maybe a little fawning would be nice.

It always made her feel... loved.

Of course, Cal didn't love her. She still wasn't sure why he'd agreed to protect her. He hadn't seemed to like her very much in the beginning, though he did seem to be warming to her.

Or maybe that was just the sex. The sex was really good.

As her lips began to curve in a smile, his gaze narrowed. Before she could say anything, though, he beat her to it.

"So, how do you want to do this?"

Her smile grew. "The normal way, I suppose. Unless you have a few more kinks that I don't know about. Would you like me to conjure up some rope? Or would you like me to tie you down this time?"

Was that curiosity she saw flash in his eyes? She'd bet her last ounce of power that the man had never been anything but the dominant one in bed.

He crossed his arms over his broad chest. "Got a secret fetish, Lady?"

Did she? "Can't say that I do. Although, I must say I enjoyed having you tie me up."

"Then maybe you should conjure up those ropes."

Oh, the man simply took her breath away when he decided to turn on the dominant charm. And she did mean dominant.

Even though he stood across the altar from her, he still loomed over her. She wasn't tall and leggy like Turan. She was petite and curved, and she'd never had any complaints from her lovers. Not that they would dare criticize her to her face, but most of her bed partners had seemed genuinely happy to bed her. In fact, they'd been so genuinely happy that most of them would have bent over backwards to please her.

Which had gotten old more than five centuries ago.

"What are you thinking, Tessa?"

Cal's soft query refocused her attention on him. Those beautiful gray eyes had a laser focus on hers.

"I'm thinking you should be naked."

"Maybe I'm thinking the same thing."

Now this was more like it. This wasn't dire consequences and end-of-the-world gloom. This was fun.

Her heart pounded in a steadily increasing rhythm as her sex moistened and clenched. She swallowed and let her lips part to draw in much-needed air. His gaze dropped to her lips and suddenly she couldn't breathe. There just wasn't enough oxygen in the room.

"Take your clothes off for me, Tessa. Start at the top and work your way down."

Her stomach clenched with desire at the heat in his voice. She had her hands on the first button of her sleeveless, white cotton top before she realized she'd reached for it.

No, she needed to slow down. They had hours before daybreak, when they would need to be back at Salvatorus's house. And this time she was determined to make the man sweat.

Without releasing his gaze, she slowly worked each button through its hole. They gave up without a fight, but she made sure the shirt didn't gap open and reveal too much before she was ready.

She wanted him to beg for her mercy.

When her fingers reached the last button, Cal finally let his gaze slip south. She swore she felt his gaze like a physical caress against her skin, trailing heat wherever it touched.

The shirt had only parted a few inches but she was naked beneath it, and she knew he could see the hint of curved flesh in that gap. Brushing her fingertips along her plump curves, she watched his eyes narrow and his cheeks flush to a ruddy hue.

With deliberate motions, she allowed her fingers to slip beneath the shirt to find the pebbled tip of her breast. She sucked in a breath at the shiver of sensation that coursed through her at the touch, the tug that tightened and moistened her sex.

Her eyelids fluttered, wanting to close as her fingertips rimmed her areole, sending shivers of electricity through her to her clit. Stroking down, she cupped the mounds and marveled at the softness of her skin on the underside of her breasts and at the way Cal watched her every move through slitted eyes.

She swore she should be able to see steam rising between them. The air itself felt heavy and hot as she drew it into her lungs, having to work harder for each breath. With one final stroke to the underside of her breast, her fingers started down, brushing against the skin of her stomach, zings of electricity piercing straight to her clit.

Her pussy heated and moistened, her sheath contracting, begging for him to fill it. She imagined the sense of fullness, the ecstasy of his possession, and her muscles clenched in anticipation.

Her lips parted to draw in air and she watched him do the same.

As her fingers reached the catch on her thin denim skirt, he blew out a hard breath, the harsh sound adding to her own arousal. Her abs tightened at the metallic hiss of her zipper releasing, and her breasts ached for his touch.

She imagined Cal putting his lips around them and sucking them into his mouth, flicking at the pebbled tips with his tongue.

The man had such a talented tongue. Just the thought of it made her weak with lust, made her lips part and—

"Push it off, Tessa. Now."

She gasped as her eyes shot open to stare up into Cal's, now directly above her. She hadn't realized she'd closed them while she taunted him and herself. She'd gotten lost in sensation, lost in expectation.

And Cal had taken the opportunity to round the altar. He stood right next to her, only inches separating them.

She gazed at him through a haze of sexual hunger, noting how lust made the muscles in his jaw clench tight and throb beneath the skin. How his gray eyes grew stormy and dark.

And how much rigid strength he held in his body. So much control. She wanted to break that control, wanted him to reach for her and tear the clothes off her body.

Her muscles quivered with need, her stomach jumping with anticipation.

Still, this was fun, too.

With her thumbs hooked in the skirt's waistband, she wiggled her hips from side to side to get the tight denim down her legs. Okay, maybe she didn't need to do the little shimmy, but Cal certainly seemed to enjoy it, if the muscles jumping along his jaw were any indication.

When her skirt fell to her ankles, it got caught on her wedge-heeled sandals so she kicked those off and stepped out of the skirt.

Now he really did tower over her, and every feminine atom in her body lit up like fireworks on the Fourth of July.

"Take the top off now."

She cocked her head to the side as she reached for her shirt but stopped short of actually touching it. "I think it's my turn to ask for something."

One side of his mouth curled up in the most mouthwatering way. "And what makes you think that?"

"Well, I have taken off my skirt and shoes."

"Fine." He reached for his belt, unbuckled it, and withdrew it from the loops of his pants with a slither. Folding it in half, he held it in his hands, giving it a slight snap that made her wonder what it would feel like tapping against her skin.

"Shirt," he said. "Now."

Ooh, the growl in his voice sent a blast of heat directly to her sex.

Shrugging her shoulders, she let the shirt slide down her arms and puddle on the floor at her feet.

Now his gaze dropped to her chest and she felt the weight of it like a physical caress against her skin. Her nipples tightened even more, if that was possible.

"You have the most beautiful tits."

She couldn't help herself. She had to laugh. "You're such a charmer."

He shook his head, his gaze stuck on her breasts. "Never said I was tame, baby."

She gave another wiggle, making sure the mounds bounced just the tiniest bit. She didn't wear a bra. Gravity didn't mean much to a goddess. She was as she would always be. Exactly one hundred and fifteen pounds and five feet, two inches, a perfect C-cup with absolutely no sag, and with a flat stomach and rounded hips.

"Tame is for dogs and accountants."

"Gods damn, you really are fucking beautiful."

Pleasure suffused her from head to toe. She'd always known she pleased men with her looks, but never had that meant more than it did at this moment. With this man. Whose cock bulged and strained against his zipper in the most tempting of ways.

Her mouth dried with wanting.

She had to swallow before she could speak again. "I think I deserve a little more than your belt."

Lifting his gaze from her chest, he stared into her eyes for several seconds before setting the belt on the altar at his side, still within reach. Then he grabbed the hem of his shirt and whipped it over his head.

And her mouth became as dry as the Sahara. Oh, Blessed Goddess, the man should have been a god himself.

He had a truly magnificent chest, broad and hard and so well defined. Even though he couldn't be in the sun, his skin held a slight tan that appeared even darker in the light of the oil lights. The muscles of his pecs bunched and shifted beneath that skin, though he wasn't flexing or showing off. He merely had to move his arms, the biceps bulging with strength, to make his body respond in beautiful ways.

Her lips longed to suck on those flat brown nipples, peaked and hard. She wanted to taste him, bite him, and when she'd done that, she'd move down to the ridges of his abs, so clearly defined.

He had a faint sprinkling of dark hair over his chest that narrowed to a line that disappeared into the waistband of his black pants. She wanted to let her tongue follow that line as her fingers worked the button on those pants. She wanted to get her mouth on his cock again, to suck on him until he came in her mouth.

"You keep looking at me like that, and I won't be responsible for my actions."

With an effort, she drew her gaze back up his body, though her smile was gone. "What about your pants?"

"You do it. Just don't touch my cock. You touch me and this may all be over."

"You have too much control for that, Cal."

"Not around you, apparently." His voice hissed through clenched teeth as she carefully pushed the button on his pants through its hole. But she didn't get to work on the zipper because Cal swore under his breath and lifted her onto the altar.

The smooth surface of the polished wood beneath her

buttocks and thighs should have been cool to the touch, but she barely noticed it as Cal put his mouth over her lips and bullied his tongue past her teeth to curl around hers.

With both hands on her face, he controlled her head, moving her into the perfect position to ravage her mouth.

Her arms circled his broad shoulders before she splayed her hands flat against his back, feeling the play of muscle under his warm skin as his tongue teased and tempted.

The heat of his body felt like a furnace blast against her skin, but she wanted him pressed against her. She urged him closer until her breasts were flattened against his chest.

Then she felt him still.

Lifting his mouth from her, he let his lips brush against her cheek until he spoke directly into her ear. "Lie back and spread your legs. And don't move."

She nearly whimpered but managed not to embarrass herself that badly. As her heart beat a mile a minute, she complied, though she took her time doing it.

When she felt her back hit the surface, she crossed her arms behind her head and waited just a few seconds before she spread her legs. Cal's gaze immediately dropped to her mound. Then he placed his hands on the inside of her thighs and spread her even wider.

"I can smell your arousal, Tessa. Spicy and sweet. I'm gonna taste you in a few minutes, but first I'm gonna make you beg for it."

His hands began to knead her thighs, his thumbs brushing higher and higher until they just swept over the delicate spot where her lacy thong covered the lips of her sex.

And because she couldn't help but rise to his taunt, she said, "Goddesses don't beg, Cimmerian."

His wicked smile made her breath catch in her throat. "You will. Keep your legs open, baby, and no touching."

Without further warning, he bent until his mouth hovered a hair's breadth away from her pussy. The lace of her thong heated, becoming a torment on the slick and already swollen lips of her sex. Moisture, thick and fragrant, slipped from her body as his tongue swiped across the lace.

He licked at her until the lace was soaked through and clung almost painfully to her sex. Her breath rasped in her chest and her hands reached back to hold on to the edge of the altar.

The scent of sex perfumed the air around them until she thought she'd go mad with it.

"Cal."

She felt him smile against her even as he flicked his tongue over her clit in fitful little glances. "Ready to beg?"

Moaning, she shook her head and bit her bottom lip. She was not that easy.

"Didn't think so. I'm not ready to finish this yet anyway."

He pulled away, and this time a little moan did escape her. She barely managed not to reach for him, had caught herself just in time. He was daring her to touch him, but he'd learn she had more will power than that.

"Damn, you're so fucking pretty here."

Her eyes closed at the reverence in his voice, a tone she'd not heard in centuries. And when he used one finger to rub against the swollen nub of her clit, she bit her lip to keep from crying out.

"Hope you're not attached to these, babe, 'cause they're about to become scrap material."

His teeth scraped against her left hip for one brief second before he tugged on the tiny bow holding her thong together. The string unraveled, making her squirm against him as he moved to do the same to the other side.

"Like opening a present," he growled against her mound, his breath ruffling the curls there. "God, you're soaking wet."

"You make me that way."

"You're gonna feel like heaven when I sink my cock in you. Just not yet."

She hoped she didn't melt into a puddle while she waited.

With her eyes closed, her other senses intensified. Her pussy clenched and ached to be filled. Her skin craved his touch.

With a moan, she arched her hips, seeking his fingers.

He rewarded her with a slight, stinging slap on her mound.

She sucked in a sharp breath. "Cal—"

"Don't move." His voice had lowered to a growl. "And don't worry. You'll get what you need. But on my time."

She felt him move again, felt his breath brush higher on her stomach, near her navel. Then his tongue dipped into the little indentation. Shivers raced through her as he licked a path back to her mound and finally, *finally*, his tongue flicked against her naked clit.

A sigh of relief played over her lips but only for a brief second as his hands slid under her ass and lifted her to his mouth. He used his teeth and tongue on her clit, working her with a single-minded purpose, dedicated only to bringing her pleasure.

His fingers clutched her buttocks, separating the cheeks then squeezing them together, stretching the tender tissues there. A short, sharp orgasm claimed her when he pressed the flat of his tongue against her clit but it cut off when he withdrew.

"Oh, not yet, baby." His voice had deepened even further, down to a husky, sexy growl. "We've got a lot of energy to build up if we want to reach through the gates to Invol."

Groaning, Tessa shook her head. "I don't give a rat's ass about Invol. Just fuck me."

He laughed, but she heard the strain in his tone. "Don't say I didn't warn you about pushing me, babe."

His mouth descended once again, and he sucked on her lower lips with a passionate frenzy that made her twist and fight against his hold so she could wrap her legs around him and hold him there.

But he proved too strong as his hands moved to her thighs again, holding her open as he ate at her.

She felt her climax build in short, sharp bursts of pleasure that continued to build into a grinding ache.

She didn't know how long he held her at the edge, but when he finally pushed her over, she cried out as a fierce, hard clenching of her sex left her longing for more when he pulled away.

The handsome angles of his face showed the sharp edges of lust. "Beg now, Tess. Come on, baby. You know you want to."

Reaching for his biceps, she pulled her head up just enough to look into his eyes. "Please, Cal. Fuck me now. I'm begging you. I need you."

With a growl that made her sex clench with painful intensity, he released her hips, ripped off his boots and pants, then caught her ankles and lifted them to rest against his left shoulder.

"You're gonna be so tight this way, Tessa. Christ, I can feel how hot you are. It's burning me, baby."

His every word made her lust burn hotter. And when he used his free hand to grab his cock and rub the head in the moisture coating her sex, she thought she'd combust.

"So fucking hot." His voice tantalized, teased.

"Stop torturing me, Cal. Please."

"Don't worry, baby. I'll make it better. I swear."

She found him to be a man of his word a second later as he began to work his cock into her tight sheath. Strong and thick,

Cal's cock stretched the delicate tissues of her pussy as he sank deep.

Tessa fought to keep her eyes open, to watch his expression harden with fierce desire as he was overcome by passion. But her own pleasure sabotaged her. The joy she got from watching him take her, the pleasure of watching him succumb, saturated her senses.

Her head fell back onto the altar and she let herself be transported by bliss. And as she did, as he slid inside her with ever-increasing motion, his thrusts becoming forceful and less measured, less controlled, she felt power rise up inside her.

It was that maddeningly elusive, heartbreakingly familiar power she'd thought she'd lost. The power that had once been so intrinsic to her nature and had been so elusive in the past few centuries.

Power this man awoke.

She barely had time to collect her thoughts as Cal groaned and began to pound into her. Each stroke cranked her lust higher and wound her hotter until finally she felt the knot of tension in her lower body snap.

She came again, and this time it was hotter, brighter, sharper. Her body bowed, her pussy taking him as deep as he could go while his cock jerked and pulsed, warmth spilling from him into her.

And just as she started to come down, she remembered why exactly they were there.

She began to murmur the ritual prayer to the Great Mother Goddess.

SIX

His cock still twitching inside her, Cal opened his eyes in time to see Tessa gasp in pleasure and arch her back, forcing him even farther into her body.

Gods damn, she was so fucking tight that he never wanted to leave her body. They could just stay here and fuck until they both succumbed to starvation.

Everywhere their skin touched, he felt her heat. It acted like crack to an addict. He craved it, soaked it in, wanted more of it. And felt his will tremble before it.

Which was one step further than he was willing to go on this journey.

Thankfully, her eyes closed and her lips began to move. He realized she'd started to pray.

He knew the ancient Etruscan language only because his mom spoke it and made sure he knew enough to understand it, if not speak it. With the after-effects of that mind-altering orgasm still coursing through his body, he didn't catch every word. Just enough that he recognized the gist of it.

But he couldn't mistake the power he felt emanating from her body like ripples on a pond. The fine hairs on his body rose.

This was stronger than he'd noticed before when her eyes had literally glowed.

As he watched, his lungs and heart rate finally starting to return to normal, her mouth curved in a smile so sinful that his cock thickened even though he'd come minutes earlier. And when her eyes opened, they were lit from within.

Damn, that really should freak him the hell out.

Instead, he couldn't help feeling a sense of satisfaction that *he* had done this to her. He'd tapped into something inside her that unleashed that power.

With more reluctance than was good for him, he slid free of her body and helped her to a seated position on the altar.

Seeing her naked skin gleaming in the firelight, he had the almost overwhelming urge to reach for her again, to pull her body flush against his so he could soak in her fascinating warmth.

Instead, he forced himself to take a step back, physically and mentally, to shut down the emotions that threatened to make him lose the edge he needed to stay sharp.

He watched her close those beautiful eyes and lay her hands flat on the surface of the altar. She continued to chant or pray or whatever the hell she was doing, but her voice had dropped below where even he could hear it.

He thought about pulling on his clothes but didn't want to disturb her, so he stood there, arms crossed over his chest.

Trying not to let his libido rule his brain, which shouldn't have been so damn hard to do.

Time passed as he stood there watching her. Watching the firelight play over her skin, watching the rise and fall of her breasts, letting his gaze stroke down her body to the juncture of her thighs.

His gaze caught and held on the perfect triangle of curls on her mound. He wondered what she'd do if he lowered her back to the altar so he could feast on her again. With an aborted sigh, he forced back the lust and waited for her to open her eyes.

Several minutes later, she drew in a deep breath and then released it on a sigh before she opened her eyes and smiled at him. That smile made muscles tighten and flex all over his body. Hell, even his dick twitched and the damn thing should have been sated.

"Finished?"

He tried to modulate his tone to hide the fact that he wanted her again. Of course, his nudity shot that all to hell because he'd already started to harden.

"Yes, thank you." She nodded but her smile had dialed down to slightly rueful. "For all the good it did. There was a time when our parents wouldn't think of ignoring our pleas. Or the pleas of their people. Uni and Tinia weren't fickle like the Roman and Greek gods. They were more..."

"Human?" Cal supplied.

"If you want to call it that." She shrugged, making her breasts bounce slightly.

And making Cal's libido crank up another notch. He really needed to watch that. Not her breasts. He watched those a little too much.

No, he had to keep his damn dick under control and not let it lead him, rather than the other way around. That meant he needed to take a step back. Focus on the problem at hand. Tessa's problem.

"So what happened? What made them retreat to Invol and hide the gates?"

Her smile disappeared completely now. "No one knows. We all have theories, but..."

Cal saw her gaze turn inward and pain creep onto her face. Some emotion he wasn't going to put a name to made his chest tighten, made him want to wrap his arms around her and comfort her.

And that would lead down a very dark path. He knew that for a fact.

At least, he *should* know that. He'd had enough experience with spoiled women, goddesses or not, to know that they really didn't give a shit about the mortals who gave the deities the power to exist.

Still, Tessa seemed... different?

Damn, he must be going soft.

Thrusting a hand toward her, he watched as she considered it for a brief second before taking it and allowing him to help her off the altar. When she stood on the floor, he released her and turned to gather their clothes.

"Cal, would it be possible to make a detour on the way back to Sal's?"

WHEN TESSA HAD TOLD Cal where she wanted to go, he'd given her a halfhearted argument but eventually he'd admitted the threat to her safety would be minimal. Now, if she were *eteri*, a regular human with no magical blood, then where she stood now would be extremely dangerous to her health.

Too narrow to allow cars, with one bare bulb shining midway down the dead-end passageway and throwing shadows all over the surrounding walls, the magical warding on this dark alley was designed to give an *eteri* a sense of extreme danger, enough to make even the most strong-hearted man turn and leave.

It beckoned Tessa to go further, to push through the darkness to the excitement that lay beyond. She wondered if Cal felt the same.

Though she couldn't see his face, she felt tension rolling off him in waves as she reached for the door handle. Like at the temple, only someone with Etruscan blood could open this door.

"Tessa—"

"Have you ever been to Downbelow, Cal?" She cut him off before he could demand she return to Sal's. She'd promised to follow his every order, and she wouldn't break her word. Still, if he forced her to run away and hide, she might never come out again.

After a moment, Cal sighed. "No, I've never been. I've only heard about it."

She turned to flash him a bright smile, which he probably couldn't see anyway. "Then you're in for a treat." She pushed open the door and stepped into utter darkness. "Close the door tight. The lights will come on in a sec."

Cal paused for a second before she felt him crowd in against her. As soon as she heard the click of the lock, the buzz of fluorescent lights crackled overhead and a dim glow suffused the hallway, a long stretch leading steadily down to an iron door nearly fifty yards away.

"The band will be on tonight," she said as she started toward the door. "They're truly amazing musicians. And I believe you'll find the place itself interesting. I can't believe you've never checked it out. Your Etruscan blood would guarantee you entry."

"I've just never gotten here."

"Because you're half Cimmerian?"

"Because I'm not much into public sex."

She laughed at his dry tone. "I think you know more about Downbelow than you're letting on. Anyway, we're still a little early for that part so we'll leave before we offend your delicate sensibilities."

He snorted and her smile spread.

"Babe, my sensibilities are far from delicate, but when I fuck, I don't want an audience."

She couldn't understand why. The man was a master of sex. But mortals could be downright prudish about things she never understood. "If you know so much about Downbelow, then you know sex magic fuels the wards to keep the place hidden."

"Yeah, I know that, too. Sounds like you come here a lot."

Her smile turned rueful. "I did. Once upon a time."

When Downbelow had first been constructed, nearly one hundred and fifty years earlier, she'd been a frequent visitor. The people, the dancing, the sex. The euphoria. It'd been better than drugs, which had no effect on her anyway, and she'd become addicted to the place.

For so many years after the Etruscan deities had followed their people across the ocean to America, life had been just that. Life. Not really living. Not like the old days, when their people had spent weeks, sometimes months, worshipping the deities, celebrating, sacrificing. Partying.

"Tessa?"

Blessed Goddess, she'd loved to party.

And the ancient Etruscans had adored her. Though she'd always been a minor deity in the pantheon—even before the Romans had risen and made most of the Etruscan deities obsolete—she'd been beloved by her people for her sweet and, yes, sunny disposition.

She'd laughed. She'd danced. She'd loved to make love. Hell, she'd loved anything that felt good.

But until Downbelow had been built, the Etruscans had lost their ability to play in the States. They'd been much more concerned with their survival, about fitting in and hiding their magic from the *eteri*.

The Etruscan deities remembered well the horror of the Inquisition and the witch hunts. With the rise of industry and science, their magic had become much easier to hide. No one believed in magic any more. Only in money and possessions.

"Tessa." Cal laid his hand on her shoulder and gave her a little shake to get her attention. But that wasn't what made her lift her gaze back to his. It was the warmth of his hand seeping into her skin. "We going in or not?"

She smiled over her shoulder at him. "Yes, sorry. Just..."

"Just what?"

She shook her head. "Nothing."

His gaze narrowed as if he might be able to read her thoughts before he turned back to the door. "Fine. Just stay behind me when we get in there. I need to get my bearings before..."

Before what?

She didn't ask. They both seemed to have thoughts they didn't want the other to know. So she nodded as she pushed the door open and then stepped aside to let him through.

She had a second to breathe in the musky, earthy scent of his skin before the magic inside the club tugged at her senses, drawing her into the heady atmosphere of the city's most exclusive club.

Cal had gone no more than a few feet into the club when he stopped. To his left, she watched his expression carefully, and though he showed no outward sign of amazement, she knew he had to be awed.

She still was every time she entered.

Who would ever guess that beneath the city of boxy brick and concrete was a perfectly formed amphitheater that looked like it'd been transported through time from ancient Etruria. Though the amphitheater was tiny in comparison to the architectural wonders built centuries earlier in Europe, Africa, and Asia, just the fact of its existence was amazing.

The builders had dug into the bedrock below the city,

creating a magnificent space—from the walls carved to look like marble columns to the ten circular rows of stone seating that encompassed the arena. Light poured down from the domed roof, which was decorated with a dazzling mural depicting the *circensis*. The mural appeared to be the source of the light, each bit of glass glowing from within, by magic, and illuminating the action below.

During the spring and summer, the arena held the *circensis*, the arena games. The Romans had devolved the games they'd stolen from the Etruscans into blood-thirsty spectacles of mass human destruction.

Those displays had always appalled Tessa and made her physically ill. She'd never lowered herself to attend the Romans' so-called "games." But she'd adored the Etruscan *circensis*. Hand-to-hand combat could get messy, yes, but neither opponent was allowed to beat the other to death. At least, not anymore.

Today, the games more resembled the *eteri*'s mixed martial-arts matches. Battles were between equally matched opponents. And no shape-changing was allowed unless both had the ability.

Still, the Etruscans enjoyed a little blood with their entertainment. Tessa believed that hard edge had kept their culture from disappearing all together.

In the center of the arena, the audience danced with complete abandon, the band on the wooden stage at the north end giving a rousing performance.

Gemma, the band's *strega*, hadn't yet started to chant the euphoria spell that would whip the crowd into a frenzy and make them furiously horny. When they paired off to have wild sex later, the energy they produced would fuel the wards on the arena and the light source.

The rest of the band played their instruments with blazing

precision as the singer, Dilby, screamed out the words to a song Tessa didn't recognize.

A tiny brunette with bright green eyes and a slender frame, Dilby could sing as sweetly as a child or scream like a metal god. To her left, lanky Caeles played his fingers over his guitar like he was caressing a woman. In contrast, Fosco raged at his guitar like a madman.

Nicolosa, on bass, had her eyes closed and no part of her body moved except her fingers, while Arruns sat cool and collected at the back, banging on his drums. Teresa held a tambourine in one hand and slapped at conga drums with the other, while Recco made his violin wail.

"Are they always this loud?"

She turned to see Cal's face screwed up in an expression of disgust, which made her laugh.

"Not your style?"

"Not really, no. Big-band swing is the only civilized music."

Her eyebrows lifted. "Do you dance?"

"You'll never find out here, Lady."

"Well, I want to dance." She fluttered her eyelashes at him and moved around him toward the floor. "So you either have to suck it up and dance with me or watch from the sidelines."

"I'll watch."

She gave him a teasing smile over her shoulder as she moved closer to the dance floor. "Your loss, big guy."

At one time, the arena would have been filled. Today, she walked halfway across the floor before she came to the outer edge of the crowd. She knew Cal followed behind her, but as she began to wade deeper into the dancers, he broke off to head into the stands.

There really was very little danger to her here. Most of these people didn't even know who she was. The Etruscans no longer worshipped her as they once had, especially the more human *Enu*.

The *Fata*, the Etruscan elemental race, led longer lives and followed the ancient traditions more closely. The *Enu* kept the secret of their lineage, but for many, the worship of their deities no longer comprised a large portion of their lives. If they even thought about it at all.

Sure, they sensed something about her as she brushed by them. Something different, something *other*. Most gave her a look, a smile, and then wondered who she was.

A few, mostly the shape-shifting *lucani*, realized who and what she was and bowed their heads as she passed by.

Her smile grew with each step, and by the time she'd reached the edge of the stage, the lingering sense of doom hanging over her head had mostly dissipated.

On stage, Dilby wrung out the last notes of the song and fell to the floor in a heap as the crowd cheered and bounced and geared up for the next song.

Dilby's head popped up, and she caught Tessa's eye. The girl's bright smile always reminded Tessa of someone, though she'd never been able to put her finger on who. And she'd never been able to figure out *what* Dilby was. *Enu*, *Fata*, or a combination of the two?

That didn't really matter in the grand scheme of things. What mattered was Dilby's uncanny ability to discern the mood of the crowd and to pick the right song at the right moment to keep the crowd on its feet and moving.

Dilby also knew exactly the kind of music Tessa loved and never failed to slip in a few of Tessa's favorites whenever she showed up. Which hadn't been often lately.

"Alright." Dilby spread her hands out to the crowd. "I know you know this one. Let's get our groove on, people!"

DISCO.

Christ, who the hell listened to disco anymore?

Cal had climbed into the stands and taken a seat high enough that he could see out into the crowd but low enough that he could be on the dance floor in seconds if he needed to be.

Tessa was right, though. Everything he'd heard about Downbelow made him comfortable enough to let her have a little space. Alright, maybe the space was for him. Fuck it all, he needed a breather.

From the moment he'd met Tessa, his life had been turned upside down. The things he thought he knew about himself were no longer true. All because of one tiny blonde of the variety he'd sworn never to have anything to do with again.

So why?

Good fucking question. Now if he only had an answer. Hell, an answer to anything would be helpful right now.

Why had Charun targeted her specifically? How could he stop a god? And why did he feel the warmth of her body?

If he stood next to her now, if he went out onto the dance floor and pulled her against him, he'd feel the heat of her skin. That close, he'd be able to see if her cheeks had turned pink as she danced. If her skin was slightly damp from exertion.

He wanted to run his tongue over her skin and taste the sweet heat of her.

Shit.

He shook his head and forced himself to check out the crowd. Young and energetic, they bounced and swayed and danced.

But his gaze quickly returned to Tessa.

She kept to herself at first, warming up. Arms over her head, she swayed as the song started, her eyes closed as if immersing herself in the music.

Hell, he wasn't even sure what it was. All he could make out was "last dance" and something about needing someone to hold her. He'd pretty much skipped the whole disco scene.

Fucking embarrassment to all mankind, if you asked him.

But Tessa must have loved it. As the song got faster, she moved even more seductively, her body a pure representation of the rhythm. Drawing men to her like bees to honey.

At first, she didn't seem to notice them. She just kept swaying by herself, as if lost in the music, even when one of those men put his hands on her hips and began moving his body along with hers.

Cal was halfway out of his seat before he realized he'd moved. Forcing himself to sit back down, he watched as she opened her eyes and looked over her shoulder at the man. Her smile made Cal's hands clench into fists. And when the asshole dancing with her turned her in his arms, Cal nearly ground his back teeth into dust.

Christ, he really was an idiot. Just because he'd fucked her didn't mean she'd pledged her undying troth. What the fuck was a troth anyway? And what the hell did it matter who she danced with?

Matters to you, you fucking imbecile. You want her for yourself.

He did. Even though he should know better.

You're an asshole.

Yeah, he had to agree with himself.

Forcing himself to stay seated, he watched Tessa bump and grind with several men through the course of the song. She didn't stick with anyone for long, and he had to admit she didn't seem to be encouraging the men in any way.

She didn't look at them the same way she looked at him,

which made the primitive part of his brain want to beat his chest in triumph and the rational part want to beat his head against the wall.

He knew which one was right. The head beating might actually do some good.

The band didn't take a break between one song and the next. They seamlessly headed into a hyped-up version of some song he'd heard playing on someone's radio. Something about being hot in here and taking off their clothes.

Benny Goodman, now that was a musician.

Shaking his head, Cal forced his gaze away from Tessa and scoped out the rest of the crowd. No one seemed to be paying her any undue attention.

Hell, he'd expected these people to be fawning all over her. She was a freaking *goddess*. Most acted as if they didn't know who she was.

Then again, maybe it wasn't an act.

Those who had made some motion of deference to her were older. Most of the people here looked like babies—

Cal stiffened as he watched a man detach himself from the back of the far edge of the crowd. The man's wry smile was so achingly familiar that Cal had to force himself to breathe through the sudden, heavy weight on his chest.

He watched the guy skirt around the crowd, smiling at friends and kissing several women who tried to cling to him. X had always drawn women like flies. He smiled. They swooned. He crooked his finger. They came running.

Blond and blue-eyed, X had a laugh that could make an entire room smile. And that covered a hell of a lot of other, less pleasant stuff.

"Caligo." The man slid into the stone seat next to Cal's, mimicking his laid-back position on the stairs. Whether on purpose or just by default, Cal didn't know.

"Extasis. You look well."

"I feel well, thanks. You look like shit."

"Yeah, well, I come by it naturally."

That made X turn his attention from the dance floor to look more closely at Cal.

"Never expected to see you here," X said after a few very long seconds of scrutiny. "As a matter of fact, I believe you once said you'd never be caught dead here."

"Have you memorized everything I ever said?"

"Only what I knew would come back to bite you later."

Cal's lips lifted in a reluctant smile. "Been to see Mom lately?"

"As a matter of fact, yes. She wanted to know if I'd seen you. Had to tell her no. Where the hell have you been, Cal?"

Cal turned to face his younger brother. X looked so much like their mom that Cal had envied him as a child. The dark gold hair, the sky-blue eyes, the upturned nose, and the sharp lines of his face. Built like a swimmer, the guy could wield a sword as well as Cal.

Though he'd never had to.

"Working." Cal knew X wouldn't be satisfied with his explanation. X had also inherited their mom's dogged determination. "What about you? How's the business?"

"Business is fine. You know that because I send you a report every six months. You do own half of it."

"I never wanted half of your business."

"You gave me the money to start it. Of course, it's half yours."

"X..." Cal sighed, shaking his head.

This was an old argument and one his brother would never let him win. Yes, Cal had bankrolled X twenty years earlier when he'd finally made the break from Cimer and moved here.

Cal had gotten him an apartment and set him up with a

bottomless bank account. Not that X had ever spent money like water. No, the kid had always been a wiz with numbers. Almost as good as he was with food.

Well, dessert, to be exact.

When X had finally decided what he'd wanted to do after those first few months out of Cimer, Cal knew his younger brother would be fine.

Today, X shipped his gourmet desserts all over the world.

"Got anything new in development?"

"You'd know if you stopped by more often."

"What am I? Your mother? Get a life, kid."

X snorted. "I've got one. You're the fool who needs one."

Cal felt his mouth curl up in a slight smile, which he crushed when X started to laugh.

"Damn, did I actually get a smile out of you? Holy shit, I can't believe you still remember how." X paused and Cal knew his brother was staring at him.

"So what are you doing here? And with someone like her? I thought you'd laid off that flavor after the last time you got your ass kicked so bad you nearly bought it. I don't want to have to patch your head back together again."

Cal didn't like to be reminded that he'd nearly bought it at the hand of some pussy-ass Greek god. Or that he'd had to call his brother for help. "It wasn't that bad."

X turned to stare at him, eyebrows raised. "Dude, your frickin' *skull* was exposed."

"When did you turn into a girl?"

"When did you become a fuck toy for someone like her?"

Damn good question. One that shouldn't make him want to take his brother's head off at the implied slur at Tessa.

He bit back the angry words before X had even more ammo to pick through and could get into Cal's head.

"Cal, what's going on?"

Looking into his brother's eyes, Cal saw confusion. And very real fear.

Cal sighed. "Nothing I can tell you about now but nothing you need to worry about. I've been taking care of myself for a long time, X. Stop acting like an old woman."

"But you're not indestructible."

"No, but I am fucking hard to kill and I'm not stupid."

As the current song wound into a crescendo, Cal's gaze tracked back onto the floor, searching for Tessa. He panicked for a brief second when he didn't see her right away, but then he caught the flash of her bright hair seconds before the lights went out.

"Fuck!" He jumped to his feet, waiting for his eyesight to adjust, ready to blast through the crowd to drag her out.

X stood next to him, his hand gripping Cal's shoulder. "Dude, calm down. It's part of the show. Pretty damn cool, too. Your lady'll be fine."

From out of the dark, the low throb of the bass made every bone in Cal's body rattle. Then the strobe lights kicked in, and he swore the entire arena began to shake as the crowd cried out. Whether in fear or excitement, he didn't know.

He didn't recognize the song, but if he had to guess, this was what the lowest level of hell sounded like. Sonuvabitch, his teeth *ached* and his sensitive ears began to ring.

"What the hell's going on?" He shouted his question in X's general direction and hoped his brother heard him.

X must have because he started to laugh. "Just watch. It's cool as hell."

Rationally, Cal knew nothing would happen to Tessa. Not here.

Still...

In the eerie flashes of the strobe light, the crowd roiled like one entity, bouncing up and down like a restless sea.

On stage, he saw the band's *strega*, Gemma, make her way to the center of the wooden platform. She stopped beside Dilby, the singer, and lifted her hands as if to appeal to the crowd. With the strobes going, the whole thing looked weird as hell, like a scene from a horror film, one where the main character had been drugged with a hallucinogen.

In the weird glow, Cal couldn't see if Gemma was speaking, but he sure as hell felt the power in the air around him begin to thicken.

Cal had no innate magic of his own, even though his mom was Etruscan. He couldn't cast worth a damn, though he was able to call power to him to open gates. Now X... He had ability, much to their father's dismay. Of course, X had just rubbed that in Cal's face like salt in a wound.

Cal slid a quick glance at his brother, his gaze narrowing at the nearly rapturous expression on X's face.

What the hell? Cal felt good. Just not *that* good.

Which was fine, because he needed his head on straight. He needed to watch out for Tessa.

His gaze shot back to the floor where the faces in the crowd had taken on the same expression. Where the hell was she?

Finally, he caught sight of her on the far side of the stage. Her face showed something different.

Power. She literally glowed with it.

Fuck. Where the hell did she get that much power?

She continued to dance with the crowd, writhing along with them. Sexy as all hell. Cal felt his body respond, blood pumping and an erection he couldn't deny. Aroused but with an increasing sense of anxiety.

No one else seemed to notice she was glowing. Most had their eyes closed as they bounced along to the music. Those that didn't stared at the stage.

They were waiting for something. Anticipation glazed the

air and beneath it, the magic continued to build. Now Cal felt it brush against his skin like velvet.

"X." Cal had to shout over the music to get his brother's attention.

"I know," his brother shouted back. "It's amazing, isn't it?"

"This is normal?"

"This is better than normal."

Shit, that's what he'd been afraid of.

His gaze locked on Tessa. She still wore that rapturous expression, but something else was going on. Something Tessa was doing affected the spell Gemma was spinning.

Maybe it was just the fact that Tessa was here. Or maybe the energy they'd created at the temple was boosting the *strega's* power.

Whatever was happening, it wasn't normal. And that probably meant trouble.

Cal stood, searching for Tessa where he'd seen her before, but the strobes wreaked havoc with his vision and he didn't see her immediately.

Shit, where the hell—There!

He caught a glimpse of her, farther away than she'd been the last time he'd seen her. Too damn far away.

Too many people were between them, and now the crowd seemed to be getting carried away. The dancers surged in one huge mass, starting to bang off each other like water bubbles in a boiling pot. Tessa was a pinball in the mix.

He had to get her out of here. Now. Before something—

An unseen force blew through the crowd like a breeze. More like a gale-force hurricane. Cal swore it went *through* his body, not just on the surface but through his actual molecules.

The dancers all faltered for a few brief seconds, as if stunned. Then they seemed to inhale as one body. Cal swore he actually heard them do it, even over the din of the music.

His gaze shot to the stage where Gemma had opened her eyes and was staring into the crowd, her expression stunned, her body frozen. The eerie sight made his skin crawl as the band continued to play, oblivious to their *strega's* distress.

Oblivious to the surging power Cal felt all around him.

Fuck.

Tessa. He had to get Tessa out of here now.

The strobes continued to fuck with his eyes. He needed help.

"X!"

His brother didn't respond; he just stared at the stage as if hypnotized.

This time Cal punctuated his brother's name with a punch to the shoulder. "X! Snap out of it. I need you."

His brother stumbled next to him, blinking. "What the fuck?"

"Something's wrong." Cal waved his hand out over the crowd. "I need your help to get Tessa out of here."

He could barely see X's expression, but he clearly heard the bemusement in his brother's voice, even over the music. "What the hell are you talking about? It's all good, man."

X acted like he was drugged. And maybe he was.

Cal had the bad feeling this ecstasy was going to come with a very big headache.

Possibly worse, if he didn't get Tessa out of here.

He was positive that whatever freaky thing was going down, it was tied to her.

"Gods damn it, X. I need to get Tessa out of here and I can't fucking see. You have to help me." He punctuated his words with another shot to X's shoulder, one that had his brother shaking his head as if coming out of a dream.

"Shit, man, that hurts... Why'd you... Whoa. Okay, you're right. Something's not right here."

"No shit." Cal felt frustration start to give way to fear. "I need you. The strobes are fucking with my eyes. I need to get Tessa out of here. Do you see her?"

They both turned to look out over the dance floor, where the audience had gotten even more frantic. The music continued to throb, but the powerful undercurrent of magic had become a constant stream. And not a pleasant one. It had taken on a life of its own.

Now. He had to get her out of here now.

"There!" X pointed, and for a brief second, Cal saw the flash of Tessa's blonde hair at the far end of the arena. Grabbing X by the arm to pull him with him, Cal plunged into the writhing crowd.

Women immediately began to slide their bodies against his, rubbing their breasts against his back and chest. A few got close enough to slide their groins against his, but he felt no desire.

He only felt the pressure against his skin. No heat. Small favor. Also helpful because when he finally felt warm skin, he'd know he'd found Tessa.

He didn't stop though hands pulled at him from all sides, trying to get him to dance with them, to create more friction and more power.

He couldn't let them get in his way. With a tight grip on X, Cal barreled through the mass of bodies. But he was practically blind and he felt panic begin to tighten his chest.

He couldn't fail her in this, in something so absolutely mundane as a rave at a dance club. But this was no ordinary club. And the power level continued to increase.

Just when he thought the fear of failing her would make him crazy, X pulled his arm out of Cal's grip, then circled Cal's forearm with his own hand, and started to drag Cal in a new direction.

Placing his trust in someone else felt weird. For so long, he'd only had himself to rely on. Cal had to force himself not to tear his arm out of X's hand, to let his brother lead him.

X pushed through the crowd, but clearing a path became more and more difficult the farther they went. Bodies mashed together so tightly that Cal and X literally couldn't get by. They had to circle. But each time, X pulled Cal along in a specific path.

The drums pounded louder; the bass throbbed harder; and Cal figured the song was coming to the end. He knew the band wouldn't stop the momentum now. They'd continue on in the throes of the power.

He hoped like hell Gemma, the *strega* channeling all that power, would be okay. His first priority, though, was Tessa.

X's pace picked up until they were practically running. Bodies bounced off them and around them, creating chaos in the midst of more chaos. The sense that time was running out forced Cal onward, even though he was practically blind.

Heart pounding, lungs burning, he drew in breath after breath of heavy air until finally he caught her scent. Just a hint of it, but he knew he was close.

Someone grabbed him, a woman by the size of her hand. She pulled him against her, making him stumble. His momentum faltered, and X lost his grip on Cal's arm.

Cal and the woman fell in a mess of arms and legs on the floor, and before he could extricate himself, the woman had her mouth on his and her tongue in his mouth. Ripping himself out of her arms, he scrambled to his feet and battled with his brain to make his eyes focus despite the strobes.

Vaguely, he heard X call his name, but Cal had seen the bright flash of Tessa's hair for a brief second. Only a few feet away.

Another strobe blinded him but he *felt* her. He put his

hands out in front of him and began grabbing body parts. If he didn't feel the warmth of skin, he moved on.

He roared in triumph when his hand felt the sweet heat of her. But this heat wasn't natural. She was burning up.

"Tessa!"

In the dark between strobes, he saw her expression. Dazed, confused. Completely out of it.

He also saw the man pressed against her back. The soon-to-be-dead man had his arms wrapped around Tessa's waist and appeared to grinding his groin against her ass as he sucked on her neck.

Fury made Cal pull back his fist. He would kill the guy for touching her.

"No! Cal, don't!" X grabbed Cal's fist and held on. "You might hit Tessa."

Cal needed a second to process X's words and a few more to get his anger under control. He shook his head to clear it then looked at X and nodded. Then he took careful aim and smashed his fist in the guy's face. The man never even knew what hit him. He dropped like a stone.

And Tessa blinked those blue, blue eyes at Cal. They shone as brightly as a lighthouse but her expression was dreamy, her mouth tilted in a soft smile. As if in slow motion, she closed the space between them, circled her arms around his neck, and pressed her body full length to his.

Lust flashed like a lightning strike as her lips closed over his. The hair on his body stood up and his cock answered her siren's call, stiffening beyond hard to painful. His arms wrapped around her waist and lifted her off her feet so his cock could nestle into the notch of her thighs.

Her taste flooded his senses, and the heat of her hands on his neck as she held onto him burned into his skin like a brand.

She moaned when his lips parted hers and his tongue slid into her mouth to duel with erotic ferocity with her tongue.

She let him overcome her, let him completely consume her as she sank into him. He ate at her mouth like a starving man, kissing her until he couldn't breathe and then kissing her more.

When he had to pull away or risk passing out from oxygen deprivation, he clamped one hand on her neck so she couldn't get away. He barely registered her legs locking around his waist or the hands she ran through the short strands of his hair. All that mattered was staking his claim.

He had to get inside her. Had to get her naked and under him. And she seemed to be in line with the program.

Her hips arched into his, rubbing the tip of his cock against her lace-covered clit. The tiny skirt she wore rode up so far that he would only need to flick the edge to expose her ass.

"Cal!"

The male voice calling to him annoyed the hell out of him. He didn't want to know anything but Tessa, feel anything but her warmth and the silkiness of her skin.

Sucking on the tongue she slid into his mouth, he tasted her desire for him.

"Cal, you ass. We gotta get her out of here."

He didn't want to go anywhere. Here was as good a place as any to fuck. And he wanted to fuck her so badly—

A punch to the kidney made him gasp in pain and release Tessa's mouth. He turned to kill whoever had dared to interrupt him and saw a face he recognized, a face he trusted.

Cal shook his head as Tessa, deprived of his mouth, began to lay open-mouthed kisses from his ear down his neck, occasionally stopping to bite and make him shudder with sensation.

As Cal blinked harder, sanity began to return.

X grabbed Cal's arm and started to pull him toward the closest exit, which was still a decent fifty yards away.

"Let's go," X yelled. And still Cal barely heard him. The band seemed to have gotten louder and pressure built in his ears, closing them.

They needed to get the hell out of here. Right now. Sex could wait. But not that long. He swore Tessa vibrated in his arms, as if she held an energy inside that needed to be released. And who knew what would happen when it did.

He only knew instinctually that it wouldn't be good for anyone in here.

Tessa's hands clawed at the material of his shirt, ripping it from his back as her teeth sank into his earlobe.

Letting X lead the way, Cal held onto Tessa as he ran for the door. Every step bumped his cock against her mound, sending him that much closer to coming.

He didn't know how long they took to reach the exit, but the frenzy behind him had reached a fever pitch. He didn't bother to look back as X ripped open the door and shoved Cal and Tess through before following them and slamming the door shut.

The absolute silence of the hallway was broken only by the rough sound of their breathing. and Tessa's soft moans. She almost sounded in pain. As if she had to come or die.

"Cal, please. I need you."

Without a second thought, Cal walked straight to the nearest wall, set her back against it to brace her, and ripped away her panties with one hand. As he fumbled for the zipper on his pants, she panted against his chest, her fingernails scoring his back hard enough to draw blood.

Vaguely he heard X say, "Oh shit," but he couldn't stop.

She needed this. She needed the release. How he knew that, he had no clue. He only knew he had to make her come before the power that had been building inside her did serious harm.

The zipper released and he shoved down his pants far

enough to free his cock. With one hand on her hips, he bent his knees and shoved inside her in one smooth motion.

Buried to the hilt in seconds, he felt her shudder around him. Her sheath enclosed him like a fist, almost too tight for Cal to move. But he did. He thrust hard and fast. Bending his head, he caught her mouth as she turned her face up to his. His kiss was almost brutal, his lips demanding and voracious.

Her head hit the wall behind her, but she only sealed their mouths together more tightly and arched her hips to take him deeper.

His body tightened, blood boiling as he fucked her. No finesse, no rhythm. Just demand. Christ, he couldn't get enough of her. Had to have more. All.

His. Her body attuned to his every move, she answered his passion with her own. She licked and nipped, attacking him with the same frenzy he felt. Her nails scraped down his back, almost painfully, until she filled her hands with his ass and squeezed. Hard.

His cock throbbed inside her.

He tore his mouth away from hers to rasp in her ear, "Fuck, Tessa. Harder, baby."

She did what he asked. She sank her nails into his ass at the same time she sank her teeth into his shoulder, hard enough to break the skin.

He felt the power coiled inside her release in a nuclear-range blast, searing every nerve ending and making him come with the ferocity of a beast. His cock throbbed and spilled inside her. Liquid heat poured from him for what seemed like hours as her pussy milked him with rhythmic contractions.

Heart pounding against his ribs like a caged bird, he forced himself to lock his knees and tighten his arms so he didn't drop her. After that totally amazing release of energy, Tessa had gone boneless against him. As if she'd passed out.

Shit. "Tessa, you okay?"

When she didn't answer, his lungs began to constrict. Fucking hell, was she hurt?

It took a tremendous amount of will to lift his head away from the wall, where he had rested his forehead against the cool concrete. The air around them still vibrated with energy, so much that he swore he should be able to see it.

Tessa's head lay on his shoulder, her face turned away so he couldn't see her.

"Tessa!"

His tone was sharper than he intended, but fear bit into his gut with sharp teeth. And when she didn't respond at all, he fought off panic. Pulling out of her still-tight sheath, he groaned at the shivers of lust that sparked through his system. He still wanted her, wanted to be back inside her, thrusting—

No time for more of that. Threading one hand through her hair, he lifted her head away from his shoulder as gently as he could and nearly collapsed in relief when she sighed and tightened her arms around his neck and laid her head back down.

"Fuck, Tessa, are you okay?"

She answered with another breathy sigh and tucked her head into the side of his neck. Her lips brushed against the sensitive skin below his ear, and lust attacked again. With an effort of will, he pushed it aside.

"Come on, babe. You gotta help me here. We need to get back to Sal's."

"Mmm, don't wanna move." She slurred her words like a drunk on a ten-hour bender. "Wanna sleep."

"You can sleep all you want when we get back to Sal's."

She sighed, her warm breath raising goose bumps. "You're lying. Can't sleep. Know that. What happened?"

She sounded tired but thinking straight. A small relief. "Not sure." Though he had his suspicions.

With one arm still wrapped around her to hold her up, he tucked himself back in his pants and zipped up.

"Loosen your legs, babe."

With a grumpy sounding sigh, she did as he asked so he could pull her skirt down to keep her decent. He had no idea where her panties were. He seemed to remember ripping them off.

From behind him, he heard another groan and realized he'd forgotten about X.

Swinging Tessa into his arms, where she settled against his chest with a sigh, he turned to find his brother sprawled on the floor, rubbing the back of his head with one hand.

And sporting a hard-on.

"Holy shit." X blinked a few times before he finally held Cal's gaze. "I feel like I'm crawling out of my skin and I'm horny as hell. What the fuck?"

Cal covered a sigh of relief. X seemed no worse for wear. Heading out, he helped X to his feet, watching to make sure his brother was steady. "We'll figure it out later. Come on, we gotta get back to Sal's."

He needed to get Tessa somewhere safe. His leg muscles felt like wet noodles and his arms weren't much better. If someone attacked them now, he didn't think he'd be able to fend them off. And knowing that scared the crap out of him. Not only did that put Tessa in danger but X, too.

And if anything happened to either of them...

"Let's go."

SEVEN

Tessa woke with a hangover. That was really strange because deities didn't get hangovers. At least not from alcohol and drugs created by mortals. Only those created by the gods themselves had the power to affect their chemistry.

Except for chocolate, of course. She loved chocolate, loved its calming properties. She wondered if it would help with this blasted headache.

Where the hell had she gotten her hands on some of Fufluns' wine? The God of the Vines guarded his stash like it was priceless, which, of course, it was. The grapes he used to make it only ripened once every hundred years and grew only in a specific and magically hidden vineyard in Tuscany.

She hadn't had a bottle in more than two centuries. So what had she been doing last night?

Groaning, she tried to open her eyes but only managed a squint into the brightness of the room. Blessed Goddess, her beloved sun had it in for her today. Covering her eyes with her hands, she rolled over and pressed her face into the cool pillow.

Drawing in a breath, she caught Cal's masculine scent on the sheets.

Cal.

She gasped and sat straight up in bed, causing her head to throb mercilessly.

Where was Cal?

The previous night's memories flooded her brain. The temple. The amazing sex. Downbelow... Those memories were a little hazy, but she knew there'd been more amazing sex there, as well.

What the hell had happened at Downbelow that had given her such a headache? Frowning, she ran through her memories. She remembered dancing. She loved to dance. Dilby, the lead singer, had played her favorite songs and then...

Then what?

The *strega*, Gemma, had started to draw power for the euphoria spell that was Downbelow's featured attraction. That spell gave pleasure to the patrons, and that pleasure, in turn, fueled the wards that kept Downbelow safe and hidden.

Last night, though... Something strange had happened.

"Hey. How're you feeling?"

Her head shot up to see Cal leaning on the doorjamb. And her temples protested with a massive jolt of pain. With a groan, she lifted her hand to her head to rub at her temples.

"I feel like I drank an entire bottle of Fufluns' wine. My head is killing me."

He nodded, his expression carefully blank. "Since I've never had Fufluns' wine, I'm just gonna assume the hangover's pretty bad. You want some pills for that?"

She tried to smile for him but was fairly sure it looked more like a grimace. "Won't help but thanks."

He nodded again but didn't move, just continuing to stare at her.

Her smile died. "Is something wrong?"

Did she have bedhead? Something on her face? Why wasn't

he coming into the room to kiss her good morning? Her gaze narrowed, as much from being perplexed as from the brightness of the sun seeping through the cracks around the window shades.

"Cal, is everything okay?"

He drew in a breath and released it on a sigh before answering. "Not sure yet."

She huffed and swung her legs off the bed so she could walk over to him. His gaze dropped immediately to take in her nudity. That brought out a bit of a true smile on those gorgeous lips, but almost immediately he dragged his gaze back to her face.

Okay, something had happened. Something that had put him off.

Hands on her hips, she stopped only a foot away from him and glared into his eyes. "Alright, Cal. Just spit it out. What's going on?"

He blinked twice, the only sign that he was having trouble holding her stare. "I thought maybe you could tell me."

She raised her eyebrows at him. "Since I'm not exactly sure what happened last night..."

His focus on her became a pinpoint beam. "What do you mean, you're not sure what happened?"

"I mean, what happened at Downbelow is a little fuzzy."

"That ever happen before?"

She rolled her eyes. "Yes, but not for about 1,500 years."

And that was no exaggeration. She hadn't experienced anything like that since she'd still had power.

He nodded, as if he'd known what she was going to say. "Put some clothes on and come downstairs. We need to talk, and when you're naked, I can't think straight."

Her smile took her off guard and eased some of the pain in her head. "Nice to know."

She'd hoped for a return smile. No such luck. If anything his expression tightened even more.

"I'll be downstairs. Don't be long, Tessa."

He turned and stalked away, leaving her to stare after him, feeling worse than she had when she'd woken.

What had changed while she slept? What had she done last night to make him look at her like that? She guessed the only way to find out was to get her butt downstairs.

In the closet, she found clothes she knew would fit her. Jeans, T-shirts, shorts, skirts, blouses, and dresses. Sal had a selection to rival the most exclusive boutique. All designer labels. All from the current season's collection.

She had no idea if Sal chose the clothing himself or if he just ordered one of everything in a few sizes. She wouldn't put it past him to simply call the designers himself.

She chose a bright blue sundress with tiny little straps, a tight bodice, and a skirt that flared at her knees. It was a Valentino. Her favorite Italian designer. It made her feel feminine. Pretty. Confident.

She needed a bit of that. Okay, maybe more than a bit.

The look on Cal's face...

Sliding on a pair of bright red, strappy flat sandals to go with the sundress, she took a deep breath and headed for the stairs, trying to figure out why she felt like a naughty schoolgirl who'd been called to the principal's office.

Her mouth quirked at the image. She wondered if Cal had any interested in role-playing. She'd get him a dark suit and a paddle and let him bend her over his desk...

Hey, after however many millennia, you did what you could to spice up your sex life.

She still wore the smile as she went downstairs, though she slowed as she heard a third male voice, in addition to Salvatorus and Cal. She didn't recognize the man, but their voices were hushed, not raised as if angry.

Who would Cal be discussing her situation with?

She picked up her pace until she stood in the entryway to the kitchen at the back of the house.

"Good morning, Lady." Salvatorus hopped off his chair, hooves clicking on the linoleum floor as he went to the counter to reach for a mug and then poured her thick, fragrant hot chocolate from a pot on the stove.

Her mouth watered as he set the mug in her hands and waved her into a seat at the small table next to Cal. "Salvatorus, you are a god among men."

"I do my best, sweetheart." He gave her a smile that would have melted the coldest heart and coaxed a laugh out of her when he bowed with a flourish.

"Well, hell, Sal. You're making the rest of us look like uncouth savages. And while Caligo might fit the bill, I don't."

She knew immediately that the man who smiled at her from across the table was related to Cal. She saw the resemblance in the shape of his handsome face and the curve of his mouth. His eyes were the dark blue of a stormy sea and held only a few of the shadows that Cal's did.

The man stood, bowing at the waist. "Very nice to meet you, Lady. My name is Extasis, but everyone calls me X."

She held out her hand and was charmed again when he kissed it. "I'm very pleased to meet you, X, though I have the feeling I should apologize for not remembering you from last night."

"No apologies necessary, Lady." His smile turned rueful. "You're not the only one with a faulty memory of everything that happened last night."

She directed her gaze at Cal, who still had that shielded look on his face. "Then maybe you'd like to refresh my memory. I'd really like to know what put that look on your face."

Cal's eyebrows lifted the slightest bit. "What look?"

X let out an amused snort that made Cal give him a brief glare. "That look. He comes by it honestly, though. Our father has the exact same one."

"Your father must be an extremely handsome man to have produced such gorgeous sons."

X's face lit up with a smile. "Ah, Lady Tessa, you have just made my day."

Returning her gaze to Cal's, she saw a look in his eyes that made her flush from head to toe. She'd never met a man who could do that, not in all her long years. And she absolutely adored it.

"X, I'm gonna send you back to our parents in pieces if you don't knock it off," Cal practically growled.

"What? What'd I do?" X's expression was all innocence, making Tessa laugh.

Cal sighed and shook his head, his expression not lightening at all, and Tessa knew this probably wasn't the time for laughter. Whatever had happened last night, it'd freaked out Cal. So she should probably be doubly worried.

She sighed. "Alright, Cal, just spit it out. What's going on?"

He looked her straight in the eyes, his expression dead serious. "I think your powers are starting to strengthen, and I think that's going to make Charun come after you even harder."

For a few seconds, Tessa just sat there blinking at Cal. Her brain stuttered to a stop before it started to spin in circles. Cal thought her powers were starting to strengthen.

Her heart began to pound in excitement. But although that would seem like good news, Cal didn't look at all happy about it. Because of the second part of his statement.

Well, fudge. He was probably right. Charun would most

likely believe this was great news for him because when he caught her and consumed her powers, it would make him even stronger.

That should terrify her. But all she felt was giddy happiness.

For how many centuries had she been mourning the loss of her powers? It seemed like forever, and she felt their loss every day like a dull ache in her chest. To hear they were strengthening was like waking to a beautiful sunrise on a warm summer day.

She took a deep breath, trying not to let the feeling run away with her. This wasn't a good thing. And maybe if she told herself that a few more times, she'd actually believe it.

"Tessa, you still with me?"

A dark mass moved into her eyesight, and she refocused her attention on Cal. Worry drew lines at the corners of his gorgeous mouth, and she reached out to smooth them away with her fingers before she realized she'd done it.

Had another man ever worried about her like this?

Men worshipped her. They didn't *care* for her, at least not in the way this man did. He *took* care of her. The difference was... Well, the difference made all the difference in the world to her.

Beneath her fingers, his skin felt warm, the shadow of his beard rough. She wanted to feel that scruff on her cheek, on her breast, between her legs.

As if he'd read her thoughts, Cal stiffened, his body becoming rigid. She swore she felt the manifestation of his control like a force field around his body, trying to keep her out.

No way would she accept that.

Stepping forward, she pressed herself against him, flattened her curves against the hard planes of his body, and laid her cheek on his firm chest. She didn't care that they had an audience. She wasn't ashamed of her need for him. And she refused to think he was ashamed of his need for her.

But when he didn't immediately wrap his arms around her, she pulled back to stare up at him.

"Cal, is something else happening that you're not telling me about?"

Those beautiful gray eyes revealed nothing, and Tessa felt a chill begin to spread up her spine.

Finally he sighed and wrapped his arms around her, drawing her back against his body and tucking her head under his chin. "No. There's nothing else."

Neither of the other men said anything so Tessa was forced to conclude this was just Cal worrying. And she understood his worry. Really, she did.

Though it'd been years since she'd seen Charun, she knew him as well as she knew each of the other members of their pantheon. His patience was legendary, as was his capacity for cruelty.

He was, after all, the Etruscan race's final judge and jury. He meted out the punishment for those who had lived their lives without regard for others. The killers and psychopaths.

Charun had to be without emotion. It was who he was. It was a role Tessa had never and would never want. It was one Charun was stuck with. She actually understood his need to get out. She just didn't want to be the fuel for his escape.

Charun was ruthless and cruel and had an amazing amount of power... And for the first time, she realized how vulnerable Cal might be. Even though he was Cimmerian, he was still only human.

What would she do if anything happened to Cal?

She pulled back to look at him, loving the way his arms tightened around her, as if he wasn't going to let her go, before he loosened enough so she could tilt her head up to look into his eyes.

She didn't know what she expected to see. He hid his feelings so well, she really couldn't see anything. And that was worse than seeing his fear.

"Why don't you drink your hot chocolate before it gets cold." He nodded toward the table but didn't release her. "I'm going to need to leave you here for a little while. There's somewhere I need to go, someone I need to talk to, and I can't take you."

His gaze lifted over her shoulder to where his brother was standing. "Will you stay 'til I get back?"

X's answer was immediate. "Of course."

Cal nodded. "Then I need to go now."

"But... the sun's up."

Cal just shook his head. "Not where I'm going. Sal, I'll need a little help."

The *salbinelli* nodded as he headed for the front of the house. "No problem, kid." Then he motioned to X. "Come on, let's go pretend we've got something to do in another room while they say good-bye."

X's deep laughter continued to ring in her ears as he and Salvatorus walked away.

She caught Cal's gaze again. "Where are you going?"

He just shook his head. "I shouldn't be gone long. Don't leave the house. I'll be back as soon as I can."

"No, wai—"

His mouth landed hard, his lips parting hers to allow his tongue to plunge between. Lust sparked immediately, the heat of his kiss and his body consuming her.

No one had ever made her feel this... all-consuming desire before.

The ever-present lust she felt for him made her sex clench,

but something other than lust was making her weak in the knees. The emotion that grabbed her lungs in a tight fist and squeezed had her grabbing onto him and holding tight.

Cal groaned, low and deep, and her answering moan had her hips arching into his. The hard ridge of his erection pressed against her lower stomach, fire-hot and demanding. They kissed until she had to pull away and suck in a deep breath. And still she refused.

When he finally pulled back, they both were breathing so hard that she figured Salvatorus and X could hear them wherever they happened to be.

She opened her eyes to find Cal staring down at her, his gray eyes the color of storm clouds obscuring the sun.

"Be here when I get back, Tessa. I don't know how long it's gonna take but I need to go."

"Where are you going?"

"Somewhere I can't take you or I would. Just stay put, and I'll be back as soon as I can."

His lips tightened, as if he would say something more. But he only kissed her one more time and then walked by her, heading for the front room. She considered following him, but the weakness in her knees made her question her ability to do so.

Instead, she folded into a chair at the table and wrapped her hand around her mug of chocolate. It was no longer steaming, so she used just the tiniest bit of power to warm it up. And felt the rush that accompanied it. A rush that made her tingle from head to toe.

A miracle?

She'd lived with magic her entire existence. Miracles were merely the result of the vagaries of power. The power that flowed through the earth and could be controlled by those with the right set of skills. Or those like herself, who were inherently magical.

Was her relationship with Cal strengthening her powers? If so, what did they do about it? And did she want to do anything about it?

Staring out the window over the kitchen sink, she let her gaze wander over Salvatorus's backyard garden.

Enclosed by a seven-foot, white picket fence and shielded from prying eyes from the neighboring buildings by a fifteen-foot oak tree planted dead center in the space, the small garden wouldn't have been out of place in any courtyard in ancient Etruria.

Though the tree shaded much of the area, herbs, roses, and vegetables thrived. Salvatorus had a green thumb, and everything he grew had a purpose, either medicinal or culinary.

Did she still have a purpose?

"So, Lady Tessa, what shall we do to pass the time until my brother returns?"

With a quick intake of breath, she looked up to find X standing in the pass-through between the dining room and the kitchen. He wore a warm grin that made him more handsome than he had any right to be.

And though he might be just the slightest bit more handsome than Cal, X didn't make her blood race like his brother. He didn't make her thighs clench or her heart pound. All those overused romance clichés she'd scoffed at previously now made her pause and consider.

Was what she felt for Cal something more than mere desire? Tinia's teat, had she actually fallen in love with the man?

Something of her shock must have shown on her face because X began to frown.

"Lady Tessa, are you okay?"

Forcing a smile, she waved to the seat across the table from her. "I'm fine. Please sit, Extasis. I would love to talk with you."

"And is there a specific topic you'd like to discuss?" His smile widened as he slipped into the chair across from her.

Her smile became more natural at X's teasing tone. "Aren't you afraid your brother will punish you if you tell me secrets?"

"I'm not afraid of Cal, and he loves me too much to really hurt me. So what would you like to know about him?"

Good question. Would "everything" sound too pathetic? She was a goddess, after all. Still, quelling her curiosity had never been her strong suit. She thought quietly for a few moments.

"Has he always been so guarded?"

X's grin turned a bit lopsided. "Well, when you grow up the firstborn son of Diritas, you learn to be... let's just say you learn to be cautious." He sighed before continuing. "Dad's not known for his compassion."

"I'll admit I don't know much about the Cimmerians, but I was led to believe they're not a warm, fuzzy bunch. Present company excluded, of course."

X's smile returned in a flash. "Thank you. I like to think I take after my mother."

"And that would be a bad thing, according to your father."

"Yeah, not much room in the Cimmerian world for those who don't enjoy a good bloody fight."

"Sounds harsh."

"Well, you either learn to fight or you're considered not much use in Cimer."

"And is that why you chose to live here?"

"Oh, I can fight, Lady."

She gave X a rueful smile. "Sorry, I didn't mean to offend—"

"No, no. You didn't. I just never developed the one trait Cimmerians prize above all others. Their inability to feel. I figure it's because of my mom. Cal and I are half-breeds. Our mother is Etruscan *aguane*. Did you he tell you that?"

Inability to feel? Feel what? She shook her head, unsure what X was talking about. "Cal told me about your mother, yes, but he never mentioned anything about a lack of feeling."

"I don't mean emotional feelings, Lady. I mean physical sensation. Cimmerians are great warriors because they feel no pain. They can fight until they literally fall over dead because they don't feel heat or cold or pain."

Shock made her blink. How had she never heard about this? "Cal never told me."

How could she not have known? Wouldn't that lack of sensation have shown in his lovemaking? She thought back over their every encounter... and remembered how he stroked her body with those big hands. Was it all for her benefit?

"What about pleasure? Does he... Do Cimmerians feel pleasure?"

X's smile loosened the knot forming in her chest.

"Yes, they do." But his smile quickly disappeared. "But... I don't want to lie to you, Lady. We're longer lived than other humans. After decades of feeling no pain, warriors tend to lose their capacity for all emotion."

Did Cal feel nothing when he touched her? Nothing at all? "Are you trying to tell me Cal feels nothing for me—"

"No. No, no, no." X waved his hands in front of his chest. "I'm not saying anything about Cal. And since I'm spilling all sorts of truths, I gotta say, sometimes I think Cal might feel too much. Emotionally." X stopped to sigh and run a hand through his short dark hair. "He's gonna kill me for spilling like this, but my brother can be a stubborn SOB and there're things I know he hasn't told you and probably never will."

When X didn't continue right away, she said, "Like..."

"Like the beating he took the last time he trusted a deity."

Salvatorus's voice made her realize he'd come up behind X without her noticing. How he managed to walk so silently on a wooden floor with those hooves, she would never understand.

"What do you mean? Which deity?"

"Venus." Salvatorus's mouth curled in a sneer. "That bitch used Cal to do her dirty work, and Vulcan smashed him to shit. Cal nearly died before X got to him and brought him here for medical help."

She shook her head. "Surely Cal knew Venus couldn't be trusted. Why would he ever go near her?'

"Because my brother has a soft spot for damsels in distress," X said, "and Venus laid it on thick. She told him Vulcan was abusing her when what she really wanted was to use Cal as a distraction while she stole Vulcan's hammer. When that didn't work out, she said Cal was the one trying to steal the hammer and she threw herself at Vulcan."

X stopped but Tessa sensed he had more to say. "Please, X. I know there's more. Please continue."

Though she was still a goddess of the Etruscan pantheon and X, though only half Etruscan, still fell under her jurisdiction, she would not compel him to answer. It just wasn't in her nature. Never had been.

Finally X sighed again. "Did he tell you why he left Cimer?"

"No."

X looked at Sal, and she swore he waited for Salvatorus to nod before continuing. "Cal was the first half-breed born in Cimer to a Cimmerian warrior and an *aguane*. He took a lot of shit growing up. I didn't come along until years later, so I didn't put up with half the crap he did. And from what I understand, it was pretty awful. Besides, my dad's not exactly a bundle of fun. He was hard on Cal. Really fucking hard... Excuse the language, Lady. And then Cal and Juliana were bound."

Her eyes narrowed at the surge of jealousy. "Bound how?"

"To be mated. Cimmerians are matched by their parents, usually after the boys turn twenty. Now, I don't know everything because I wasn't there, but I guess Dad was worried none of the other men would allow their daughters to tie themselves to Cal because he was a half-breed. And there aren't that many Cimmerian women born, so competition for them is huge."

"Sounds barbaric."

X grimaced. "Yeah, but I guess the old way where they fought to the death over a woman was much worse. Anyway, Juliana said she wanted Cal and her father agreed. I'm pretty sure there was money involved, but again, this was before my time and my parents don't talk about it. From everything I've heard, Cal loved her. And when she died, Cal left Cimer and vowed he'd never go back."

This story was getting worse by the minute. "How did she die?"

X shook his head, though she didn't think he was refusing to answer. "The official story? One of Cal's rivals for Juliana killed her in a jealous rage so Cal killed him and left, giving up his post as a Watchman. I can count on one hand how many times Cal's been back to Cimer since then."

"You say the 'official story' like you don't think that's what really happened."

"Depending on who you talk to, the story changes." X sighed again and rubbed a hand through his hair. "It came out later that Juliana's father, who was a member of the Elders' Council, had bound her to Cal because he wanted to exploit Cal's ability to travel though the planes without the use of the gates. Cal refused.

"The Cimmerians have strict rules against using the gates for personal gain, and Cal was a Watchman. He didn't break rules, not ever. Since Cal now knew the guy's plan, Cal was a liability. So Juliana's father hired a Sentinel to kill Cal.

"Juliana stepped in front of Cal just as the assassin tried to take him out. No one ever knew if she did it to save his life or if she was an innocent bystander. After he killed the assassin, Cal nearly beat Juliana's father to death. Cal's never talked about it. Not ever. Not even to me."

Her brain raced, full of scenarios about how that scene would have played out. If Juliana had been the innocent dupe, that would explain Cal's white-knight syndrome. If she'd been involved in her father's plans, that would explain why he hadn't wanted to help her in the first place.

So many questions. Too few answers.

And—

Dear Goddess Thesan, I pray you attend the birth of my child. I ask for your blessing to keep my child safe from harm and to ensure his safe passage into this world.

The summons whispered through Tessa's head, its strength a testament to the speaker's dedication. There was no desperation in the request, only urgency.

The urgency of a first-time mother about to give birth.

"Lady Tessa, are you okay?"

She blinked up at X, who frowned at her from across the table. And when she smiled, his frown turned bemused.

"I'm fine, X. But we're going to need leave immediately."

"What! Oh, no—"

"Aw shit, Tessa." Salvatorus's disgruntled growl made her smile widen.

"—you can't go anywhere. Cal will kill me if you leave the house." The look on X's wasn't exactly fear but it wasn't far off the mark, either. And he looked frozen to the chair.

Salvatorus, on the other hand, had jumped down and

stomped into the front room, grumbling, "Cal's gonna have my ass," under his breath. But he didn't say no.

She rose and X's expression turned panicked. "Lady, seriously, I'm not as strong as my brother. If you leave the safety of this house, I can't protect you as well as Cal. Where do you need to go? Isn't there some way—"

She laid her hand on his arm. "X, I know what Cal said, and I do realize what I'm asking. But I've been summoned and I will not disappoint Flavia."

"Summoned?"

"Yes. One of the duties I still perform as the goddess Thesan is midwife. We need to leave for Hamburg immediately. A *gianes* at the Hawk Mountain enclave is ready to give birth to twins."

Deliberately skirting around X, Tessa headed for the front room, where she knew Sal was getting ready to transport her and X to Hamburg.

"Come along, X. Flavia's had a hard pregnancy and I don't want her to worry."

Behind her, she heard X sigh long and hard. "Lady Tessa, I'm begging you to recon—"

"The Hawk Mountain facility has safeguards of its own." She refused to back down on this. "I doubt Charun even knows about it, and even if he did, I doubt his minions will be able to breach the security there. I must go.

"I am still a goddess of the Etruscan pantheon. I may not guide the sun into its position every morning as I once did, but I love my people. And I will not allow Flavia to deliver these babies without my presence."

X straightened as if she'd kicked him in the ass, and a look of respect flashed across his expression before a smile curved his lips. He really was a gorgeous man.

Yet, seeing X's smile only made her wish Cal was here by

her side. She hated breaking the promise she'd made Cal that she'd not to leave here without him. And once he learned she'd left, he might refuse to return to her.

"X, please don't make me renege on the promise I made her to be there."

After several seconds of holding her gaze, X tipped his head back as his eyes closed, and he sighed. "You know I'll never hear the end of this."

Looking down at her again, he bowed slightly, arm across his waist, and then waved his hand for her to continue into the living room.

"After you, Lady. But when Cal gets back, please put in a good word for me. Maybe he won't be tempted to tear me limb from limb. Maybe he'll only take a few fingers."

EIGHT

Well, shit.

Cal stomped through the forest surrounding his cabin, heading for the oldest stand of trees on the property. The old oak there would be perfect for what he needed.

Even though the tree canopy diffused most of the light from the sun inching closer to the center of the sky, he wore jeans, leather gloves, and his lined sweatshirt with the hood shading his face.

Not ideal for the middle of August. Even though he didn't feel heat—except for Tessa's—he had to be careful not to succumb to heatstroke.

Where he was going, he wouldn't have to worry about the sun. But until he got there, he couldn't let any inch of his skin be exposed to its rays. The burn would be a bitch and he didn't have time for setbacks. He needed to return to Tessa as quickly as possible.

"Jesus Christ, you sound like a fucking, weak-ass sycophant. This is what you get for working with a goddess."

But he knew that just working for her wasn't the problem. He'd started to care for her.

"*Idiot.* You're a fucking idiot." He stomped on a branch in his path, needing to feel something break beneath his feet.

When Sal had zapped him back to his trailer, he'd immediately felt like he'd been kicked in the gut. He hadn't wanted to leave her. He couldn't shake the feeling that, as soon as he was gone, Tessa would be in danger.

"This is why you don't screw around with the people you're supposed to protect. Gods damn, Dad was right about something."

His father had been harder on Cal than any other father had been on their son. Diritas had known Cal's *Fata* blood would be a liability. Hell, he'd thrown it in Cal's face every other day.

And Cal, like most sons, had wanted to please his father.

"Yeah, well, you know where that got you."

Banished wasn't the right word because he'd left on his own. Still, after what had happened...

He felt rage bubble low in his gut and squashed it back into the deep hole where he usually kept it. Anger wouldn't do him any good where he was going. In fact, he may have to grovel or, at the very least, be civil to whoever met him on the other side.

Depending on who that was...

"You know, if you'd been born a pure-blooded Cimmerian, you wouldn't give a shit about Tessa."

He could tell her to go to hell, literally, and that would be the end of it. But for the second time in his life, he'd let someone get close.

"And you know how well that worked out the first time."

Shit. He really hated when he was right.

With a sigh, Cal stopped to get his bearings, squinting through heavily tinted sunglasses to make sure he was headed in the right direction. And spotted his target only a few feet in front of him.

Hell, someone could've jumped him, and he probably wouldn't have heard them coming. What the fuck kind of protector did that make him?

"A pretty fucking bad one, that's what."

No, just one who'd fallen for the wrong woman. Just like his dad.

Yeah, and look at your parents now.

Shit and double shit.

Shaking his head, hoping to clear it at least for the time being, he closed the distance to the huge old oak tree that was his target.

The tree was at least a hundred years old and rose a good thirty or forty feet in the air. He couldn't span its trunk with his arms, and when he pressed his ear to the bark, he heard the sweet music of nature pulsing through the tree's core.

The *Fata* blood in his veins, so despised by purebred Cimmerians, had given Cal an unexpected talent none of the other Cimmerians had, one many wished they did. And had killed to have.

Yeah, he really didn't need to be thinking about that right now.

Typically, a traveler had to pass through specified gates throughout the world to get to Cimer. Those gates were few and far between, making them easier to defend and harder to find.

But not Cal. He could build a shortcut to Cimer, which floated in the mist between the planes of existence, or between this earth and the other realms such as the Greek deities' Mount Olympus, the Mayans' Xibalba... and the Etruscans' Invol and Aitás.

Cimer's unique position gave the Cimmerians leverage over those who lived on the other planes and wished to use the gates to travel back and forth. About a millennia earlier, the Involuti, the founding gods of the Etruscans and those from whom all other Etruscan deities were descended, had made a pact with the Cimmerians: Shut down all access to the gate to Invol, and you would never want for anything. Guard the gate with your lives, but never reveal its whereabouts under penalty of death.

Cal had never questioned why the Involuti had brokered that deal and had never cared enough to ask. He only knew that the pact had never been broken.

At least not until now.

Taking a piece of chalk from his pocket, Cal stepped in front of the tree and kneeled at the base. With the chalk, he drew the shape of a rounded door on the oak's trunk. He made sure to start his chalk on the ground before drawing it up and over the bark and then bringing it back down to the ground.

He'd already taken off his boots and socks, making sure the tops of his feet were shaded. Then he curled his toes into the soil at the foot of the tree, the entire soles of his feet in contact with the dirt. Placing his hand in the center of the outline on the bark, he closed his eyes, gathered his will, and pushed open the door.

He felt the rough bark of the tree trunk swing back, away from him, and without opening his eyes, he stepped through into the void.

Even though he'd braced himself, the displacement from one plane to another was a shock to his system. It felt like he'd pulled his body through a sieve, each molecule having to break apart from the others and reform on the other side.

He fell to his knees, gasping for air, his stomach rocking. If he'd chosen to travel more than a hundred miles to get to the nearest gate, he wouldn't have had such a severe reaction. Of course, he hadn't been to Cimer for several years so maybe the reaction was worse because of that.

When he was finally sure he wasn't going to toss the contents of his stomach, he took a deep breath, feeling the clean air of his homeland filling his lungs. Damn, after so many years of living on earth, where the air was constantly polluted with noxious fumes, this was... well, this was like breathing in a little bit of pure ecstasy.

He kneeled there for a few minutes, letting the dew on the grass seep into his jeans. When his stomach settled, he shook his head and stripped off the hooded sweatshirt, leaving it in a ball by the tree he'd connected to from earth. He'd have to use the same tree to get back.

Looking around, he noticed that not much had changed since he'd been there years before. Too damn long ago.

He wanted to stop by his parents' home and at least say hi. But the circumstance under which he'd left made that difficult, and he'd only managed to get home twice in the past eight decades. If anyone saw him—

"I see not much has changed for you, Caligo." The mocking voice came from above. "Let me know if you need a hand up, boy."

Fuck. Just... fuck.

Even without turning around, Cal knew exactly who stood behind him.

Drawing in a deep breath, Cal pushed to his feet, even though he could have used another few minutes on the ground. Minutes he didn't have because he needed to get back to Tessa as soon as possible.

With a concerted effort at a neutral expression, he turned to face the guardsman behind him. Cal bowed his head just enough to pass for respect. "Greetings, Elido."

Broad as a bus, with a right hook that could send a man flying at least 20 feet—and yeah, Cal knew that from personal experience—Elido had the dark hair and sharp features that were so markedly Cimmerian. He could have been a poster boy for the entire race.

Eli smirked and leaned on his staff, as if Cal didn't warrant being on guard against. Not that Eli thought of Cal as a friend. Not anymore.

"Long time, no see, Caligo. Maybe not long enough. What're you doing here, half blood?"

Ah, yes. Some things never changed, for good or worse. "I need to get to Invol."

Eli's eyebrows rose, shock evident on his features. "And why the hell would you want to do that?"

"You don't need to know. Just get the fuck out of my way."

Eli snorted, shaking his head. "Yeah, well, I don't think you want to take that tone with me, boy. You know the rules. No one goes to Invol and no one comes out. Even a half blood like you should be able to understand that. What makes you think you're special?"

Cal didn't think he was special. Never had. Too many people had been oh, so happy to tell him how very not-special he was growing up.

This was why Cal stayed away, though he knew his absence hurt his mother.

Well, that was going to change. Why should he let the assholes dictate his life any longer? He was older now. Stronger. Possibly stronger than most because of his mixed blood.

But now wasn't the time to do a self-psychoanalysis. When he'd made sure Tessa was safe, then maybe he'd set a few new rules at home.

For right now, though, he'd start small.

Shaking off the remaining nausea, he stepped right into Eli's face. The other man barely came up to his nose. Huh. Cal had never realized that before. Something else to thank his mom for.

"Get outta my face, Sentinel. I've got somewhere to be."

Cal's use of Eli's title was deliberate, and Eli stiffened at the insult. Before Cal had left Cimer, he'd risen above Eli in the ranks of the Cimmerian guard. Yeah, he'd been that good.

That's right, buddy. I was farther up the food chain than you, and you know it.

Cal's rank rubbed most of the guard the wrong way, but his dad remained a high-ranking officer and few would willingly cross him. When that mess with Juliana had happened, not even his dad had been able to control the shit storm and he'd never questioned Cal's decision to leave Cimer for earth.

But Cal still held the rank of Watchman, one step above Sentinel.

So suck on that, Eli.

Apparently Eli didn't like the taste because his mouth pursed and his expression turned sour. Suddenly, Cal didn't want to play this game anymore. He just didn't have the time for it.

"Eli—"

"Yeah, fine, whatever." Eli moved to the side, staring out into the forest, his expression blank. "It's your funeral, Cal."

"Yeah, well, it's not my death I'm worried about."

Fuck, he had a goddamn big mouth. Eli's gaze sharpened on Cal again.

"What have you gotten yourself involved in? And why do you need to go to Invol because of it?"

Cal very nearly told Eli to go fuck himself, but before the words could escape, he bit them back. Many years earlier, he and Eli had been friends. Good friends. Eli was a few years younger, but they'd grown up together, trained together. Eli had been one of the only people, in addition to his parents and a very few others, who'd stuck up for Cal before he'd left. That was probably the reason Eli was still stuck as a Sentinel.

Cal needed to remember that not everyone had turned their backs on him. And that they'd suffered consequences as well.

He shook his head. "I can't talk about it, Eli. I just need to get there unnoticed and then I have to go back. A life depends on this."

Eli snorted. "You always did have a soft heart, Cal. It's gonna get you killed one of these days."

No, he didn't have a soft heart. His heart was titanium.

Except for one small spot where a gorgeous blonde Etruscan goddess had slipped into it.

"Fine, just... be careful, Cal," Eli said. "Invol's not for the faint of heart. You can be lost there. Or so I've heard."

Cal paused, hearing no trace of sarcasm or bitterness in Eli's voice. "Thanks for the warning." He meant that sincerely because he was about to break a pact that had held for two millennia, and he probably would get himself killed doing it. "But I can't *not* go. It's too important."

"Then I hope you accomplish whatever it is you came to do."

Before he realized what he was about to do, Eli dug the end of his staff into the ground.

A loud crack rent the air, and a lightning bolt appeared out of nowhere to strike the ground at the spot Eli's staff had marked. The jagged edges of the lightning didn't fade. Instead, they widened until the brilliant flash became a constant blinding glow.

When the gate was finally big enough for a man to step through, Cal caught a whiff of the stench pouring through. The light and the smell combined to make his eyes tear up. What the hell was that smell?

"Damn it, Eli. You're gonna take a lot of shit for this if anyone finds out you opened this gate for me."

Eli just shrugged. "Then I guess you better not tell anyone. Here, take this." Eli whipped something out of the pack on his back and held out a cloak, complete with hood. "You're gonna need it."

Shit. That's what he smelled. Ozone. Fucking ozone. His gaze narrowed as he watched the sunlight pour out of Invol, gilding everything it touched.

You'll be toast if you walk through there, you idiot. You're crazy. You've finally lost it.

But if he didn't, Charun would eventually catch up to Tessa and he'd take her. And she'd be gone from Cal forever.

He knew he wouldn't want to live if that happened. He was screwed either way. At least if he walked through that gate, Tessa might live.

Hell, what was life without one really bad sunburn?

"Try not to get extra crispy, Cal." Eli's mocking words held an undertone of caution. "And stay close to the gate. I'll hold it open for as long as you need me to, but I won't be able to come in after you. I don't have another cloak."

"If I'm not back in fifteen minutes, assume I'm not coming. And Eli... thanks."

Eli just nodded. "No skin off my nose. Don't do anything stupid and maybe you can save your ass."

"ARE you positive this is something you absolutely have to do?"

Tessa huffed as X asked the same question for the tenth or eleventh time. Sal stood in the center of the living room, arms crossed over his chest, waiting for Tessa to give him the word. She didn't want to force X to go with her, but neither did she want to go alone.

Besides, she was a little worried about what Cal would do when he got back and found out she'd left. She didn't want to leave X to bear his brother's wrath and she could admit, at least to herself, that neither did she want to face Cal alone when he caught up with her.

If that made her a coward... well, okay, she could live with that.

"X, it's two in the afternoon. Charun doesn't attack during the height of the day." At least she hoped he wouldn't. "I'll be fine."

Which should be true. Especially where she was going.

X just stared at her for several very long seconds before he sighed.

"Alright, Sal. You heard the Lady." X crossed his arms over his chest. "Beam me up, Scotty."

"Always the comedian," Salvatorus grumbled. "Watch out, kid, or I'll ship you to Antarctica. Without your clothes."

X didn't even flinch. "Yeah, well, that'd be kinder than what Cal's gonna do to me."

"Oh, suck it up, kid."

X opened his mouth to respond but Sal already had his spell in motion. In the blink of an eye, X was winked away from the space where he had been standing to Frentani's. At least she assumed that was where Salvatorus had sent him. She wouldn't put it past the *salbinelli* to give X a detour through a snowbank somewhere.

When he turned to her, she gave him a smile. "Thank you, Salvatorus. I do appreciate everything you've done for me these past few days."

Smiling, he swept a low bow. "Lady Tessa, sweetheart, it's always my pleasure." When he rose, though, his expression was deadly serious. "That said, don't go doing anything stupid. X is right. Cal will go ballistic if anything happens to you. The man has more than a passing fancy for you, and that's something he doesn't have often. Be safe."

A little glow from the thought that Cal cared about her as

more than just a job suffused her body with heat. She bent down to press a kiss to Sal's stubbled cheek. "Thank you. I'm sure everything will be fine."

Salvatorus nodded as he touched the center of her chest just above her breasts, and the world flickered around her and went black.

When color returned to the world, she blinked and brought everything back into focus. And gasped when she realized X had his hands in the air as if he was being robbed and Dr. Eric Frentani held a gun aimed at X's head.

"Nice of you to arrive in time to save my head from being blown off, Lady Tessa."

She rolled her eyes at X's smart-ass remark but turned to face the doctor with a smile. "Please forgive my late arrival and my unannounced guest. And I apologize in advance for his mouth. Eric, this is Extasis. X, this is Dr. Eric Frentani."

Eric lowered the weapon immediately, gave X a short, sharp nod as a greetingthen turned to her with a more much warmer expression.

"I'm just glad you were able to get here, Tessa," Eric said as he took her hand and led her through the dimly lit halls of the underground facility that served as the hospital for the *Fata*. "I've put Flavia closer to the surgery room in case there are complications. She's had a rough time, as you know."

The cool yellow walls, the color of the first light of day, reflected the low light and created a calm, tranquil atmosphere that never failed to make Tessa smile.

Several rooms branched off the main hall, none of them occupied at the moment except for the one at the end, where Tessa could hear Flavia's heavy breathing.

"How far along is she?" Tessa asked before they reached the door.

"Eight centimeters. And it's taken a damn long time for her

to get there. I told her she might want to wait to call you but she's scared. I asked her if she wanted to call a friend to wait with her but... Well, I still haven't been able to get her to tell me where she's from."

"No need to push her, Eric. She'll come around to trusting us eventually."

At least Tessa hoped she would. The little *gianes* had shown up at Salvatorus's door about two months earlier. Timid, underweight, and barely vocal. She refused to say where she was from, where her family was, or who the father of the baby was.

At first Sal had thought maybe she'd sustained a head trauma that could explain her reluctance to speak. But when she'd refused to see a doctor, he'd called in Tessa.

The wood elf had immediately known who Tessa was, bowing and calling her by her proper name. But the girl still wouldn't tell Tessa any more than she'd told Salvatorus.

"She'll be glad to see you, Tessa. I was afraid she was going to give me a hassle when it came time to push if you weren't here."

Knowing X had trailed along behind them, Tessa turned to motion him forward. "Maybe you'd like to rest in one of the other roo—"

"Don't even think about it, Lady Tessa." X shook his head. "When Cal catches up to us and finds out I let you out of my sight, I'm a dead man. Don't condemn me to that, please."

She laughed at the exaggerated expression of fear on his face that contrasted with the twinkle in his eye. "You're as bad as your brother. You just have sneakier ways of getting what you want. Fine, just stay out of the way, okay, X?"

"Is there something going on you want to tell me about, Tessa?"

Eric stared down at her, concern darkening the light blue of his eyes. Born to *Enu* parents—the human branch of the two magical Etruscans races—and blessed with the Goddess Gift of healing, Eric was a gorgeous man.

Tall and broad, he exuded health and confidence. He never got angry or flustered, never raised his voice. His features were sharply masculine and devastatingly handsome. The scruff of a golden brown beard gave him a rakish edge, and his always-in-need-of-a-trim caramel brown hair had subtle waves women wanted to sink their fingers into.

If she was looking for a hunk, he'd fill the bill. *If* she was looking. Which she wasn't. At least, she hadn't been.

Until Cal.

She gave Eric a friendly smile, not wishing to encourage him in any way. Since the first time she'd met him, he'd made it perfectly clear he was interested in her. Not as a goddess, but as a woman.

His eyes held the same heat Cal's did. But Eric evoked none of the passion one look from Cal managed. Thinking about Cal made her tension level ratchet up another notch, and Flavia couldn't afford for Tessa to be distracted.

"Nothing we need to discuss now, Eric. But thanks for asking." She gave him another smile to soften her rejection. "Now, I think I'll just go talk to Flavia."

CAL WOKE to the sound of a child's laughter.

At least, that's what he thought it was. Or possibly the blinding light that surrounded him was screwing with his brain.

With a start, he checked to make sure his body was completely covered by Eli's cloak, no skin exposed to the brutal sunlight pouring down all around him. He couldn't be sure because he could barely see, but he didn't smell burning flesh so he figured he was okay.

"You're not supposed to be here."

The voice startled him so much that he nearly tilted his head back to find the source. He caught himself just in time. It was a young voice, and he couldn't tell whether it was male or female.

"I've come to ask for your help," Cal said. "One of your own needs help."

"One of my own?" A pause. "What does that mean?"

Cal's head had begun to pound as the bright sunlight and the nausea that accompanied travel between the planes combined to make him feel like shit. But this was too important to allow his physical failings to deter him.

"It means Thesan, Lady of the Golden Light, is in danger and needs your help."

Another pause, this one longer. "Who are you?"

Cal thought maybe the tone of that voice had gone just a little bit cold and decided to be a little more courteous. He dipped his head. "My name is Caligo, and I'm protecting Thesan from an attack by Charun."

Dead silence.

With his eyes closed, Cal strained to hear anything, a rustle of clothing that would pinpoint the position of the person he was talking to, a whisper of breath, any sound at all.

He heard nothing.

"Hello? Did you hear me? Thesan needs your help."

"You don't have to shout. I am still here."

What the fuck? "Then maybe you could tell me what you can do to help."

"Help? How?"

Okay, this was getting weird and he was getting pissed off. Probably not a good thing to do when you were talking to a deity. "Maybe by getting Charun off Tessa's *ass*."

"And how would you want me to do that?"

Cal opened his mouth to respond, but he didn't have a clue what to say. Weren't the deities supposed to have all the answers? This one sounded like a child who wouldn't be able to find her, or his, way out of a paper bag.

Okay, maybe he was going about this the wrong way. "If you don't mind my asking, who is this that I'm speaking to?"

His teeth clenched around the need to bite off his words. Or possibly snarl at the clueless wonder he was conversing with. But that was definitely a shortcut to getting his cloak ripped away and frying to a crisp before he could make it back to Cimer. Though he didn't feel heat, cold, or pain, he certainly felt the internal heat of his frustration at the moment.

"I'm sorry," the voice said, palpable sorrow in the tone. "That's a question I can't answer."

Okay, this was just too freaking weird. Maybe Eli had pulled one over on him. Maybe this wasn't Invol. Hell, he could be anywhere…

"I'm sorry I can't be more help. It's… complicated. And you must leave now, Caligo. It's not safe for you here."

"No! Wait—"

He felt himself being pushed toward the gate and was powerless to stop it. Air rushed by him as he flew through the gate at amazing speed. So fast he didn't have time to experience the disorientation of passing through the planes.

And when he landed wherever it was he landed, he felt like he'd fallen to earth from the top of the Empire State Building.

Really fucking hard. On asphalt.

Not in Cimer.

The only lucky thing was that half of him fell in shade.

Cal heard the sizzle of his own skin and pulled his legs into the safety zone afforded by a dumpster. The stench of overripe garbage made his stomach heave, and he rolled onto his side, waiting for his breakfast to return.

After a few minutes of taking deep breaths through his mouth, he figured he wasn't going to blow chunks.

That still left the little problem of where the hell he was and how the hell he was going to get back to Sal's.

Cell phone. Where the hell was his cell?

And now he was rhyming and he wanted to laugh. Damn, must have hit his head harder than he'd thought.

He stuck his hand into his pocket and breathed a sigh of relief when he felt the smooth plastic of his phone. That was quickly followed by a low groan of disgust when he realized the damn thing was in pieces.

He must have fallen on it and crushed it all to hell.

Luckily, he still had the cloak. But he was gonna cause one hell of a scene on whatever street he happened to walk out onto. He'd be lucky if the cops didn't pick him up.

Where the hell was he?

He looked around at the narrow alley surrounded by brick buildings. They looked somewhat familiar, but he couldn't immediately place them. Might have something to do with the fact that he was still seeing double. Probably a slight concussion from the fall.

Not too far away, he heard the rumble of traffic. City traffic, lots of cars, horns beeping, loud music. Was he in Reading? Or had he been tossed somewhere halfway around the world. You never knew with deities.

He tried to force his eyes to focus, but before they did, he heard the distinct sound of a door opening and the wall in front of him parted.

A gasp and then the sound of footsteps approached. "Hey, are you alright?"

He couldn't help himself. He rolled his eyes and shook his head. "Do I look alright?"

Distinctly feminine laughter made his eyes narrow, because

he thought he recognized that laugh. Tipping his head back, he tried to bring the face now peering down at him into focus.

When it did, he wondered if he should just take off the cloak and let the sun have its way with him. "Shit. This just isn't my fucking day."

"AS YOU KNOW, this could take a while, Lady," Eric whispered. "Why don't you have a rest while Flavia's sleeping?"

Trying not to sigh in Eric's face, Tessa forced a smile and rose from the side of Flavia's bed. The *gianes'* labor had appeared to stop and she hadn't had any contractions for the past hour. Flavia had even managed to fall asleep a few minutes earlier.

It had to have been hours since Tessa had last seen Cal, and though her entire attention had been focused on Flavia, a small part of her brain had been waiting for Cal to walk through the door. And every minute that passed that he didn't, the knot in her chest drew a little tighter.

"I'm fine, Eric, thank you. I just need to stretch my muscles. I think I'll take a little walk."

Eric nodded and she turned toward the door, knowing he followed her with his eyes the entire way.

Shutting the door behind her, she sighed as she leaned back against the solid wood. She closed her eyes and took a couple of deep breaths, trying to stave off the panic that wanted to make her heart pound out of control and her lungs gasp for air.

Where was Cal? Why wasn't he back yet? Had something happened?

"Lady Tessa, are you okay?"

She gasped and her eyes flew open to see X grimace as he leaned against the wall on the opposite side of the hall.

"Shit. Sorry, didn't mean to startle you."

"Have you heard from Cal?"

X shook his head, his expression turning grim. "No, not yet."

Damn it, that's really not what she wanted to hear and she didn't want to discuss this within Eric's hearing distance.

Pushing away from the door, she motioned for X to follow her and then walked the length of the hall to another room where they wouldn't be overheard.

As soon as she'd closed the door behind her, she asked, "Should it take this long?"

X had already started to pace. "I honestly don't know. Travel between the planes can be tricky, even for Cimmerians. It could take minutes or it could take hours."

"And if something goes wrong?"

X's expression didn't change, but she swore she saw his brain working before he finally spoke. "Cal's too good for something to go wrong."

"That's not an answer, and you know it."

"It's the only one I have." He shook his head. "I don't—"

A knock at the door dropped silence over them like a veil. "Tessa, there's someone at the outside door to the house asking for you," Eric said. "I think you need to talk to... them."

She exchanged a look with X before she opened the door to address Eric. "Who is it?"

Eric just shook his head. "I have my suspicions, but they asked to speak to you and I don't think my pay grade's high enough to turn her away."

"Her?" X spoke before she could ask the same question.

Eric gave him a quick glance. "There are two people outside. I only know for sure one is a female. The other is covered in a cloak—"

X shot out of the door and ran for the end of the hall before he realized he didn't have any idea how to get where he needed to go.

It only took a few seconds for Tessa to reach him and point out the door that led to the stairs to the upper level, the ranch house that served as Eric's home and provided camouflage for the clinic.

They ran up the stairs, Tessa taking the lead as she headed for the front door. A small monitor by the door showed the two figures, one covered head to toe in a dark cloak. The other...

"Shit."

X's hand froze on its way to the door handle. "Tessa? What?"

She sighed. "Open the door, X. Just be prepared for the sugar overload."

X raised his eyebrows but turned the knob and stepped back.

"Geez, I thought you were never going to open the door. Long time, no see, Thesan. How've you been? Keeping busy, I hope. I have something who says he belongs to you." The strawberry blonde who walked across the threshold didn't look like she was struggling to hold up the much bigger man at her side.

"He's a little worse for wear, but I can see why you might like him back. Very nice. Doesn't have much to say, though."

Tessa's breath caught in her throat as she caught a glimpse of the man's face beneath the cloak. "Cal! Oh, thank the Blessed Mother Goddess."

X had already reached for his brother, slinging Cal's free arm over his shoulders and taking his weight from the woman as Tessa moved to his other side.

"It wasn't very hard to find this place, you know, for somewhere that's supposed to be secret." The other woman continued on without taking a breath. "When Cal asked me to bring him to you, I only had to call Salvatorus and he told me where to come. You might want to think about that. Not that I would ever say anything, of course. I wouldn't. It's just that if you don't want anyone to know about it, you might not want to tell guys like this. I mean, if I he told me, who knows who else he'd tell."

As the other woman babbled on, Tessa and X helped Cal to the couch, and he fell into it with a rough sigh. His head dropped back onto the cushion, the hood falling away to reveal his haggard features. He just breathed for several seconds while Tessa struggled to get the cloak off him so she could check him for damage.

"He wouldn't tell me what he was doing in the alley outside Ichy's club in Philadelphia. He said a few really rude things and then demanded I bring him here to you. I think he thought I was Venus at first. At least, that's what he called me. If he hadn't said your name, I just would've let him expire. I don't think he handles the sun very well, and if you ask me, that could be a problem, considering what you are."

Cal groaned low in his chest as Tessa finally wrestled the cloak open so she could check him for injuries. She didn't see any visible burns or bleeding but that didn't mean he didn't have internal injuries, and from what X had told her about Cimmerians, he might not even know he was injured until it was too late to help.

Tessa cupped her hands around his face, the stubble on his cheeks rough against her palms. "Cal, talk to me. Are you okay?"

"Wow, this place is *really* not what I expected when he asked me to take him to you. Do you need money, Thesan? I know things have been hard since I took over—"

"Jesus, X." Cal's voice was barely audible above the other woman's incessant chatter. "Just shoot me now. She hasn't shut up since she dragged me out of that alley."

As X choked back a laugh, Tessa breathed a sigh of relief then threw her arms around his shoulders and clung.

"Whoa. Hey." His arms circled around her, pulling her tight against him. "I'm fine, Tess. Really. Just a little unsteady from the travel but I'll be fine in a few minutes. Unless my brain explodes because she won't *fucking* shut the fuck up."

Pressing a kiss just below his ear, Tessa felt him shudder just the tiniest bit in reaction and pulled back with a smile on her face. Not even the other woman's noise could bring her down right now.

But Cal was tired. He needed rest, and he'd never get any with *her* here.

Standing, she faced the woman who was still talking and tottering around on four-inch heels, dressed in slinky black capri pants and a skin-tight red tank. She wouldn't look out of place in a backwoods *Grease* road show, Tessa decided and then silently chided herself for the nasty thought.

Aurora had brought Cal back to her, after all. That had to count for something.

"I know we don't see a lot of each other anymore, and I know—"

"Aurora."

"—you really don't like me that much but—"

"Aurora!"

The other woman blinked and came to complete stop. Tessa had the sneaking suspicion that the other goddess couldn't listen and walk at the same time.

That's just mean.

And, unfortunately, possibly true. The deities of the Roman pantheon were, for the most part, spoiled rotten, bitchy, egotistical, and completely self-centered. And a few were... not quite up to speed.

Tessa walked over to the other woman with a friendly smile,

as if approaching a hyperactive child. The stunned look on Aurora's face immediately blasted into a wide grin. She was like a puppy, so eager to please. If she hadn't usurped Tessa's beloved job, Tessa might actually have been able to like the woman.

And, really, after so many millennia, she should be over this petty jealousy shit.

"Thank you for bringing Cal back to me. I truly appreciate it."

Aurora's smile widened so much that Tessa thought the goddess's face might split open. And, unlike her sister, Venus, Aurora didn't have a mean bone in her body. That smile shone as bright as the sun on a summer day.

"Oh, you're so welcome. When he said he needed to get back to you, I wasn't sure if I could trust him. I mean, I know you're not celibate or anything, but it's been a while since I've heard through the grapevine that you'd taken a lover and—"

"And I'd love to spend time catching up with you," Tessa broke in before she gave into the fast-building urge to strangle Aurora, "but I really need to get Cal into a bed. X, could you please show Aurora the way out?"

She turned to see a look of blind panic cross X's face just before the other goddess turned on him like an evangelist in sight of a new convert. The look X shot her should have made her blister and wither under its heat. Tessa just smiled and walked back to Cal. X was a big boy. He could take care of himself.

"Hi, X. Wow, you're a big one, too. I like that in a guy. What does the X stand for? Have you ever read the Black Dag—"

Tessa blocked out the rest of Aurora's one-sided conversation as she sank onto the couch beside Cal. Her hands immediately reached to cup his face, their gazes linked. His moonlight gray eyes still held traces of pain but his expression lightened as he looked at her.

"Are you really okay?"

Cal didn't want to lie to Tessa. Physically, he'd be fine. Yeah, he was a little weak right now, but that had more to do with the travel between planes than it did with any physical injuries. Still, he had to tell her his trip had been a bust, and his chest tightened to the point of pain thinking about it.

They needed to talk. He needed to figure out what to do next. Where to hide her. Cimer would do for now. They'd stick to the forest, away from the towns by the river—

"Cal." Tessa's voice drew his focus back to her, back to the blue of her eyes. "Tell me. What happened?"

She stared at him, her gaze steady. Trusting. Damn it, he really wanted to live up to that trust.

If anything happened to her...

He took a deep breath, drawing her sweet scent into his lungs. "I'm still not real sure what happened. No," he held up a hand as she opened her mouth to speak, "I'm not putting you off. Just... give me a few seconds to clear my head."

Giving a soft sigh, Tessa rose from the couch and stretched out her hands to him. "There's a spare bedroom in the back of the house. Why don't we get you somewhere away from that... woman's manic energy. I swear it lingers for days and makes me crazy. You need a little quiet time."

Cal's lips twisted into a wry grin. "Sounds great. Let's get the hell out of here before X returns and wants to wring your neck for pawning Aurora off on him."

It took more than a little effort on her part to help him off the couch and back to his feet, which just pissed him off. At first, his legs refused to hold his weight and his knees bent in protest before he forced them to hold steady.

Damn, that's not right.

Travel between the planes usually didn't affect him like this. Hadn't since he'd been a green kid learning how to slip his body through the spaces between the planes. Of course, being tossed through a couple of planes at the same time probably hadn't done him any good.

Tessa stood by his side, her top lip caught between her teeth, watching his every move with wide eyes. She held her hands at her sides but the muscles in her arms tightened each time he moved, as if she was anticipating him falling on his face.

That just made him feel that much worse. Christ, he must look pretty fucking bad.

Forcing his feet to move, he nearly did exactly what she expected. He stumbled forward until she slipped her arm around his waist and aligned her side with his. The warmth of her body seeped into his, causing his heart to kick into a faster pace, and he sucked in a deep breath. Her sweet scent made his mouth water.

Damn.

How pathetic was it that he couldn't walk straight but still wanted her so badly he couldn't think straight either? And on top of the desire was the guilt. And the fear.

As they trudged down the hall to the back of the house, he tried to figure out how to tell her he hadn't learned anything at all on his trip.

Total bust.

Gods damn it.

The knot in his gut tightened even further. What the hell did they do now? That trip had been his Hail Mary pass.

"Cal! Hey, don't pass out on me."

Tessa gazed up at him with worried blue eyes, but the worry wasn't for herself. No, the worry was for him. She had no idea how badly he'd failed her.

"I'm not gonna pass out on you." He forced the words from his mouth but bit back the curses that wanted to follow.

"Glad to hear it. But I'd feel better if you didn't look at me like that. You're worrying me."

He was worrying himself. And not just because he'd failed. His lungs seized, squeezing out air in a painful rush.

"How am I looking at you?"

"Like you're about to keel over."

Shit. He shook his head, trying to school his features into some semblance of... well, anything that didn't resemble fear. Which was exactly what he was feeling. And that really sucked.

Cimmerians didn't feel fear. That went against their whole philosophy of life. No pain, no fear. Well, he'd gotten the first part right, at least. He wasn't in any pain. Unless you counted the agony of a constant hard-on around Tessa.

He thought about pushing her away. About not leaning on her. He didn't really need her help to walk. But he liked the feel of her body against his more than he cared to admit. Even through the fear, her proximity made lust boil in his blood.

"Here, sit down."

Looking up, he realized they'd come to a stop in front of a bed. Not as big as he was used to but big enough. And now that he had sex on the brain, nothing else mattered.

Tessa began to pull away, but he grabbed her arm and held her in place.

"We need to talk."

He meant every word but the bed was too damn close.

She nodded, her expression soothing, as if she was talking to a child. "Absolutely. As soon as you've—"

Wrapping his arms around her shoulders, he pulled her against his chest and cut off her short gasp with his mouth.

As soon as his lips touched hers, the lust that'd been boiling in his gut spilled into his blood. His need for her broke free, swamping his good intentions and better judgment in waves of searing heat.

Her body stilled against his for several seconds and he wondered if she'd push him away. Then her fingers sank into his biceps, and elation thundered through him.

Her lips opened for his tongue, and when he sank inside her mouth, she moaned low and deep in her throat. The sound forced an answering groan from him as he twisted them and propelled her backwards onto the bed.

They landed in a tangle of arms and legs, hands reaching for buttons and hems.

He tasted her desire for him in the urgency of her movements and the heat of her breath. His tongue plunged into her mouth, lapping at her spicy flavor. Her tongue slid against his, enticing as she shoved her hands beneath his shirt and scraped her nails up his back, hard enough to leave marks.

Damn, if he wasn't careful, he'd become addicted to the burn he felt only with her.

His fingers wrapped around the hem of her dress and yanked it up, out of his way. The tiny scrap of lace she called underwear gave way with a tear. He had a brief second to wonder how many pairs of her panties he'd ruined before she moaned into his mouth and arched into his hand as he cupped her mound.

Warm, silky skin, wet with her desire, slid beneath his fingers. Groaning, he coated his fingers in her juices, spreading them over her clit and the lips of her sex.

"Cal." His name sounded like a plea on her lips. "Hurry."

She didn't need to tell him twice, but the heat of her distracted him. He didn't think he'd ever *not* be distracted by her heat.

With a rough snarl, he kneeled on the bed between her legs and ripped at the button on his pants. The zipper nearly broke as he yanked it open and then shoved his pants down his legs. Somewhere along the line, he'd lost his shoes. Two less things to take off.

As soon as he was naked , she reached for him, wrapping her hand around his shaft, and proceeded to pump him.

His breath caught in his throat and he stilled. Her touch mesmerized and seduced. His blood flowed hot and heavy, and he had to force his lungs to breathe.

He stared at her face as she watched her hand worked his cock with a steady motion. The smoothness of her palm slid over the skin of his shaft, which ached for her to stroke him harder.

His hips thrust forward, wanting more pressure, a faster pace. But Tessa had her own agenda, which seemed to be to make him crazy.

Her hand slowed to a glacial pace, and she used her free hand to reach between his legs and cup his balls. His head fell back on a rough sigh as she stroked and tormented. His balls drew up tight, the blood pumping thick and fast, and he let himself melt under her touch.

How long could he let her touch him like this? How long could he withstand her torment without ravaging her like a beast?

Not fucking long, it turned out.

His cock twitched and swelled in her hand, and he knew if he didn't get inside her soon, he'd come all over her hands. Not a bad way to go, but not what he wanted.

He wanted to be wrapped inside her warmth when he finally blew. Reaching for her hips, he lifted her until her entrance was on a level with his groin.

Arching her back, she rubbed her pussy on his shaft, spreading her warmth, her moisture to his cock. Their breathing rasped in the silence of the room as she angled the tip of his cock until it brushed against the swollen lips of her sex.

"Put it in, Tessa. Come on, baby. I can't wait any longer."

He barely recognized his voice, so deep and hungry.

Her lips curved in a purely wicked smile at the sound, and she stretched one finger from his balls along his perineum and scratched the skin there, not hard enough to hurt. But enough to make his cock threaten an explosion.

"I have faith in you, Cal."

And she did. He saw it in the soft light of her eyes.

Fuck, he wished he deserved it.

Before he lost himself in the truth of that, he took matters into his own hand. Putting one hand over hers, he aligned the tip of his cock with her slit and thrust until just the tip of him was lodged within her.

Her hands fell away so he could go deeper, and with both hands on her hips, he withdrew then plunged again, harder this time.

"Wrap your legs around my waist, Tess. That's good, so damn good."

She did what he told her, and each movement worked him deeper. His cock felt larger with each thrust. The tight fit of her pussy squeezed him as tightly as her fist and he lost all desire to think. Instead, he let sensation sweep him away.

With their gazes locked, he felt caught in a spell, every motion heightening his pleasure. And hers, if her expression was anything to go by.

She stared up at him, her eyes half-lidded, her teeth caught in her bottom lip. A pink flush covered her cheeks, and he let his gaze slide down her body to where they were joined.

He watched his cock disappear into her body then reappear, slick and ruddy red. Each time he thrust inside, the need grew to do it again. And again. His gaze traveled back up, over the slight swell of her belly to her breasts. He wanted to feel those soft mounds pressed against his chest.

Pulling out of her tight sheath made Tessa cry out and reach for him, but he had to move her, had to shift her so he could lie on top of her, covering her completely. The hardened tips of her breasts dug into his chest as he set his elbows into the mattress on either side of her shoulders and burrowed back into her body.

Deeper this way, especially when she lifted her legs and wrapped them around his waist. Her low moan made him shift, go deeper.

Her eyes drifted shut as he lowered his head to kiss her, letting his hips take up a rhythm of their own. She opened her mouth to him, spread her legs just the tiniest bit further, and gave herself up to him.

Yes. As if that was what he'd been waiting for, he let himself go, driven by the need to conquer.

She was his. Lifting his mouth from hers, he wanted to hear her cry out his name in ecstasy, to see her eyes go dark with lust and her body respond to his every move. His hips drove him deep, speed increasing on every thrust in time with her every gasping breath.

He heard himself saying, "Come on, baby. Come on. That's right. Let go." Felt the deep-seated tension in his lower body coil even tighter as his orgasm approached. Felt her body tighten in anticipation, the arch of her neck, the tightening of her pussy.

And finally the keening cry that signaled her release and the tight clench of her muscles around his cock, squeezing him, milking his response.

He tried to hold out, but she controlled the action now. Each movement of her body dictated his. She demanded he join her and he did with a harsh grunt, pumping his seed into her and collapsing over her with nothing but bliss on his mind.

NINE

"I can practically hear you thinking, Cal. Whatever it is, whatever happened, it'll be best if you just spit it out."

As Cal slipped to her side, Tessa rose up on one elbow so she could stare down into his eyes. He wanted to look away but kept his gaze locked on hers.

As his lungs still tried to breathe normally, Cal knew he couldn't put off telling her any longer. The fear he'd managed to keep at bay while he'd been inside her body began to tear at his stomach.

But, damn, he loved her eyes. They reminded him of the bright noon sky he hadn't seen in eight decades.

She smiled when he didn't say anything right away and ran one finger down his cheek, as if coaxing the words out of him. "Come on, Cal. It can't be that bad."

Yeah, it could. Hell, it could be worse.

"Tess—"

Bang, bang, bang.

"Hey, guys, you gotta get up." X's voice barely carried through the thick oak door. "The doc's looking for you, Lady. I think Flavia's finally ready."

Tessa's smile spread as she pressed a kiss to Cal's lips and then scrambled off the bed to gather her clothes.

Cal shook his head when he realized he still had no idea where he was or what she was doing here.

"Who's Flavia and what is she ready for?"

Tessa tossed his pants at him, nearly hitting him in the face before he grabbed them out of the air. "To have her babies."

"And you're here... why?" Sliding off the bed, he pulled on his pants and then enjoyed the show as she shimmied into the underwear he could have sworn he'd ripped but that now looked whole. Her breasts jiggled just enough to have his cock twitch in response. "I told you to stay at Sal's, Tessa. What if someone had followed you here?"

With a breath-stealing shake, she tugged the sundress she'd been wearing over her head. "I couldn't. I promised Flavia I would be here for the birth of her children, and when she summoned me just after you left, I couldn't refuse. And don't blame X. I gave him no option but to come with me."

The fear cranked up a notch but he tried not to let it show. "And where exactly are we?"

"Well, right now we're in Dr. Eric Frentani's home on Hawk Mountain." She stopped at a mirror to check her reflection, tried to finger comb her hair into behaving, and then gave up with a little shrug. "Below us is the medical facility he runs for the *Fata*."

"Hey, guys." X's voice came through the door a little bit louder this time. "Why don't we discuss this on the way downstairs. Frentani said it's gonna happen in, like, minutes."

Tessa hurried to the door, hopping from one foot to the next as she pulled on her sandals, and opened it as Cal yanked a T-shirt over his head.

She turned back to wave at him as she hurried through the door, giving X a quick once-over as she passed him. "You don't look any worse for wear. You got rid of Aurora nicely, I hope."

"My brain's bleeding, trust me." X shook his head. "That one never shuts up. And I don't think Aurora would've noticed if I told her to fuck off. Hell, I barely got a word in edgewise."

Cal caught his brother's gaze and held it as he attempted to keep up with Tessa. "You and I need to have a talk about what I mean when I say, 'Don't leave.'"

X just rolled his eyes. "Try the tough guy act on someone else, big brother. And you know there was no way I could've kept her at Sal's."

"Fuck me, X—"

"If you two are going to resort to name calling, I'm going to go downstairs and lock the door so you can't follow me." Tessa paused in the doorway midway up the hall. "Don't be angry at X. It's not his fault. I'm irresistible. You would've given me what I wanted, too."

Knowing she was right but still figuring he should punch X for the principle of it, Cal settled for a quick jab to X's shoulder as Tessa rolled her eyes and pushed through the door. Cal nearly didn't get his foot in the crack before the door closed and automatically locked him and X up there.

X gave him a brotherly shove through the door, and they followed Tessa down a bright stairwell to another bright hallway. No harsh fluorescent lighting down here. Recessed lights gave the illusion of sunshine, even though he knew this entire place was underground.

And though it smelled mainly like a hospital—that disinfected, sterile, chemical scent—he also smelled flowers. And not a fake, perfume scent, either. It smelled like—

The unmistakable sounds of a woman in pain came from down the hall. He and X froze as Tessa picked up her pace and disappeared into the room at the end of the hall.

"Shit." Cal looked at X, whose face had paled just the slightest bit. "There really is a woman about to give birth down there."

"Yeah, there is. But trust me when I say that you want to get your ass into that room." X leaned closer and spoke in a tone barely above a whisper. "Frentani's got a thing for Tessa. I'm warning you now so you don't go off the deep end when you meet him."

He shook his head. "Son of a bitch, I don't need this now."

"Cal, what happened? Were you able to talk to anyone in Invol?"

"Yeah, for all the good it did. I haven't told Tessa yet. Hell, I don't know *what* the hell to tell her. It was fucked up."

"What do you mean?"

"I mean, something wasn't right with the person I spoke to. It was... almost like they didn't know who they were or where they were. Just fucking weird."

"Well, shit." X's expression screwed up into a frown. "Now what?"

From the end of the hall, the woman moaned again.

Gods-freaking-damn. He hadn't signed on for any of this shit. Not for blue-skinned demons or trips to Invol. And definitely *not* for pregnant women.

"Cal?"

But he wanted his woman. A real-life goddess. He wanted her more than was healthy, considering he'd nearly been burned to a crisp.

"Yeah, yeah. I'm going."

Taking a deep breath, he started down the hall, pausing as he got to the door before he walked through.

"Push, Flavia," Tessa said. "You're so close to meeting your first child. You just need to push."

The woman on the bed barely noticed Cal's entrance, but

Tessa, standing by her head, her arms around the woman's shoulders, gave him a quick glance and a smile before her attention returned to the action.

The man sitting in front of the woman on the bed—which actually looked more like some funky huge chair with no actual seat that he could see—had time for a scowl before turning back to the laboring woman.

Cal moved to stand behind Tessa, careful not to move too fast. He wasn't squeamish about childbirth. At least, he didn't think he was. He'd never actually seen a baby being born, but he'd seen men die in bloody, awful ways. He'd killed some of those men with his own hands. Surely, the birth of a baby couldn't be that bad.

Cal couldn't help himself. He looked down.

Maybe he needed to revise his opinion. Holy fuck, that looked painful as all hell.

Tessa's calm voice soothed the other woman. Hell, it soothed him and he wasn't the one giving birth.

"Okay, here comes another one. Push, Flavia. The baby's crowning." The doctor smiled down at the sweaty, pale-faced female on the bed.

Cal had watched enough *ER* repeats to know this meant the baby was close to being born. He found himself moving closer to Tessa and the bed so he could see the baby. Just not close enough to really see what was going on down there.

Hell, the woman should have some privacy.

Tessa stood next Flavia, her body supporting the smaller woman, and breathed in rhythm with her. Frentani said something that Cal didn't catch because he was fascinated by Tessa. She wore the most peaceful expression, damn near beatific. She was completely in her element, her voice a low, comforting hum.

The little *gianes* had a death grip on Tessa's hands. She breathed when Tessa told her to breathe, pushed when Tessa told her to push, and relaxed when Tessa told her to relax. Actually, she looked more relaxed than Cal would have ever imagined possible.

He knew a lot of that was Tessa's doing. Cal felt some kind of power flowing between the two women, something that must have acted like a sedative on Flavia.

"Okay, Flavia," Frentani said. "Push now."

Cal kept his gaze on Tessa. He saw her smile grow wider, and then he saw that flash in her eyes, the glow he'd seen earlier when they'd made love. Her goddess powers had kicked in.

A thin, high wail jerked him out of his thoughts, and his gaze shot to the end of the bed where Frentani held a tiny, wriggly infant in his hands.

"A girl, Flavia." The doctor smiled up at her. "A true beauty, like her mother."

With a choked little cry, Flavia reached for the child and Frentani laid her in her mother's arms.

Damn, the baby looked really... gross. All white and red and splotchy. Thin arms and legs waving and a little round belly. The baby had no hair at all, and with its mouth open and screaming like it was, it looked like one of those alien babies from *The X-Files*.

Flavia stared at it with the most amazing smile on her face, as if it were the most beautiful thing she'd ever seen. After seeing what she'd gone through, Cal would've thought she'd want to rage against that little bit of flesh that had given her so much trouble.

Instead, Flavia crooned something under her breath. It sounded like a lullaby. Or a prayer. Then he realized Tessa had joined her. He knew enough Etruscan to realize that's what they were speaking but not enough to know what they were saying. But he did feel the emotion behind the words.

Then Flavia gasped.

"Tessa, take the baby." Frentani positioned himself at the end of the bed. "All right, here we go again, Flavia."

Cal's eyes flew open as he looked at the guy.

Again? What the hell?

"Here." Tessa turned to him, and before he could protest, placed the now blanket-wrapped baby in his arms. "Hold her for a few minutes. Don't drop her."

He looked down into the tiny face of the baby in his arms.

"Ah, Tess, I'm not sure—"

Flavia cried out as her contractions began again and Tessa returned to her position next to her. He looked back at the baby, its little face screwed into a scowl before it let out an ear-piercing howl.

Oh shit.

CAL STOOD over the bassinettes next to Flavia's bed, hands in his pockets, his gaze locked on the two babies.

Tessa had been watching him for the past few minutes while Eric finished up with Flavia. The second birth had been more difficult than the first, and Tessa's leg muscles ached, as did her arms and shoulders.

All worth it.

She walked over to stand next to Cal. "How're you holding up, big guy?"

Cal looked up, his gaze locking onto hers. "Are you okay?"

She tried to dredge up a smile for him, but weariness hung on her like an ill-fitting coat, heavy and uncomfortable. "I'm fine."

"No, you're not." His gaze cut toward the bed. "How's Flavia?"

"She'll be fine."

"Thanks to you."

Oh, this man was way too observant. "She's young and strong. I just helped her along."

"No, it was more than that. This little guy," he lowered his voice as he nodded toward the baby boy who'd given his mother so much trouble, "probably wouldn't have made it if not for you."

She shook her head. "No, that's not true. Eric is a wonderful doctor—"

"But you made the baby breathe. I saw what you did, Tess."

Her lashes lowered as she remembered those few second when she thought she might lose the boy. He'd had an obstruction in his esophagus that had cut off his air supply. With the tiniest surge of her power, she'd dissolved it before he'd suffocated.

There were so few *Fata* in the world, so few being born. They couldn't afford to lose the babies. "I didn't realize you were watching so closely."

"I was watching you."

She smiled in spite of her fatigue. "You say the nicest things."

He moved closer and bent his head close to her ear. "No bullshit, Tess. Are you okay?"

Truthfully, she wasn't, but she couldn't allow Eric or Flavia to know that. First rule of being a goddess: Never let 'em see you sweat.

"I could do with a recharge."

His eyes flared with heat. "I'll recharge your battery any time, Goddess."

Sweet Mother Goddess, the man could turn her on with just a few words. What she wouldn't give for a few hours alone with him. Hell, right now, she'd take a few minutes. As if he'd read her mind, he took a step closer. Then another.

She had to tilt her head back so she could keep eye contact, her breasts barely brushing his chest. The look in his eyes suggested he was about to ravage her, and she wasn't about to turn him down.

Instead, he wrapped his arms around her shoulders and pulled her against him, tucking her head under his chin. His hands slid under her shirt at the waistband and splayed across her back, his cool skin warming against hers. She'd meant to ask him why his skin always felt chilled but she'd never gotten around to it. There was always some other drama.

"Tessa."

Eric's voice tried to cut between them, but she held on to Cal as he stiffened. "Is something wrong?"

"Flavia would like to speak to you alone."

She pulled back to give Cal a smile. "We'll finish this later."

He nodded but didn't say anything. Instead, he shot Eric a look. Something passed between the men and they headed for the door in unison.

Damn, the testosterone show was about to start. Too bad she'd have to miss it.

"TELL me again who you are and why you're here."

Frentani had led Cal down the hall to an office and shut the door before turning on him with a scowl that probably intimidated other men. Cal fought back a sneer. The good doctor felt he had a prior claim on Tessa. Tough shit.

But this was Frentani's domain, and Cal was not an unreasonable man. He was willing to trade some information. And Tessa obviously trusted the guy, so he couldn't be that bad.

"I'm Tessa's protection."

Frentani scowled harder. "And why does she need protection?"

Cal crossed his arms and leaned against the door at his back. "You'll have to ask her that. If she tells you, fine. Now, I need to know if you've got a drug that'll knock her out so she can sleep but not dream."

"Why?"

"Because she needs the rest."

The doc's eyes narrowed. "Yeah, I can see that."

For a few seconds, Frentani stared at him and Cal thought maybe he wasn't going to answer, which would just piss him off. Then the guy surprised him.

"No. I don't have anything that'll work on her. The deities look like us, but their physiology combined with their magic makes them damn near immune to everything except certain, specially made drugs. Only those created by the deities themselves.

"Since the Etruscans were cut off from Invol, they've been unable to get the ingredients for any drug they might have made to help themselves. As far as I know, none of the medicinal herbs had been brought over from Invol . Only Fufluns' vines produce grapes capable of being made into wines that can intoxicate a deity, and he can only grow those in a specific area of Tuscany."

"You know an awful lot about deities."

"I've made it my business to know."

Yeah, Cal bet he had. Probably because of one beautiful blonde goddess still in the room with Flavia.

"Look, maybe if you tell me exactly what's going on, I may be able to help."

Cal hesitated, but he knew in his gut that the guy would do anything for Tessa. Then again, so would he. And right now, she needed to get some rest.

"Tessa's being hunted by Charun while she sleeps. So far he hasn't caught up. But when he does, he'll consume her powers and may be powerful enough to leave Aitás. Apparently, this would be a very bad thing for the world, but my main concern is Tessa. She needs to rest or she's going to burn out while I figure out how to get Charun off her ass."

Frentani paced a tight circle as he listened, scrubbing his hand through his hair as if he wanted to tear it out.

"Why the hell didn't she tell me?"

Because she's a goddess and you're still just a man.

Cal had enough sense not to say that out loud, considering the same could be said for him. "Doesn't matter."

Bullshit.

Alright, yeah, it mattered, but Cal didn't want to get into a pissing match with the guy, especially since Tessa would be pissed. And she didn't have the strength to be pissed at him right now.

"Look," Cal continued, "I'm running out of options. Do you have any suggestions?"

Frentani continued to pace, rubbing a hand along the back of his neck. "One, but she's not gonna like it."

"Depending on what it is, she wouldn't have to know."

The doc sighed as he came to stop in front of Cal. "Find one of the Roman deities and ask for Nectar. The Etruscan and Roman deities are closely related. Physically, the Romans are pretty much copies of the Etruscans, although they'll never admit it. Their Nectar should have the same sedative effect on the Etruscans that it does on the Romans."

Damn. Why the hell hadn't *he* thought of that?

And double damn, who the hell did he approach?

They'd just sent the obvious choice packing. Aurora had seemed eager enough to be helpful.

Where the hell had she gone and could he track her?

"If I go after Aurora, Tessa will need somewhere safe to stay. She needs to rest. She hasn't had more than a few hours sleep in the last week."

"I think I might have a solution."

Cal shook his head. "'Might' isn't good enough."

Frentani looked right into his eyes. "This facility is only known to the *Fata* at the Hawk Mountain enclave and to Sal. Any others who come here are brought by Sal. It's built directly over the ley line that runs through most of this county. My mother laid the wards herself, and she's a *strega*. Do you know what they are?"

Cal nodded. "Yeah, I know about *streghe*." Etruscan women blessed with magical goddess gifts such as healing and visions, they were closely in tune with the earth and its power. Witches, by most standards.

"Then you know the wards will hold. Plus, I have a room—"

Cal's eyes narrowed, hands clenching, and Frentani gave a rueful laugh. "Yeah, ya know, I kinda figured it was like that between you and Tessa, but I didn't..." He cleared his throat but held his ground as Cal continued to glare at him. "So like I was saying, I've got a safe room."

"And that means...?"

"That means it's sunk into the earth and lined with lead."

Cal's breath caught in his throat for a second. "Impenetrable to magic?"

"Yes."

"Has it been tested?"

"Yeah."

"Does Tessa know about this room?"

Frentani shook his head. "Need-to-know only. And those who've stayed there usually don't want anyone to know they had to use it. It's a well-kept secret even among the Etruscans."

"And Charun won't be able to find her there?"

"No."

Cal looked into Frentani's eyes, trying to see just how certain the guy was. The doctor didn't blink.

Alright. Alright, he could do this. He could leave her here, just for an hour. Or three.

She'd be fine.

"I'LL BE FINE, Cal. Everything will be fine."

Tessa stood next to him, a sweet smile on her lips as he stood next to the solid iron door, closed to give them a few last minutes of privacy. As far as Cal could tell, the room was everything Frentani had promised. Tessa should be safe here.

He couldn't allow himself to believe otherwise because he needed to leave. Now. The sun had set, and he could move around outside without fear of getting toasted.

But it also meant Tessa was at her weakest. It'd scared him that she hadn't put up a fight when he'd told her what he had planned.

"I'll be gone a couple of hours, four tops." Fewer if he could manage it, but something told him this wasn't going to be a hit-and-run mission. "Get some rest."

Tessa smiled at him as if he were a puppy. Hell, he wouldn't have been surprised if she'd patted his head and told him he was a good boy. And he'd lap it up like a good dog.

Shit. When had the tables turned? When had he become the one who needed reassurance? And when the hell had he started to worry about his jobs like they were important to him?

When you started sleeping with this job.

Yeah, that had probably been a mistake, but it'd been the best damn mistake of his life. One that threatened his sanity.

He didn't want to leave her, and he couldn't tell whether he had a legitimate reason to worry or if he was just being paranoid. Not all paranoia was a bad thing. Too much, though, and you started to lose focus.

Tessa couldn't afford for him to lose his focus.

As if she'd read his mind, her smile dimmed until it became a bit sad. "Be careful, Cal. I'll be very upset if something happens to you."

He saw worry cross her expression, and he couldn't help wondering if she was concerned about what would happen to her if he failed. If she cared about his safety. Then she leaned in and kissed him as if she couldn't bear to see him go. Her mouth opened over his, and her tongue touched his lips, asking for entrance.

Like he'd ever deny her.

Wrapping his arms around her waist, he pulled her flush against him. Her hips tilted into his; her breasts pressed into his chest; and the pressure stoked the fire in his blood. And this was no slow-burning ember. Hell no, this was an inferno that threatening to escape his tight control.

Lust flooded his senses with heat and made his nerves pop and sizzle. His brain short-circuited when her tongue slid past his lips to tangle with his. He felt the warmth of her fingers on his scalp as she threaded them through his hair, each one a brand.

Christ, he was about to incinerate.

With a groan, he pressed her against the door and lifted her. Her feet left the floor as she wrapped her legs around his waist, pressed her mound against his erection, and short-circuited his brain.

Right here, right now. He needed her. Right fucking now.

Turning, he pressed her against the door and thrust so hard that he heard the door creak behind her.

"Shit." He pulled back to look at her. "Did I hurt you?"

Christ, he didn't want to hurt her. He tried to draw back even farther but she refused.

"You're killing me, Cal. Hurry."

She curled her hands around his neck, brought his lips back down to hers, and opened her mouth to him again.

Not hurt. And so hot for him.

The heat of her skin, of her sex, seared him even through their clothes. He had to have her. Forcing a hand between their bodies, he pushed her skirt up with rough hands, causing her to moan his name.

"Tess, unwrap your legs, babe."

She didn't hesitate to do exactly what he told her, and he stripped her underwear down her legs as fast as he could with one hand. As soon as they hit the floor, her legs wrapped back around his waist and his hand clawed at the button on his jeans until it parted. Or it tore. He didn't care.

His engorged cock made it interesting getting his pants down one-handed, but finally he managed to bare enough of himself to get inside her. They groaned in unison as he filled her in one motion, his need for her allowing no hesitation. He had to be right here, right now, and he froze, absorbing every sensation.

But Tess was impatient and started to ride him, pulling up and sinking down like a pole dancer. Only way better.

She felt so good, so fucking good, he let her have the control. Her tight sheath made every movement heaven and hell, the friction enough to make his eyes roll back in his head.

He had to break their kiss to drag in air and buried his face in her neck, drawing in her sweet, sun-warmed scent as she rode him faster.

Her quickening breath brushed over his shoulder, warning him of her imminent release. He pumped into her on her next downward stroke and felt his release hit him like a gunshot to the lower back. His hips thrust forward, nailing her to the door and making her cry out as she came all over his cock with a rush of heated wetness and a tight, rhythmic clasp.

For several minutes, they stood there, panting, hips locked, her legs tight around his waist, their arms wrapped around each other. And a powerful sense of rightness settled in his chest, which shook him to his gut.

Tessa turned her face into his neck and her breath brushed his ear. He shivered at the sensation of warmth.

"Cal?"

He stepped away from the door, expecting her to unwind her legs. But she didn't. "Cal, are you okay?"

No. "Yeah. Are you?"

"Yes." Her smile brushed his cheek. "Even better now."

"Good."

She finally unwound her legs, and he set her on the floor then stepped away and pulled his pants up. "I gotta go."

"I know."

Forcing himself to meet her eyes, he saw that familiar glow. And her trust in him.

He wanted to be worthy of it.

She bent to pick up her panties and shimmied them up her legs. Blood swelled back into his cock as she wiggled, but he forced back the desire and shook his head to clear it.

He wanted to say something, something about how he felt, how she made him feel. But didn't know what that was because it was nothing he'd ever felt before.

She must have seen something in his eyes of what he wanted to say because she smiled.

"Be careful. Come back to me soon."

Then she stepped back and away.

He turned and headed out the door, making sure it was closed tightly behind him. Every step he took away from her felt wrong, but he forced himself to keep going. If he wanted to keep her safe, he had to do this. He just didn't have to like it.

X had agreed to remain here until he got back and that eased the worry. Some.

Once outside the building, camouflaged beneath an ordinary-looking home in a wooded area on the side of a hill, Cal started walking northeast, heading farther into the woods. The moon had just risen and, out here, away from the city lights, the crescent glowed brightly.

Hoping like hell that he wasn't about to make a huge mistake, he pulled out his cell phone and dialed a number he'd sworn he was going to delete. When the line connected, he took a deep breath.

"I need to cash in that favor."

TEN

"So Cal filled you in?" Tessa asked as she sat on the bed, watching Eric pace near the door.

"Yeah, he did." Eric stopped pacing to look at her. "Why didn't you come to me first, Tessa?"

She didn't answer right away as she let her gaze travel around the room. The bed frame and the side table were made of iron. The plain walls and silk bedding were snow-white, which helped repel any magic that might get through the iron-lined walls.

All that white made her blink, so stark in comparison to the warm gold of the sunlight she longed for. Down here, below the ground, she felt the absence of the sun. And she felt no residual power at all from the reflected sunlight off the moon.

It made her feel cut off, alone. And with Cal gone, the fear she'd been keeping at bay started to creep back into her stomach and to lie there like a cold, hard ball.

"Tessa?" Eric called to her as if she were far away. And maybe she was. "Are you okay?"

No, she wasn't. But she wasn't going to say that to Eric.

She hadn't come to the doctor for just the reason that he'd

wanted her to. She liked Eric, but not in the way he wished she would. He wanted her. Hell, he seemed to genuinely like her as a person, as opposed to just wanting to get it on with a goddess.

But she'd never felt that spark with him. Not like the forest fire of emotion Cal lit in her.

Which could be more of a problem than she'd bargained for.

Blessed Mother Goddess, if you can hear me, please keep him safe.

"I needed a warrior, Eric. Not a doctor." She flashed him a look and caught his scowl. Catching back a sigh, she knew it was time to change the subject. "How are the babies? Will they be okay?"

He shook his head, and she knew he wasn't going to take her not-so-subtle hint.

"Tessa, what do you really know about this guy? I understand Salvatorus recommended him and you trust Sal. Hell, I trust Sal. But I don't want you to fall into something because you're scared."

"I'm not in danger of falling into anything." Because she'd already fallen. And hard. "The babies, Eric. Will they be okay?"

He sighed, ran his hands through his hair, and finally shook his head. "Yes, I think they'll be fine. They're small, but you expect that with twins. And the boy's lungs aren't as developed as I'd like but, yeah, they're going to be okay."

She nodded and forced a smile. "Good. Now, I'm going to lie down. Would you tell X to let me know if he hears anything from Cal? And can you dim the lights on your way out, please?"

He sighed again, this time with resignation, and turned toward the door. "I have to shut the door tight but there's a call button on the table. Press it if you need me. Try to get some rest, Tessa. You need it."

As the door snicked shut and the lights powered down to a dim glow, she sat on the bed, pulled her knees tight to her chest, and took a deep breath before releasing it slowly. But the growing weight on her shoulders wouldn't budge.

Worry ate at her stomach. Worry for Cal. Worry for herself. Worry about the babies and Flavia. All that stress jumbled together into a hard ball that made it increasingly difficult for her to breathe normally. And impossible for her to rest.

She knew, theoretically, that this room should hide her from Charun's reach. Iron's ability to repel magic was well documented among those who used magic. Still, sometimes the rules didn't apply to deities.

Sometimes… hell, most times the rules didn't apply to deities. When that worked to her advantage, it wasn't such a bad thing. When it didn't…

"Oh, Uni's ass, just lie down already."

With a sigh, she did, curling onto her side and wishing Cal's big body was curled around her. She hoped he'd get back soon.

THE REDHEAD PACED the length of her palatial bedroom as Cal stood in the corner, his gaze flicking between the door and the female.

He'd taken a huge risk, letting her bring him here. But he really hadn't had a choice. If any of the others caught him here…

"This isn't a favor, Caligo. What you're asking could get me skewered by a lightning bolt, you idiot. I can't believe you would even have the balls to ask me it. You know I can't give it to you."

He crossed his arms over his chest. "I know exactly what I'm asking. You owe me, Venus. Vulcan nearly killed me and you let him. You're lucky I never told him exactly what you were up to, playing him off against Mercury."

Her beautiful face screwed into a cold scowl that made Cal wonder how he'd ever been taken in by her looks. Her green eyes gleamed like cold glass, and her lips curled into a hateful sneer. Even her hair rubbed him the wrong way, brassy and too bright.

"Don't piss me off, mortal." She tossed that too-bright hair over her shoulder in a move she probably thought was enticing. Not so much. "What you're asking for is forbidden."

Hell, everything about her rubbed him the wrong way. Especially the way she curled her lip. If she were a man, he'd punch her. Just once. Just to take care of that constant sneer.

"I know that." He spoke each word slowly and carefully, as if speaking to someone with mental disabilities. Which he wouldn't be surprised if she had. "Which is why I'll make you a promise. I won't tell if you won't tell."

Her gaze could slice a man in two. "Don't be juvenile. What do you want Nectar for anyway?"

Besides the fact that it was a powerful aphrodisiac to humans? And its healing powers legendary? "Let's just say it's not for me."

Venus' eyes narrowed. "Then who is it for?"

He shook his head. "Doesn't matter. I need it and you're going to give it to me. You owe me."

That perfect nose, which Cal thought was too damn straight, went up in the air. "You presume too much, Cimmerian. I don't *have* to give you anything."

"Then I will beg an audience with Jupiter and tell him all about your little scheme."

Probably be suicide. Jupiter had a habit of slinging thunderbolts at people for fun in his specially designed throne room on the first level of this ostentatious estate. But if it was the only option left to him, he'd do it. For Tessa.

Venus huffed and tossed her hair over her shoulder again. "He'll kill you."

Cal shrugged. "You can only hope he does. Because if he

doesn't, Daddy's not going to be too happy with his little princess when I tell him why you wanted Vulcan's hammer."

Not that he knew for sure. He'd only had a suspicion but when pure hate showed in every scrunched line of Venus' face, he knew he'd guessed right.

Damn, if looks could kill, he'd be sliced, diced, and fricasseed. But she didn't lash out at him. She couldn't use her powers here. Jupiter had added that safety device so the deities couldn't attack each other while they slept.

The Roman pantheon really was more like a pack of jackals than a family.

Still, she could pick up a knife and shove it in his heart. He'd be just as dead, and none of the other gods or goddesses would bat an eyelash. But she'd have to reach him first, and he was faster and stronger. He'd fight her to the death over this.

And he was right about what Jupiter would do to her if he found out why she'd wanted Vulcan's hammer.

Venus' head tilted back and that straight nose pointed even higher. "You don't have a clue what you're talking about."

He let his brows rise slightly. "You really want to take that chance? You know, you'd be surprised what you pick up when you hang out in a bar with lots of disgruntled gods, most of whom have been fucked over by you. And there've been a lot of them, haven't there, babe?"

The muscles in Venus' shapely arms quivered as her hands curled into fists at her sides.

Yes, he was playing a dangerous game and he had to be careful not to tip his hand. But Tessa needed the gods-damn Nectar, and Venus would give it to him whether he had to beg, borrow, or steal it. Without losing his life.

Like the remaining Etruscan pantheon, with the exception of those who'd withdrawn to Invol, the Roman deities lived on earth. Unlike the Etruscans, they lived like one big, incestuous, redneck family. But they did it in one of their multimillion-dollar compounds in the Hamptons, in Gulf Coast Florida, or on the outskirts of Rome.

This one was in the Hamptons. Cal recognized the view from the windows as the Atlantic Ocean. The Atlantic had that dull, blue-green color whereas the Gulf always sparkled. Almost like the fury in Venus' eyes right now.

Maybe he'd gone about this the wrong way.

Deliberately softening his expression and forcing down some of the tension in his body, Cal sighed. "Look, Venus. I'm not asking for an entire bottle. I'm asking for a couple of tablespoons. Just enough to knock out another deity."

Her eyes narrowed and her mouth pursed. "Someone I know?"

He squashed a smile. "Of course it is."

"Who?"

No way was he going to tell this bitch goddess about Tessa's situation. She'd find some way to take advantage. Cal refused to put Tessa into a worse situation than she was already in.

So he lied. "Let's just say Voluptas has it coming."

The smile that lit Venus' face would have frightened off a gorgon. Voluptas, the Roman Goddess of Pleasure, had been a thorn in Venus's side for centuries.

The goddesses overlapped in their duties, especially where love and pleasure collided. And both were bitchy enough to want to make the other's life miserable.

"Well, now," Venus practically purred, "that could be a different story. I might be convinced to provide you with what you need."

Cal bowed his head, biting back his victorious grin. "It won't be going to waste, I can assure you."

With a drawn-out sigh, Venus rolled her eyes. "Fine. Stay here. This could take a little while."

Something in the way she said that sent a chill skating up his back. He didn't trust this one not to stab him in the back, even though he was doing something she wanted. Hell, he didn't trust any of the deities not to fuck him over, which made the feelings he had for Tessa all the more unusual.

As Venus left the room, he heard the snick of the lock.

Bitch.

He tried not to think about the fact that he was now locked in. Not that he would have gone wandering around the Roman deities' home uninvited. He didn't have a death wish.

Besides, it wasn't like he could just walk off the property. He'd needed Venus to bring him here. He'd need her—or one of the other deities—to get him out. He hated that. Hated the sense of being trapped.

What if something happened to Tessa while he was gone?

He took a deep breath, leaned against the wall, and prepared to wait.

TESSA COULDN'T SLEEP.

She tried for at least an hour, tossing and turning in the bed. But she couldn't get her brain to shut off enough to allow her to rest. She kept thinking about Cal.

Was he okay? Would he be able to convince Venus to give him the Nectar? They didn't even know if it would work on her. What if he'd put his life in danger for nothing?

Cal was human. Only human. Breakable. A mortal who would eventually die and leave her. As had all her human lovers. Which was why she hadn't taken one in centuries.

"Screwed up here, didn't you?" Her voice sounded overly loud in the silent room, as did her sigh. "And now you're talking to yourself. Great. Just great."

If she didn't find something to distract herself, she was going to go crazy in here. Because now that she had time to think, she knew she couldn't stop.

Since there was no clock, she didn't know long she spent waiting and worrying. She only knew it seemed like an eternity.

So when the door lock clicked open, she sighed with relief. Until X pushed through the door. His expression made her heart crash against her ribs.

"What happened? What's wrong?"

"Aurora just texted me. We have to go. Cal's in trouble, and you need to go claim him. She said Mercury's gonna kill him if you don't. She said he's already hurt. Bad."

X's words were clipped and tight as he took her arm and practically pulled her out the door and down the hall. "I don't know what the *fuck* he's doing in the Romans' Hamptons compound because nobody *fucking* tells me anything, but Aurora said if we don't get there soon, he'll be dead."

Tessa tried to swallow but could barely get past the lump in her throat as she hurried alongside X. "He went to get Nectar for me. To help me sleep."

"*Shit.*" X practically ripped the door to the second floor off the hinges to get it open. "We gotta hurry, Lady. Cal's a tough son of a bitch, but he can't put up with a beating from a god for long."

"How are we going to get there?"

"Aurora said she'll transport us there. I just have to text her back."

They were running by the time they hit the first floor, even though Tessa had no idea where they were running to. When they reached the living room, X stopped and pulled out his cell phone. The seconds felt like hours as she waited for the line to connect.

"It's X. We're ready."

On the other end of the phone, Tessa heard Aurora's unusually subdued tone and worried even more. She couldn't make out what the goddess was saying, but whatever it was, she knew it wasn't good. X's expression became grimmer by the second.

"I understand," X said. "Yes. I'm sure. Do it."

He grabbed Tessa's hand, and before she could blink, she found herself standing in the circular foyer of a grand home.

She'd never been to the Romans' Hamptons estate before but she never would have mistaken it for anything else.

The statues completely gave it away. The twelve, life-sized marble renditions of the main Roman deities lined each side of the foyer in two half circles. Jupiter and Juno flanked the wide doorway straight ahead. Beyond, she saw a palatial-looking sitting room.

She didn't see any living being, though, and the panic started to eat at her. She turned her head, looking for another room, looking for Cal, but saw nothing. If she had to search the entire complex, she'd do it and face whatever consequences came.

"There you are." Aurora stepped into the opening to the next room and Tessa felt the overwhelming urge to kiss her. "We have to hurry. Your human is getting the crap kicked out of him, Thesan, and I know you'd rather he wasn't irreparably injured."

Aurora held out her hand and Tessa willingly took it, allowing the other goddess to lead her and X deeper into the house. She barely noticed her surroundings, only that they were gaudy. Probably expensive as all hell because the Romans did everything to excess.

That had never been the Etruscan way. The Etruscans were more level-headed, less likely to fly off the handle. More compassionate.

The Romans had a mean streak a mile wide. And Cal had walked straight into their midst. For her.

"Here." Aurora stopped by a door midway down a hallway. "Quickly. I can't go in or Mercury will know I helped you. Don't show any weakness, Thesan. Mercury will use it against you. And you can't take X with you. It will just give Mercury more ammunition. Go. Now."

"No," X said. "Wait, Lady—"

Without any idea of the situation she was stepping into, Tessa grabbed the cut-glass door handles, noted the buzz of power running through the handles, and pushed through.

CAL WAS DAMN sure he was about to go down for the last time when the door to the room opened.

He'd put up a decent fight, but the winged messenger of the Roman gods fought dirty. And Mercury drew his power from the air around him, making him damn near impossible to beat down.

Hell, the god barely looked winded and Cal was sucking air like a jet engine. Though he couldn't feel any pain, blood ran from his mouth and from the cuts on his cheeks. His left arm had definitely been fractured; his right hand had shattered bones; and his right tibia threatened to give out at any moment.

He'd been so close to getting the hell out of there with his prize. Venus had been about to send him back to Tessa when the door to her room had burst open and Mercury had stomped through like a bull on a rampage.

Hell, the guy's black eyes had been glowing red like a freaking B-movie demon.

Cal had barely had time to shove the small vial of nectar Venus had given him into his back pocket before the enraged god had swung one large fist at his face. The impact had spun him around like a character in a Bugs Bunny cartoon.

After that, the fight had more resembled the beating taken by Sylvester Stallone in the first *Rocky* movie. Except this wasn't going to end in a draw.

Mercury was going to punch the shit out of him until he broke every bone in Cal's body and his heart finally stopped beating. And the only thing Cal could think about was Tessa. If he died, X would die trying to save her and Charun would take her anyway.

So when the door opened and Mercury turned to see who would dare interrupt his fun, Cal took the opportunity to make a break for it. Not that he got far. He tripped over his feet and went down to his knees. Probably looked funny as hell. Wished he could laugh about it.

He felt even less like laughing when Tessa walked into the room. He wondered for a second if he was seeing things or if it really was her.

Yeah, she was wearing the same blue dress she'd had on when he'd left her. And it wasn't like she looked any different than she had that morning. But there was something about her, something in the way she held herself. Her spine was rigid, her lips in a flat, straight line, her eyes cold.

She resembled Aurora more now than when he'd first seen the two of them together. It was all about the way she held herself rather than her appearance. She *looked* like a goddess about to kick some ass.

And she'd come for him. It hurt, but his lips curved in a smile.

"Touch him again, and it will take a century for your skin to grow back after I burn it off."

Mercury turned with a snarl, lifting his arm to backhand

her. Cal forced himself to his feet, even though he knew he'd be too late to save Tessa from being hit.

The bastard would pay for daring—

Mercury's arm froze in mid-strike. His eyes widened in shock, his mouth a ring of complete disbelief.

"What the fu—"

"And I really don't want to listen to you whine," Tessa said, "so be a dear and shut up."

Okay, now Cal's mouth was hanging open as much as Mercury's. How the hell had she done that?

"Cal, you have some explaining to do, I think." With a slight turn of her beautiful neck, Tessa glanced at him and he was stunned to see her eyes glowing as well. Her powers were in full force. "But that can wait for later. Now, it's time for us to leave."

"Thesan? Is that you?" Mercury's gaze narrowed as he stared at her.

"Yes, it is actually. Sorry for the hit-and-run visit but you have something that belongs to me and I need it back."

Her normally warm voice had an edge of ice to it now, but it toned down Mercury's expression from furious to curious. Hell, the guy looked happy to see her. And that was *not* something Cal wanted to think about.

"This mortal is yours?" Mercury gave Cal a glance, his lip curling in a sneer. "Are you sure you really want him back? Not much of a man, if you ask me. Can't take a few punches."

"Yes, well not everyone is as perfect as you, Merc." Her sultry smile made Mercury's eyes narrow with lust. "Unfortunately, I need this man in one piece."

The gaze she turned on Cal made his balls want to crawl back into his body. Hell, if he wasn't so sure she was playing Mercury like a pro, he'd want to crawl in a corner and whimper like a whipped puppy.

"He's only useful to me if he's fully functional, unfortunately," she continued. "I'm so sorry he's been a bother. It was nice to see you again, but I'll take him off your hands now."

There was no mistaking where the word "mercurial" came from as the god turned on a charming smile. "Are you sure you need to leave so soon?"

With a strut like a peacock, Mercury crossed the room to sidle up to Tessa. If the guy so much as attempted to touch her, Cal would break his fingers. When he could walk again, of course.

And if Tessa smiled at Mercury one more time, he'd bust the guy's ruggedly handsome face into itty-bitty pieces. With his good hand.

"Unfortunately yes." She snapped her fingers in Cal's direction without taking her eyes off Mercury. Damn, that turned him on. Strange but true. "I have business to attend to, and I need Caligo to complete it."

"And what exactly do you need a Cimmerian for, Thesan?"

Cal stiffened as Venus entered the room through a door behind him. *Shit.* His stomach tightened into a hard ball of knots.

Not good. *So* not good.

Tessa turned to face the bitch goddess, and Cal worried for a brief second that Venus would chew her up and spit her out. Tessa was too sweet, too kind. She had a warm heart.

Venus had acid in her veins and a stainless-steel pump in her chest.

But when Tessa looked at Venus, Cal saw no warmth in her expression. No hint of her true personality in the cool blue of her eyes. This was the Goddess Thesan, the deity who'd been worshipped by millions, who'd commanded the sun and channeled its power for her own purposes.

It'd been easy to forget.

"For no reason that concerns you, little doll."

Cal wasn't the only male in the room holding his breath.

What the hell was Tessa doing? Antagonizing Venus was a fast track to getting your head bitten off. But Venus didn't attack. Her chin tilted up slightly, as if she'd taken a hit.

What the hell?

"I only ask because your mortal may have a hidden agenda. He came to me for a... favor." Her gaze darted to Mercury for a brief second, and Cal knew Venus wouldn't reveal that she'd given him the Nectar. She didn't have a death wish, and giving Nectar to mortals was a death sentence. "I wouldn't want to see you get injured, Lady."

Lady? Venus was calling Tessa "Lady"? Cal felt liked he'd slipped into the Twilight Zone. None of this made sense. Well, he understood why Mercury would want to hit on Tessa. The woman was gorgeous. But Venus kowtowing to Tessa?

Tessa bowed her head slightly and shrugged one perfect shoulder. "I'm sure I can handle whatever he may come up with. Now, if you don't mind, we really need to be going. I have an appointment I can't miss. Caligo, attend."

She snapped her fingers in his direction again, and with a lurch, he forced himself to his feet. Just because he couldn't feel pain didn't mean that he didn't realize the damage he was doing to his body. And there was a lot of fucking damage to his body. He was fairly sure he had a punctured lung and possibly kidney damage.

But he had to obey. For this plan to work, they had to walk out of here. And fast.

He made sure he was steady on his feet before he attempted to move. Wouldn't do to keel over now. He took a step toward her. Then another and another until finally he stood next to her.

Tessa's expression showed no sign of compassion. A sneer marred her beautiful lips. "You'd better hope your injuries don't interfere with my plans, Caligo."

"I'm sure they won't, Lady."

"Yes, well, we'll see, won't we? We can see ourselves out, thank you."

Tessa turned to Venus one more time, nodded, then flashed Mercury a smile that made the god's lips curve in a lustful smile. That Cal really wanted to wipe off his face.

Never gonna happen, buddy.

They made their way out of the room then. Tessa never looked back, and neither Mercury nor Venus followed. That was a damn good thing because Aurora was waiting for them, standing in the shadows of an alcove near the front door, which was the size of a fucking castle gate. It was barred with a thick wooden beam and black iron hinges at least a foot long.

Christ, did the Romans do nothing on a normal scale? What the hell were they compensating—

"Holy shit." He knew exactly what they were compensating for. "Big fucking shoes."

Tessa spared him a quick glance, and this time he saw fear in her warm blue eyes. Now, *there* was his Tessa.

Even though they were nowhere near being in the clear yet, all the blood began to rush to his cock. Well, at least something still worked. And that was definitely not what he should be thinking about now. He had to concentrate on getting his legs to work so they could get the fuck out of here.

"Thesan, hurry."

Aurora's stage whisper echoed through the entry hall, loud enough to be heard through the ringing in his ears. That worried him. So did the numbness in his left leg.

Still, he kept moving. They had to get out of here and fast, before either Mercury or Venus decided they needed to converse a little more. Tessa took his arm, probably because he stumbled and nearly fell, and he sighed in relief as he felt her warmth seep into him. His heart beat just a little faster and he swore the ringing in his ears eased.

Still his Tessa.

"Aurora," she whispered, "we need to get out of here right now."

"I know. Jupiter's asking questions and that's a very bad thing."

Tessa stopped and took a second to enfold the other woman in a hug. Hell, Tessa even looked like she meant it. "Thank you. For everything."

Aurora's smile was nearly as bright as Tessa's. "You know you only have to ask." Then Aurora shocked the shit out of him by curtseying to Tessa before straightening with an impish smile and giving a little finger wave. "Later."

With a snap, Cal's vision went black. When it cleared again, he realized they were back at Frentani's.

"Cal!"

He heard X shout his name and heard Tessa gasp. He wanted to reassure her that he was fine, but he was pretty sure that was a lie.

Then he passed out.

"LADY, why don't you take a seat? You look like you're going to fall over."

Tessa shook her head, unable to take her eyes off Cal. She and X had carried him downstairs to the medical facility after he'd passed out and put him to bed in the safe room.

A minute ago, Eric had hurried in, taken one look at Cal, and started to swear under his breath. That terrified her. But no more than the ash-gray color of Cal's face.

"I'm pretty sure he's bleeding internally, and I'll have to

operate to stop it." Eric's voice seemed to come at her from far away. She could barely make out his words as she stood next to the bed, staring at Cal. "I'm going to need someone to assist. It'll take the nurse a few minutes to get here, and I don't think we have time to spare."

Cal was dying. She knew it without having to be told. She swore she could feel him slipping away from her with each passing second and every labored breath. Leaving her alone. Nothing she could do to stop him.

Powerless—

No, not powerless. She blinked, her body shuddering as if with shock.

She looked at her hands then lifted her gaze to Eric. "You need to leave. You and X. Right now."

Both men whipped around to stare at her as if she'd lost her mind.

"Lady, what—"

"Tessa," Eric cut off X. "This man needs immediate help or he's going to die within minutes."

"I know that." She turned to X. "I can fix him. But if anyone else is in the room when I do, they could drain my power. You have to leave."

"What?" Eric looked stunned. And unconvinced. She couldn't blame him. He didn't know about her returning powers. "Tessa—"

"No. No arguments." X nodded at her, his expression set. "Do it. I know you can." Then he turned to Eric. "Let's go, Doc. Now."

"Wait." Eric's shell-shocked expression nearly made her smile. "Just wait a minute. Tessa, you don't have the power to—"

"Yes, I do. I won't let him die." She shook her head. "Not like this. I can do this, Eric."

Eric didn't believe her. She saw the doubt in his eyes. It didn't matter. *He* didn't matter. Only Cal mattered right now.

She had to fix Cal.

As X practically dragged Eric out of the room and shut the door behind them, Tessa walked to the side of the bed.

She barely saw the rise and fall of Cal's chest as he took a breath. His color had become even more ashen. She was almost afraid to touch him, but Eric had been right. They couldn't wait even a few minutes.

She had to do this, and she had to do it right the first time. If she was wrong about her power... If she couldn't do this...

He's mortal. They all die eventually.

It was the one immutable fact of their existence.

And though he would return again, reborn into another body, he'd return with no memories of his previous life, possibly centuries in the future. And she was selfish. She didn't want to lose him. Not yet.

This had to work. Placing her hands on his chest, over his heart, she closed her eyes. And tried to feel each beat of his heart. She strained to hear it in her hands and feel it echo in her own chest.

There! Faint but there.

Though she'd helped to deliver hundreds, maybe thousands, of babies, and she'd fixed defects ranging from cleft palates to heart murmurs, she'd never attempted to fix damage such as this in a full-grown man.

And there was a lot of it.

She heard the air escaping from the puncture in his lungs. Heard the bile leaking from the tear in his spleen and the acid from his ruptured kidney. Each fracture in his bones registered as a white-hot pulse of pain in the corresponding area of her body.

At least she knew he felt no pain.

But with each passing second, he slipped farther and farther away from her. She refused to allow it.

"You will not get away from me that easily. I won't allow it."

Digging deep, she sought out the part of herself where her power resided. It'd been dormant so long that she wasn't sure at first that she could remember how to call it.

It'd come to her unexpectedly at the club. She'd done nothing to encourage it, hadn't even realized she was using it. It'd been so long since she'd been able to. Now, she forced herself to remember. She had to. Cal's life depended on it.

At first, she felt nothing. Nothing but his pain. It burned inside her, so she dug deeper, knowing that each passing second put him closer to death.

Blessed Goddess, what if she couldn't do it? What if—

"No." She forced herself to focus, to block out that inner doubt demon. "You can do this. You *have* to do this."

And she would. She just needed—

With a gasp, she felt the power rise up, so strong it caused her vision to go dark around the edges. It burned hot and bright in her blood and brought tears to her eyes.

Blessed Mother Goddess, she'd missed this! Missed the heat as it consumed her, the fizzy elation,

and the sense of completeness that came with her power. For so many years, she'd felt like she was missing a part of herself. And she had been. Maybe one of the most important aspects of herself.

At least, she considered it important. And right now, she figured Cal would, too.

After that first rush, when the power wanted to have its way with her, to burn her up from the inside out, she wrestled it back under her control. And forced it to do her bidding.

She had to heal Cal. She wouldn't be able to bear it if anything happened to him.

"I pray to you, Mother Uni. Give me the strength to do this right." She took a deep breath and began to focus all that energy. "Please don't let me screw this up."

CAL WOKE to the sounds of a storm.

Loud booms of thunder followed by flashing light. Cool. He loved thunderstorms. He tried to open his eyes... and found he couldn't. Damn, he was tired.

He must have fallen—

Images rushed through his head. Tessa, Venus, Mercury. The Roman deities' Hamptons estate.

What the hell?

He needed to open his eyes but they felt like they had weights attached to them. His body felt unnaturally heavy, too, which just freaked him out even more. He began to struggle, to make his foot, his arms, his fingers move. Anything. He struggled against the darkness that confined him.

At first, nothing happened. His body refused to respond, as if he was paralyzed. No. That wasn't possible. Yeah, he'd taken a beating, but it hadn't been *that* bad. It couldn't have been.

Move, damn it.

Panic began to set in and he knew that if he let it, it'd take over until he couldn't think straight. He needed to think, to command his body to listen to his brain.

Forcing himself to calm, he focused on his breathing. On the motion of his lungs as they filled with air and then released it. On the beat of his heart, a little fast with panic but strong. Steady.

Okay, let's try this again.

In the darkness, he visualized his big toe, imagined wiggling it. Yes! It moved. Now his legs.

Boom, boom, boom.

With a firm grip on his emotions, he worked his way up his body until finally he got to his head. And he opened his eyes. From total blackness to complete whiteout.

He blinked a few times. The white never changed, but he noticed variations in the color now. His hands clenched. Sheets beneath him. And warmth throughout his body.

He turned his head. "Tessa."

She lay across his torso, her head pillowed on his chest. Not moving.

"Tessa. What—"

Boom, boom, boom.

What the hell was that?

The door. Someone was banging on the door to the safe room in Frentani's clinic.

Though his body felt sluggish and uncooperative, he forced himself to sit up. He hoped to hell he didn't have any broken bones but he couldn't take the time to check.

Tessa wasn't moving. With his heart in his throat, he shook her shoulder gently.

"Tessa, sweetheart, wake up. Tessa, please."

At first, she didn't move, and the tightness in his chest became a stranglehold.

She appeared to be breathing but—

Groaning, she lifted her head and turned to face him.

"Cal?" He barely heard her whisper. "Are you okay?"

"Jesus, Tessa, what the hell's going on? Are you okay?" The dull sheen over her normally vibrant blue eyes made the bottom drop out of his stomach. "What did you do?"

Shaking her head, more to move her hair than as an answer, she cupped his jaw in both hands, her gaze traveling all over his face then down his body.

"How do you feel? Are you—"

The pounding on the door started again, and Tessa shot a quick glance in that direction. "Don't move. I'm going to tell your brother what's going on. I'm sure he's worried sick."

"No." He reached for her but overestimated the control he had over his body. His arms moved but not fast enough to stop her. "Damn, what the hell happened?"

She took each step toward the door as if feeling her way along a dark alley. He made a move to get off the bed and follow her, but the effort was just too much for him. Damn, whatever the hell had happened, he had to get over it fast.

She looked wiped out, weak. Why?

Opening the door, she spoke in a low voice then heard X answer back. He couldn't hear them but it didn't matter. Their tones were low, concerned.

Shit. Whatever had happened had been bad. He lay back, trying to think of the last thing he remembered. He remembered taking a hell of a beating from Mercury. Remembered Tessa coming to his rescue. Vaguely remembered Aurora having something to do with getting them out of there.

After that, nothing.

"Cal."

Tessa's voice pulled him back to the present, and he looked up to find her standing by the bed.

"You need to tell me what happened." he demanded. "Why do you look like you're about to pass out?"

She smiled but it lacked conviction. And brightness.

"I'm fine—"

"No, you're not." In fact, she looked worse than he'd thought a minute ago. And he felt better. "Tessa, what the hell happened?"

Sucking her bottom lip between her teeth, she nibbled on it for a second before releasing a tired sigh. "What's the last thing you remember?"

"Everything's a little fuzzy after Mercury started to use me for a punching bag, but I vaguely remember Aurora sending us back here. After that, nothing."

"You were badly injured, Cal. I wasn't sure you were going to make it."

She blinked, her gaze skittering away for a second before returning, tears dampening the corners.

He wanted to pound on his chest like Tarzan at the obvious concern in her expression, but he managed to contain the barbarian instinct. "Hey, babe. I'm fine. No harm, no foul. Did Frentani put me back together?"

He didn't want to owe the guy, especially not for his life, but a debt was a debt and he paid his. So when Tessa shook her head, he couldn't help but feel a little grateful that he didn't have to thank the doctor.

"Then who—" His gaze narrowed on her dull eyes and the ashen pallor of her skin. "You healed me."

She hesitated for a second before nodding. "Yes. I've never done a healing on that scale before. It was... a strain."

Yeah, he could see that. "Damn it, Tess." He reached for her, wrapped his hands around her upper arms, and felt the subtle quivering of her muscles beneath his hands. "You practically drained yourself, didn't you?"

She didn't have to answer. He saw all he needed to in her face.

"Gods fucking damn it, Tessa. I'm gonna kick X's ass for letting you—"

"Letting me?" She stiffened beneath his hands and would've pulled away if he hadn't had such a firm grip on her. "Don't presume to think you can control me, Caligo."

Putting a stranglehold on his inner caveman before he really pissed her off, he tried to throttle back his anger. But the anger was coming from fear, and he had a shitload of that zapping through his body. "I'm not presuming anything. Shit, Tessa, I'm worried about you."

Her lips trembled but she firmed them a second later. "There's nothing to be worried about. I just need some rest."

Rest. The whole reason for his trip to the Hamptons.

He released her and reached for the pocket of his jeans where he'd stuffed the tiny vial of nectar that Venus had given him. Only he wasn't wearing his jeans. Just his underwear.

"The Nectar. Did you find it? I had it in my jeans."

She shook her head. "No, I didn't find it but I wasn't looking, either."

"So where are my jeans?"

She took a deep breath, as if she needed to gather strength just to turn her head. "I left them on the floor. I was a little too worried about you to care where they landed."

Her eyes drifted closed, and fear hit him low in the gut.

"You need to lie down, babe. And I need to find that Nectar."

She nodded, a listless bob of her head. "Maybe just for a little. But I don't think I should take the Nectar now. I'm afraid..."

Afraid didn't cover the emotion roiling in his gut. Without waiting for her to move, he picked her up and rushed back to the bed. Laying her down, he cupped her fragile jaw in his hands and stroked his fingers along that soft skin. "What? What are you afraid of, Tess?"

Her eyes flicked partway open. "I'm afraid it'll make the lethargy worse and that I won't..."

She shook her head as if she didn't want to go on.

"Won't what?" he prompted.

"That I won't wake up."

A chill skated down his spine. "Is that a possibility?"

"I don't... I'm not sure. And I'm afraid if I go to sleep, Charun will find me, regardless of the room."

Shit. Just shit. "Then we'll figure something else out."

Her lips curved but couldn't quite form a smile. "I... I think I drained myself pretty badly."

Yeah, he thought that, too. "Then we'll just have to..."

He paused, thinking, knowing exactly what should work to restore her powers. Reaching for band of his underwear, he stripped them down his legs.

Tessa's brows lifted in amusement. "Cal, you know I love—Oh." Her mouth curved in a weak but knowing grin. "Sex. You think sex will restore my powers."

"Got it in one. I always knew you were smarter than the average goddess."

He reached for the hem of her dress and pulled it up her legs, exposing beautiful, sun-kissed skin. Her thighs, the pretty female space between. Then her stomach and finally her breasts. When he'd pulled the dress over her head, he tossed it over his shoulder and let his gaze simply take her in.

So damn beautiful.

Especially the smile curving her lips, the one that made his cock begin to fill. He'd had a brief moment of panic that he wouldn't be able to perform, that his fear would trump his desire for her.

Guess he didn't have to worry about that. Even drained, pale, and listless, she managed to make him horny.

Which was probably sick. He paused, his gaze meeting hers, and he pulled his hands away from the temptation of her skin.

"Tessa... You know, maybe this wasn't such a great idea. You're not—"

"Oh, no you don't." She reached for his wrists and dragged his hands to her waist. "You don't get to stop now. I think it's a great idea. Don't wimp out on me, Cal."

Well, when she put it like that... "Fine." He forced a cocky grin to his lips. "Since you're forcing me to have sex with you, then we need to go slow."

Her smile made the embers of his desire flare. "Slow is not always a bad thing."

"Glad to hear you think so. No," he said, when she reached for his hand, "you just lie there and think of the old country."

Her smile held a little more heat, a little more life. Yet, her complexion continued to pale. "I'd rather be thinking about where you're going to put your hands next."

He bit back a groan. "Close your eyes, Tessa." She could barely keep them open anyway, and the dullness of their color made him think about things other than sex.

"Aren't you afraid I'll fall asleep?"

He cursed silently at the fear in her eyes. "No way will you be able to sleep through what I'm about to do to you."

Her smile widened as her eyes closed. "Awfully sure of yourself, aren't you?"

Not at all. Not with her life in his hands. "I know what I'm doing, babe. Just concentrate on feeling, Tess."

"Then touch me already."

His lips quirked but he didn't move to immediately obey. Had to have some control, after all. Instead, he leaned forward and blew a stream of air across her bare stomach.

She drew in a quick breath then held it as he pulled away. Waiting.

"Breathe, Tess."

She obeyed immediately, her lips parting to draw in much-needed air as her fingers dug into the sheets at her sides. "Do you get off on torturing me, Cal?"

Her breathy tone made his blood burn and his cock thicken. "I didn't even get to the good stuff yet, babe. Just wait."

He watched her throat convulse as she swallowed, the slim

column inviting his touch. Lifting his hand, he brushed the tips of his fingers against the skin just below her ear. Smooth, warm. So damn soft.

The need to taste her had him leaning forward, close enough that he could flick her earlobe with his tongue. Not enough to really get a good taste of her but enough to make her shiver. And when he leaned in again for another, she tilted her head so he could have better access.

Each time he breathed in, her scent made his breath catch in his lungs. His body urged him to go faster, to put his hands on her. The need was almost painful.

Too bad. Suck it up. Stick to the plan.

And he did have a plan.

This time, after a short lick, he nipped the flesh just below her ear. "You taste like candy. Sweet."

"I don't think you got enough of a taste to really know for sure. Why don't you try that again?"

He pulled away. "That sounded like an order, Lady."

She smiled and didn't try to cover it this time. "I would never presume to do that."

"No, of course not."

He bent his head and laid his lips on her skin, just above her left breast. Her heart beat just below his lips, the heavy rhythm a comfort and an enticement at the same time.

Stroking his lips downward, he made sure he stopped just above the nipple. The darker pink flesh puckered into a hard, pointed tip that he couldn't resist. He let his tongue graze over it, and a shudder ran through him as she arched her back, trying to get him to take more of her into his mouth.

This time, he didn't draw back. Her sucked her into his mouth and drew hard on the nipple. He knew her breasts were sensitive and deliberately let his teeth graze the pebbled skin.

Her gasped moan made the hair on the back of his neck lift, and he had to force himself to slow down. To savor the moment.

But he had to get closer. She drew him like honey drew bears.

"Move over. Just a little, hon."

She obeyed without question, and he repositioned himself until he straddled her hips. On his hands and knees now, he sucked her neglected nipple into his mouth, alternately tonguing the stiff peak and sucking on it.

Lifting his right hand, he plumped her breast, kneading the soft flesh. The woman had a body to be worshipped. And much more of it to explore.

Tearing himself away from the perfection of her breasts, he placed a row of stinging kisses down her sternum. When he reached her belly button, he flicked his tongue in the little depression before continuing his way down her stomach.

He had to rearrange himself farther down her body to get where he wanted to go and, when he did, let his breath ruffle the pale curls on her mound. Her breathing quickened, now coming in labored pants, and her stomach quivered and contracted.

But she didn't reach for him, and she didn't open her eyes.

Bending forward, he placed a quick kiss on those neatly trimmed curls as a reward. "I'm going to put my mouth on you here. Same rules apply."

She shivered, a delicate little convulsion of her body. "Such a taskmaster."

"Just wait, babe. You have no idea what I'm capable of."

"Oh, I think I have an idea."

"Then let's see if you're right."

He let her hang on the edge of anticipation for a few more seconds before he moved. Sitting back, he placed his hands on her knees then slowly dragged them up her thighs.

Smooth skin slid under his rough palms, making his heart

race and his cock pulse with leashed desire. Hard and insistent, it strained to be inside her. He wondered if she realized he was torturing himself just as much as he was her.

When he reached the tops of her thighs, he started back down again, kneading her sleek muscles, curving his hands behind her knees, and stroking down her calves.

The sigh that escaped her lips was equal parts arousal and pure female contentment. His goddess loved to be stroked. To be touched. And he lived to touch her.

He spent several minutes just running his hands up and down her body, making sure he caressed every inch of skin—except those few delicate inches between her legs. He avoided that with tormenting precision. No matter how much he wanted to touch her there, to stroke that warm, moist flesh. To put his mouth on her clit and flick at it with his tongue.

Just thinking about it made every muscle in his body tense.

"Cal." Her voice held a sultry quality, causing his cock to pulse with desire. "Please."

He paused, though his hands shook with the effort not to touch her. She hadn't opened her eyes but the color in her cheeks was brighter, pale pink instead of that terrifying ashen color.

"Please what?"

She had to take a breath before she could answer again. "Please fuck me now."

He swore she'd reached inside his body, grabbed his lungs in both hands, and squeezed all the air out of them. "I still don't think you're ready."

Moving to the end of the bed before she had a chance to move, he flipped her onto her stomach, startling a choked cry from her.

After brushing that golden hair out of the way, he let his eyes feast on the smooth expanse of her back, those rounded hips, and her gorgeous ass. He wanted that ass. Wanted to completely own her by fucking her there, tunneling inside that tight channel while he had his fingers in her pussy.

Just the thought had precum seeping from his cock and his hands clenched into fists.

First things first.

Starting at her shoulders, he massaged the knotted muscles there. He'd never given anyone a massage before, though he knew the general concept. He'd never had a relationship with a woman that made him want to touch her more than just for sex.

That should have given him pause. Instead, he completely ignored the thought.

He started slow, not wanting to hurt her. Her bones felt so damn fragile beneath his that he actually worried he'd hurt her. Until she sighed in what sounded like utter bliss.

"Oh, Blessed Goddess. Cal, you have magic hands."

Damn, he loved that she enjoyed what he was doing. Leaning over, he nipped the side of her neck, his cock brushing against the smooth skin of her ass. "That's not the only thing magic on me, baby."

She laughed, a small sound that made all the hair on his body rise. "You're so damn sure of yourself."

Not always. But it was nice to hear from her. "I've got good reason to be." Leaning back, he gave her ass a very slight smack, just enough to make her shudder and her skin flush a very pale pink. Then he started working his hands down her back until he reached the firm, smooth globes of her ass.

"You have the prettiest damn ass I have ever seen."

The words were out of his mouth before he realized he'd said them. Not that they weren't true. Still, for some reason, they embarrassed him. They were crude and she deserved better—

She sighed. "I think that may be the sweetest thing you've ever said to me."

The bare hint of a smile that he saw on her lips eased his idiotic embarrassment, and he smoothed his palms over those plump curves before cupping them in his hands and squeezing. The faintest impression of his hands remained.

It looked right. His.

"Gods damn, Tessa. I want your ass. Will you let me have it?"

She sighed and her muscles went liquid beneath his hands. "You can have anything you want, Cal. Don't you know that yet?"

She turned her head just enough that she could look up at him over her shoulder, and he knew right then that she meant every word. He could barely breathe through the tightness in his chest, and he couldn't wait any longer to have her. "On your knees, Tessa. Face down."

She obeyed without pause, lifting her ass in the air, her face turned to the side, one cheek pressed to the mattress.

His restraint cracking at the seams, Cal spread her legs with rough hands and then cupped her mound. His fingers slid through her slick sex, drawing her moisture forward to her clit and back to her rear entrance.

"Cal. Please."

"Yes." He would please her. He had to. There wasn't any other option.

Moving on his knees between her legs, he widened her stance by another few inches. With her open before him, his gaze followed his hand as he spread her lower lips and then speared two fingers into her sex. He slid in easily because she was so wet. And tight.

Gods damn, she was tight. His cock ached to feel her stretched around him. Instead, he forced himself to stroke her, to work her arousal higher. Wet heat. He felt it on his fingers and could smell her desire for him in the air around them.

No more waiting.

Sliding his fingers out, he grabbed his cock in one hand and her hip with the other. Then he aimed and thrust deep into her sex.

He didn't stop until he felt his thighs hit hers. She closed around him, tight as a fist, and her gasp of pleasure as he forced the last few centimeters inside made his hips buck.

Sucking in a deep breath and holding it, he froze, soaking in the sensation, feeling her inner muscles contract around him, tugging at him, milking him. He could've come just from that alone so he froze, forcing back the orgasm. Not ready. Not nearly ready.

Her broken sigh pushed him even closer. "You feel so good, Cal. Please. Move."

"Your wish is my command, Lady."

He pulled back and thrust. Hard. He didn't worry about hurting her. He knew he wouldn't. She could take whatever he dished out. And she liked it.

The pace was just this side of brutal—a rough, hard ride that neither of them wanted to stop. She backed into him every time he pushed into her, seemingly taking more of him each time. The drag of flesh against flesh stoked his desire until his blood felt like it was boiling in his veins and heat covered him in a fine sheen of moisture.

Sweat. He'd never felt heated sweat coat his body before. Never felt it drip down his back and off his balls. He'd never felt the actual heat of a woman's pussy as it surrounded him, not before Tessa.

His cock shuttled into her body in a wicked rush, his fingers gripping her hips like talons. Tessa's soft sighs of pleasure increased to husky groans, and his gaze once again slipped to her ass. He had to have her there. Had to have her completely beneath him.

Pulling out, startling a cry from her, he grabbed a pillow and stuffed it beneath her hips, pulling her legs out flat. He leaned down so his mouth was right at her ear. "I want your ass, Tessa. Can I have you there?"

Her breathy moan was answer enough but her head bobbed in agreement. It lit a match to his already flaming desire.

Coating his cock in the moisture flowing between her legs, he made sure he was slick before he pressed the tip to the small puckered entrance. Coming down on his hands, he covered her with his body as he began to invade that tight space.

Her muscles tried to reject him even as she pushed back against him. Turning his head, he sank his teeth into her shoulder. The taste of her sweat made his hips plow forward.

Gods damn. His cock pushed through that first tight ring of muscle and he continued forward, wanting more. Wanting everything.

With his body over hers, she could barely move. He controlled her, yet she still owned him. Every inch he gained, she claimed more of him. Until there was nothing more for him to give her.

Then he pulled out, not enough to slip free but far enough to make his forward thrust worth every second of the torture of her tight passage. And it was wonderful torture. She milked him with each motion, every breath. He wasn't going to last long but she hadn't come yet.

And that was priority one.

With his chest plastered to her back, he slid one hand beneath her hips, arrowing straight to her clit. Her gasp let him know he'd hit the right spot. He stroked her, teased her, and flicked that little nerve bundle between his fingers until she writhed.

She couldn't go anywhere, not with his bulk surrounding her, but she bucked against him, making him sink deeper.

"Cal, make me come."

"Absolutely, baby. You'll get to come. But when I say so."

Then he moved his fingers, pulling back until he could thrust them into her pussy. He fucked her with two fingers, her sheath so damn tight because his cock in her ass stretched her to the limits.

She moaned when he began to work her in both passages.

"I'm gonna get a dildo made just for you, Tess," he rasped in her ear. "A big one. And I'm gonna take you like this again."

Shuddering beneath him, she could only gasp out his name. And that was all it took.

Her pussy clenched around his fingers as she came, a tight grip that was matched by the contraction of her back passage around his cock. Heat blasted him like a furnace, though he wasn't sure if it was hers or his. He only knew he felt lit up from the inside.

He came, pouring his seed into her in devastatingly slow pulses that he swore went on for hours. He barely felt the wave of power that coursed through her, he was so blown away by his own orgasm.

Still, he had enough sense to realize what was going on. And enough pride to smile.

After several minutes—or it could have been an hour, he wasn't really sure—he rolled to his side, drawing her with him so he could wrap his arms around her and hold her tight against him.

He felt each of her shuddering breaths mirroring his own as he tried to calm his racing heart. Her hands had wrapped around his arms when he'd shifted, as if she was afraid he was going to move away. And even when it became clear he wasn't moving, she let them rest there. Returning some of that amazing energy.

It only took a few minutes for him to feel completely renewed. Refreshed. And for the anxiety to kick in again.

Double-edged sword.

Her power had saved her. And would also condemn her.

She turned in his arms, staring into his eyes. He knew she was thinking exactly the same thing. "Now what?"

He shook his head. "Hell if I know, babe. But I'll think of something."

ELEVEN

Tessa sat by Flavia's bed, holding the baby girl yet to be named.

Like all *gianes*, this little sweetie had river-blue eyes that would not change color and pale brown hair that would eventually darken into a beautiful golden brown with green highlights.

That distinctive trait was one of the reasons *gianes* rarely ventured into the more populated areas of the world. Besides, the major waterways of the so-called civilized world were largely polluted, and Etruscan wood elf needed clean, fresh water coming straight out of the earth to live.

Luckily for Flavia, a group of *Fata* had built an enclave not far from there in a thickly wooded area of the Oley Valley. The land was private, a clean stream ran through it, and the protective wards ringing the property had been erected by Selvans, the God of the Woods himself.

Flavia and the babies would be safe there, and they'd have the support of the other *Fata* who lived there.

From the next room, she heard the low rumble of Cal and X talking, though she couldn't make out what they were saying.

In the bed, Flavia sighed in her sleep, her arms cradling her son, who also slept. The little girl, however, was blinking up at Tessa, though her eyes were shut more than they were open.

"As much as I love holding you, baby girl, I think it's time for you to get some more rest." Tessa stood, setting the baby in the bassinet attached to the side of the bed. Flavia would be able to see the baby immediately when she woke up.

Instead of leaving, Tessa sat back in a chair. This new, little family brought a smile to her face.

Tessa had never had children, though not for lack of trying. Many centuries ago, she'd been almost frantic in her pursuit of a child. She'd had sex with gods, demigods, humans, *Fata*, men of all races. She'd begged, pleaded, and bespelled. Nothing had worked.

Her sister, Lusna, Goddess of the Moon, had conceived her son, Tivr, many centuries ago and under circumstances she'd never spoken off. Not even when Tessa had begged her to tell her the secret.

Tessa had heard something in Lucy's voice as she refused that made it clear she'd never speak of it. That the experience had been traumatic, though she never treated Ty with anything other than a mother's complete and occasionally overbearing love.

Tessa had wanted to share that connection with another being. But she'd had to give up that dream. She'd made certain never to want anything that badly, to never ache with desire until she couldn't see straight, to never weep with the knowledge that she'd always be alone.

Until Cal.

Just the sound of his voice soothed her and made her want him at the same time.

Leaning her head against the chair back, she let her gaze wander to the wall that separated her from Cal. The paint color was a soothing blue-green, reminding her of the waters of the Mediterranean. Of home.

She hadn't returned to Etruria in years. America was her home now, but that didn't mean she still didn't long for the hills, the forests, the ancient and deep-seated power in the land. Not that America didn't have power. The ley line running beneath this part of the country had been pure and largely untapped when the Etruscans had decided to settle here more than two centuries earlier.

The green forests, the Schuylkill River, the fertile fields... all these things had drawn them. Still, maybe when this was all over, she would return.

She longed to let her hands run along the bark of centuries-old oaks and her feet sink into the soil that nurtured the greatest vineyards on the planet. If she closed her eyes, she saw the villa she owned outside of San Gimignano. If she breathed in, she could smell the rich scent of the earth and the tang of ripe grapes on her tongue.

The vineyards would be gearing up for harvest in September. It was a joyous time.

"You miss it, don't you?"

She knew that voice, knew it should terrify her. And somewhere inside, deep in her gut, she was.

But not for the reasons she had been before.

She knew she shouldn't engage him, shouldn't answer, but something in the tone of his voice made her pause.

"Of course, I do. It's home."

"True. And yet you've wandered. You've traveled the world. You've seen so much more than I have ever dreamed while I rot here."

She was dreaming and she knew it, caught in that place between awake and full sleep. And trapped with the god who hunted her.

She needed to snap out of this, to wake. But she was so tired. And so damn curious.

"You rule an entire plane of existence, Charun. Here... Now... we are obsolete."

"We wouldn't have to be."

Yearning hit her square in the gut at his softly spoken words.

"We could rule again," he continued. "The humans are clueless. They understand so little of how the world works. They don't believe in magic, even though it's all around them. They're petty and greedy and small-minded. It would take so little to have them under our thumbs again. Worshipping us. We only need to work together."

She shook her head. "It would be chaos."

"It would be wonderful. We would rule and not just a small part of the world but the entire world. When I open the gate and leave Aitás—"

"After you consume my powers and leave me to rot there."

Charun paused. Though she couldn't see him, could only hear him in her mind, she knew he was considering his response carefully.

She couldn't remember the last time she'd actually seen Charun face to face. It'd been well before the Involuti had sealed Charun in Aitás then hidden Invol away as well.

She wasn't even sure what had prompted the Involuti to lock Charun in his realm. She only knew she couldn't blame him for being pissed off about it. She just didn't want to be his sacrificial lamb. And this conversation was leading him right to her.

Wake up. Now.

Her heart pounding, she tried to rip herself out of the dream. Only she couldn't quite manage it.

"Oh, come now, Thesan. You know you're not strong

enough to fight me." Charun chuckled. "You've managed to hide yourself well enough, but you always knew—"

"Tessa! Tessa, wake up!"

Gasping for air, her eyes flew open and she looked up into Cal's sharp gray gaze. His hands tightened on her shoulders as he shook her, her head snapping back and forth painfully before he pulled her tight against his chest.

"Jesus fucking Christ, Tessa. What the fuck happened?"

She blinked a few times, trying to catch her breath, but the anxiety, the *fear* she sensed from Cal made it almost impossible. Staring into his eyes, she forced herself to focus on breathing, on bringing down her heart rate. But she needed him to help her.

"Cal." She lifted her hands to cup his cheeks in her hands, feeling his anxiety like a swarm of angry bees against her skin. "We need to get out of here. Now. I can't put Flavia and the babies or Eric at risk."

Cal stiffened and glanced behind her. Tessa realized he was holding her in his arms in the hallway. He must have gotten her out of Flavia's room while she'd been asleep.

Good. The last thing she wanted to do was terrify Flavia.

"Fine." He set her on her feet, grabbed her hand, and pulled her toward the stairs to the upper floor. "Let me tell X where we're going, and then we're getting the hell out of here."

"YOU'RE GOING TO DO *WHAT*?"

Cal wasn't about to repeat himself. They didn't have much time, and he wasn't sure he could force the words out of his mouth again. The first time had been bad enough. And if X didn't get out of his way, Cal was going to have to move him. Forcefully.

"You heard me, X. Now move your ass."

His brother stood in front of the door leading to the outside, his mouth open, speechless. Cal would have to remember that when he needed to shut X up, all he had to do was shock the shit out of him.

Cal decided that was a good thing. If he'd shocked X, maybe he'd get the same reaction when he went to grovel for help from the only man he thought had the power to help him and Tessa now.

X started to shake his head and then couldn't seem to stop. "And you actually think Dad's gonna go for this? After what you said to him the last time you saw him?"

Cal winced. That had been a bad scene.

Alright, maybe bad wasn't harsh enough.

The last time he'd seen their dad, Cal had said some truly unforgiveable things and his dad had responded in kind. Since then, neither of them had said anything to the other.

For Tessa, Cal would talk to his dad.

She stood behind him, her hand wrapped around his like a vise. She hadn't said a word since he'd grabbed their stuff and practically dragged her up the stairs to the first floor and toward the front door. Her skin held a sickly pale hue, but it wasn't because she was drained. She was scared. Maybe terrified was the better word.

He needed to find a way to get Charun off her back permanently. So far, he hadn't come up with one damn idea. Taking her to Cimer should buy them some time.

He'd wanted to make a clean getaway, but X had caught up to them before they could.

"I think going to Cimer is the only option we have left until I can find a way to get Charun off her back."

"But... you know..." X started shaking his head again, flashing a look at Tessa. Cal knew exactly what X was thinking.

There'd be no sun in Cimer.

Tessa's hand tightened convulsively on Cal's and he turned to look into her eyes. They were round, her pupils dilated, and he swore she'd turned a lighter shade of pale.

Yes, he knew exactly what he was asking her to give up. But only for a short time. A year, maybe two. He wanted her safe. Wanted her where he could best protect her. This was the best he could come up. It would have to be enough because nothing else had worked up to this point.

"I understand what going to Cimer means," she said. "And I'm ready."

Damn, she made him want to wrap her in his arms and not let go. To put his mouth over hers and kiss her until he couldn't breathe any more.

"I won't let anything happen to you, Tessa. You know that, right?"

"Yes." She nodded, a slight smile curving her lips. "I know you will do whatever you can to protect me. But right now, we need to get out of here before Charun sends one of his demons. The sun is setting. We don't have much time. Once we're gone, Eric can shut the wards tight."

There was that trust again. Shining in her eyes. But he had to be sure she knew what she was getting into. "You know what that means, right? There's no sun in Cimer, Tessa. You'll be weakened. You—"

"I'll have you."

The ferocity of emotion that shot through him made him ache to kiss her, to lay his claim to her. Right here and now, in front of his brother. Hell, he wouldn't care who was watching.

The strength of that emotion didn't scare him as much as it would have only a few days ago. And if he had the time, he'd even admit to knowing exactly what he felt. But they didn't have time. He knew in his gut they were running out of it.

And really, it was what he should have done when she'd first come to him. He'd just been too damn arrogant and stubborn to do it. If he had to go crawling back to his father for help, he would.

"Yes. You'll have me."

"And me. I'll go with you."

X started away from the door but Cal caught his arm to stop him.

"You need to stay here. Help Frentani with security. I don't think—"

"I'm not helpless, Cimmerian." The doctor stepped out of the stairwell from the basement, not looking at all happy. "This place was warded by one of the strongest *streghe* I've ever known. Tessa, are you really sure this is the right course of action?"

Tessa nodded. "Absolutely. If Cal says this is what we do, then this is what we do."

Frentani sighed, his mouth flattening into a line as he looked back at Cal, a warning in every taut muscle.

Cal didn't have time for a pissing match. "X is staying. I don't doubt your wards, Doc, but what if? What if a demon gets in here? Do you really want to be the only one protecting Flavia and the babies? X is a damn good fighter. Together, you two can hold this place. I don't think there'll be an attack because I think the demon will follow Tessa. But... wouldn't you rather have the extra pair of hands?"

Cal didn't wait around for either X or Frentani to answer. They'd wasted enough time as it was. He headed for the door, Tessa following behind him. After a brief hesitation, X moved away but laid his hand on Cal's shoulder.

"Be safe, Cal." Then he shifted his gaze to Tessa and smiled. "I'll see you soon, Lady."

Her answering smile wobbled a little but it was there. "I

look forward to it, Extasis." Then she turned to Frentani. "I'm sorry for bringing this to your door, Eric. I didn't—"

"No, Tessa. None of this is your fault. Just... be safe."

Then Frentani's gaze slid to his, and Cal saw a warning there. He nodded once before opening the door and leading Tessa out into the twilight.

"CAL, are you sure I'll be welcome in Cimer?"

Tessa couldn't contain her question any longer. They had only started making their way through the forest surrounding the doctor's home. Cal seemed to be following a path only he could see.

He didn't falter. "I'll make sure of it. Don't worry, Tessa."

Ah, if it were only that simple.

"What about your father? I know you and he are... estranged. I don't want to be the cause of any further problems between you."

Cal snorted. "Sweetheart, my dad and I don't need any help from anyone to find something to argue about. We do just fine on our own. My mom will be thrilled to see you. And so will the other *aguane*."

Her foot caught on the edge of a tree root and she tripped, just a little stumble. Cal caught her arm and pulled her close. He'd never let her fall, but she knew she should shut her mouth and concentrate.

But nerves and fear made her chatty.

"You never did explain to me how the *aguane* came to be living in Cimer."

She wasn't sure he'd answer at first but then he slid a glance over his shoulder at her. Even in the dark, she could tell he was assessing her state of mind. And yes, she really did need to hear his voice.

"They've been there for little more than a century now," he said. "Cimmerian females are born so rarely that when our father was growing up, there were none of mating age available. So my father and five other men led a raiding party into Italy. I heard my dad say once that they chose Tuscany because they figured the women would be able to cook."

His snort of laughter surprised her, and she wished she could see his smile more clearly in the fast-falling dark. "They got their wish there. They just didn't expect the Italian temper that came with the cooking ability. Anyway, about two days into their scouting trip, the men were on their way to Florence when they came upon a hunting party. Only the hunters were *Malandante* and they were kidnapping the *aguane*."

Tessa caught her breath. The *Mal* were Etruscans who'd been born with a gene to be bad. Evil, deadly, magically bad.

"They'd already killed one of the women because she put up a fight," Cal continued. "My dad and the other men killed the *Mal,* and according to who you ask, the women either threw themselves at the men in gratitude or the men made them an offer they couldn't refuse and brought them back to Cimer.

"My guess is the truth lies somewhere in the middle. Whatever really happened, the outcome was the same. There are now six *aguane* living in Cimer."

"And they're happy?"

Cal's hesitation was slight but noticeable. "I've never heard my mom complain. And even I have to admit our father is different around her. Almost... gentle. But," he sighed. "I gotta warn you. I figure as soon as my dad opens the door, we're gonna start in on each other. And it could get bad."

Then something else occurred to her. "Do you... I mean, do

the Cimmerians have a pantheon? I've never heard you mention any gods or goddesses."

"My people have never been much for deities. About a millennia ago, we had a complex polytheistic system like the Etruscans, Romans, and Greeks. But our gods were vicious, just like we'd been, and they massacred themselves centuries ago. In a weird way, their destruction saved our culture. Without gods to cause division among the rank and file, we learned to live together, if not always in harmony. You won't have to worry about any—"

He stopped, going so silent and still that she swore he wasn't breathing. She froze as well, though she couldn't quite contain her gasp of surprise.

Cal's hand closed over her mouth, and she barely had time to panic before he put his lips right against her ear.

"We're gonna have to run." A pause. "Now."

As if her body knew what he wanted her to do even before her brain did, Tessa was ready when Cal took off.

She leaped forward and poured every bit of her energy into making sure she didn't slow him down too much. She knew he had to shorten his stride for her, but he kept their hands locked together and pulled her along.

Brush cracked and popped beneath her feet, so loudly she swore it could be heard in the next state. Whoever or whatever Cal had sensed was sure to hear them.

And Tessa was no sprinter.

At first she heard nothing but the beat of her heart in her ears and the harsh inhale and exhale of her breathing.

Cal ran silently.

It was dark enough that she could barely see where they were going, but Cal had no problem maneuvering and she stayed as close to his path as she could. Still, she was running blind in a forest. At night. And fear made for a lousy run partner.

When Cal came to a stop, she didn't stop in time, slamming into his back and nearly making him fall. He kept to his feet only through sheer force of will and caught her around the waist to stop her forward momentum.

He didn't bother with an explanation, and in the very dim light of the rising moon, she saw him dig into his jeans pocket and then withdraw something small and white.

When he turned to the huge old pine in front of him and started to draw something, she had to bite her tongue to keep from asking questions. She didn't have a clue what he was doing, and now that they'd stopped, she heard—or thought she heard—whatever it was that'd spooked Cal.

The soft *shush* of air moving was her only warning. Then a dark mass hit her and took her to the ground.

She hit hard and couldn't help her short scream. The demon had its arms wrapped tightly enough around her upper arms and chest to make it hard for her to breathe. But Tessa wasn't about to play helpless victim this time.

"Tessa! Hang on!"

"Finish it, Cal!" He obviously needed more time to do whatever he was doing, and she'd give it to him.

"Hello again, Lady of the Golden Light." The demon who'd tried to take her two days ago breathed in her ear. "How—*Ugh*."

Tessa swung her head back hard and heard a satisfying crunch when her skull connected with the demon's face. Of course, pain burst through her own head, making it difficult for her to think clearly.

Luckily, her flight response worked just fine. She scrambled away on her hands and knees, back to Cal. She knew he wasn't far. She just—

"Tessa, over here!"

She course-corrected without thought, forcing herself onto

her feet. She couldn't see, fear making her blind. Her outstretched hands groped in front of her but she couldn't find Cal.

Behind her, she heard the demon moving. They had to get out of here. Now.

Cal grabbed her hand and yanked. And then they were falling.

TWELVE

Tessa fell, this time from a great height.

At least, she thought she did. The sensation of falling seemed to last forever. But when she hit the ground, she didn't hit as hard as she'd thought she would. Part of the reason for that might have been because she fell on Cal.

He was ready for her, but she must have landed on a sensitive body part because the noise he made sounded... painful.

She tried to roll off him, but his arms came around her and held her tight. "Don't move, Tess. Just... give me a minute."

He sounded winded, which was exactly how she felt. Winded and tired. No, not tired. Drained.

Shit.

Looking around, she only saw mist. A blanket of it so thick that she could barely make out the hand she held in front of her face.

"Cal, I..."

Damn, what the hell could she say?

"What? What's wrong? Are you hurt? Tessa, what's wrong?"

She felt him shift beneath her, felt him reposition her, and then his hands began to slide all over her body. Checking for injuries.

This was no blind fumbling. He could see her just fine. She couldn't see anything but the mist. Was it because of her weakening powers or just the fact that Cimer lay between the planes of existence?

"Cal, I can't..."

"Can't what?" His hands had reached her legs, and when he got to her feet, she heard him breathe a sigh of relief at not finding any broken bones or gaping wounds.

"I can't see anything."

"Nothing at all?"

"Well, no. It's just all gray mist."

Another sigh. "That's okay, babe. You're all right. You'll get your vision back in a few minutes. Sometimes it takes a little while to adjust when you first come through. Especially the way I do it."

"And that's different from how others do it?"

"Yeah. Turns out the Etruscan blood gives me a unique way to travel between the planes. I can make shortcuts though a tree but it has to be at least a hundred years old. Not too many of those left in this area. We got lucky. The demon couldn't follow us through, and if we're really lucky, the thing will need a little while to figure out where we went and how to follow us. All of the gates into Cimer are well guarded. If it tries to come through another gate, the Sentinels will know."

Good. All good. Except for that pesky energy drain.

Cal moved again, this time away from her. Her heart stopped for a brief second before he laid his hands on her shoulders and helped her to her feet. "We gotta get moving. I know you can't see it yet but we're on a path. We can follow this all the way to my parents' house. It'll take a little while but the mist will clear."

She heard the confidence in his voice and forced a smile, hoping he wouldn't see the strain behind it. "Then I guess we should be moving."

He paused. "Do me a favor and close your eyes for a minute."

Her lids fell closed immediately, and she had a brief second to wonder at how willingly she did anything he asked before his mouth closed over hers.

Heat flared, immediate and overwhelming. Maybe it was the fact that she couldn't see him. Or maybe it was the fact that she'd fallen in love with him.

His lips touched hers, and she lost herself in his taste. Hot male. Dark, spicy and all Cal.

Her arms wrapped around his shoulders and she clung, uncaring if it made her seem weak. He had strength enough for both of them. When he pressed open her lips and let his tongue slip inside her mouth, licking and teasing, she felt that strength seep inside her.

She sighed into his mouth, pressing closer. Her nipples hardened and peaked, rubbing against his muscled chest. She arched her back, needing more of him, and his hands swept from her shoulders down her back and to her ass as he lifted her to himself and against his bulging erection.

Her hips moved, her clit needing that pressure. If he rubbed just enough, at just the right angle, she'd come.

And, just that fast, she needed to come. She was panting for it, begging him for it with each gyration. He seemed to want the same thing, thrusting his cock against her, mimicking the sex act until both of them were panting.

When his hand fell to the button on the slim black pants he'd given her to wear, she leaned back just enough so he could open it and pull down the zipper.

Quick and dirty. She wanted to come with him buried deep

inside her. Didn't want to screw around with foreplay. She wanted him to fuck her.

Cal appeared to be on the same page.

He shoved down her pants and her underwear as his mouth ravaged hers. Then his hand left her and brushed against her thighs as he ripped at his pants. She could barely breathe but refused to give up his mouth. She had one hand cupped around his jaw, though he didn't seem to be going anywhere. He kissed her with the same frantic passion she felt vibrating through her.

Tearing his mouth away, he spun her, guiding her hands forward until she braced herself against a smooth tree trunk.

"Bend forward, baby." Cal's hands gripped her waist. "Damn, you're gonna be tight this way."

With her pants around her ankles, she couldn't spread her legs too far. Just far enough to let him in. He didn't waste time with preliminaries, and she didn't want him to.

She was wet and he was ready—

He thrust inside, sinking so deeply that she swore he couldn't go any further. He proved her wrong by pulling out and doing it again. He set a hard pace, the sound of his thigh slapping against her ass erotically charged. His fingers dug into her hips, the sharp bite making her gasp. She loved it. Met him thrust for thrust. Wanted more.

He gave it to her. Every hard, wonderful inch.

Her breath sawed from her lungs, and she let her head hang down as she took him. Sensation popped and crackled through her nerves, muscles tightening as she drew closer to orgasm.

And drew more power from their joining.

"God, Tessa. Tell me you're close." Cal's rough, deep rasp made her sheath clamp down on him, eliciting his groan. "I can't last much longer."

"Just don't stop." She heard the plea in her voice... and the breathless anticipation. "Please."

He thrust harder. "Never. Gods damn, you feel so damn—"

With a gasp, she came, her body spasming with the strength of it. Pure bliss. Nothing had ever felt so right or so wonderful.

Until Cal groaned out her name and poured his seed into her.

She didn't know how long it took for him to empty into her. For her orgasm to wind down to occasional spasms.

She only knew that when her arms wavered, Cal wrapped his arms around her waist and held her against him. Cal's chest labored against her back, the fast-paced thudding of his heart arousing and comforting at the same time.

Her fingertips stroked along his arms as she felt her power returning.

A double-edged sword.

Opening her eyes, she now saw shades of gray instead of a solid blanket of it. After a few more minutes, she could actually make out forms.

Around them, trees towered up from the forest floor, the trunks dark brown, limbs reaching for a dusk-gray sky. Beneath them, grass grew, soft but not green. More like a pale brown.

With her head pillowed on Cal's hard shoulder, she had no desire to move. But she knew this was only a temporary respite.

"Tessa. You okay?"

Cal capped his question with a bite to her earlobe. Just hard enough to bring up a quick lash of pain. She shivered and his arms tightened around her.

"I'm fine. I'm better than fine."

"The trip through the gate took a lot out of you, didn't you?'

She nodded, unwilling to tell him that the first rush of fuel from their sex was already starting to wane.

He didn't ask any more questions, but he did hold her a little tighter for several more minutes. Making her heart ache just a little more with each breath.

Then, with a sigh, he turned her around so they could adjust their clothes. She felt his gaze follow her, sensed his worry in the heaviness of his breathing and the tenseness of his muscles.

Which merely heightened her own sense of impending doom.

"Tessa..."

When he didn't finish his thought, she forced a smile, knowing he could see it, and lifted her hand to caress his cheek. "We should go. I'm anxious to meet your parents."

He nodded, but she could tell he was still chewing over something in his head. "The village is about an hour's walk from here. Sorry I couldn't get us closer."

"Cal." She rested her fingers over his lips, cutting off anything else he might say. "You got us away from the demon and you got us here. That, in itself, is amazing."

With a short nod, he grabbed her hand, pressed a kiss to her palm, and started walking.

THE VILLAGE, when it finally came into view through the trees, reminded Tessa of home. Of Tuscany.

Set into a slight hillside, the single-story homes sprawled away from their original footprints in haphazard directions, as if whoever had built them hadn't cared one bit for aesthetics. Which they probably hadn't.

Made of stone, the buildings had doorways but no doors and no glass in their many windows. Everything was open.

What light fell from the sky shone brighter here, and the mist that had settled over the forest dissipated until it could almost be considered bright.

They hadn't spoken much on their walk, but Tessa couldn't help asking, "How does the light get here?"

Cal stopped before they left the cover of the trees, holding onto her hand so she didn't walk ahead. "It seeps in from the other planes. We have night and day, just like above. It's just... diffused down here. Filtered."

Which was why her strength was draining. Not a huge drain, only barely noticeable. But it *was* noticeable. She couldn't help but wonder what she'd feel like in a week. A month.

And if she stayed here, safe and untouchable, would Charun move onto one of her sister goddesses?

Yes, they'd been warned, but what if Charun caught one of them? What if, instead of running and hiding like a coward, she should have stayed with them? Would they have had better luck banding together and trying to find some way to get Charun off their backs? To convince him his plan was destructive and possibly world ending?

"Tessa?"

Cal's urgent tone had her lifting her head to smile at him, but the dark look on his face wiped her smile right off.

"Let me do the talking," he said. "Everything's going to be okay."

She wanted to believe that. She really did. But she knew it wouldn't be.

"Caligo. What the hell are you doing skulking around the perimeter of the village? Good way to get yourself killed. I taught you better."

Cal didn't turn from her right away. He stiffened and took a deep breath, his gaze locked to hers. Only when she gave him another smile did he finally turn to face the speaker.

Tessa couldn't see around Cal and would have been content to wait until he introduced her, but when Cal said, "Nice to see you, too, Father," she leaned to the right.

And felt her mouth drop open for a brief second before she could catch it.

Well, now. Weren't all the men of Cal's family just too handsome for words. The man had dark hair so black that it had blue highlights and eyes a deep charcoal gray.

His face had more rugged angles than X's or Cal's did but, Great Mother Goddess, the man was gorgeous. She absolutely saw what had made his mate give up her place in the sun for him. Especially when Diritas's mouth quirked at one corner. Yummy.

He still looked pretty pissed off. But, if she had to guess, she'd say the bad-ass stance was mostly a front because his eyes looked happy. Happy to see his son.

Then Diritas sighed and shook his head, arms crossing over a broad chest. "What are you doing here, Caligo? What trouble are you in?"

Cal stiffened, sucking in a short, sharp breath. She could tell he wanted to refute his father's assumption, but he couldn't.

"Actually, *I* would be the trouble." Tessa slipped past Cal, her arm stretched out to shake his father's hand. "Hello, Diritas. I'm Tessa."

Diritas didn't look at her right away. He kept his gaze on Cal, but when Cal did nothing, Diritas looked at her.

He let his eyes travel the length of her, not in any sexual way but missing nothing. He stopped at her grass-stained pants for one brief moment before lifting his gaze back to meet hers. And when she smiled at him, he let his lips tilt upward in an answering half-grin.

Then he shocked the hell out of her by bowing.

"Lady of the Golden Light. Welcome to Cimer."

CAL HAD NEVER SEEN his mom flustered.

Serena had always lived up to her name. Today, she flittered between fussing over Cal and fretting over Tessa.

His dad... Hell, he didn't know what the hell to think about his dad. Never in a million years had Cal ever thought his dad would give an Etruscan goddess the kind of respect he'd shown Tessa.

Cimmerian men weren't exactly known for their manners. Most looked like over-muscled thugs with too little brains. While that last part wasn't true, except in a few aberrant cases, their lifestyle typically made them less than polite. And, yes, Cal knew he could count himself among them.

Maybe his mom had finally succeeded in civilizing the man she'd mated more than a hundred years earlier.

"So, when did you start fucking goddesses?"

Or not.

Luckily for his father, Serena and Tessa sat at the dining table inside the house while Cal and Diritas had taken their talk outside. Cal's hands curled into fists before he forced them to relax.

He was strong but his dad was stronger and wouldn't have any problem beating his son to a pulp. And Tessa couldn't afford to have her guardian damaged.

Who said he wasn't growing and learning?

Cal looked his father straight in the eyes. "What business is that of yours?"

"It's my business when you bring your trouble home with you."

"Are you telling me we should leave?"

Diritas snorted. "And where would you go? I assume you've exhausted all other options if you've shown up here after all this time. Now, are you ready to tell me what's really going on?"

True, they pretty much had run out of options. But did he

hear the slightest hint of affront in his dad's tone?

Nah, had to be imagining it.

"I already did."

"Horseshit. You told me she was being chased by a demon. I don't believe a son of mine can't take care of one lousy demon. Tell me the rest."

Cal considered telling his father to shove his questions up his ass but... the guy was no idiot. Maybe he could provide some insight, find an angle Cal had missed. Which was why Cal had come here in the first place. To ask his dad for help.

Funny how old habits died hard. Even when you hadn't spoken to your father in almost eighty years.

His father didn't interrupt when Cal laid out the situation, beginning with Tessa's arrival at his door and ending with their arrival in Cimer. He only left out the parts about the sex. There were some things that Cal could never imagine discussing with the man called Cruelty. Sex topped that list.

"So," Diritas said when Cal had stopped, "why not just walk her to the gate to Aitás, pat her on the ass, and get rid of her? Let the deities take care of their own messes. Why get involved?"

Cal opened his mouth to answer but found he couldn't. Because the only answer he had was that he didn't want to be rid of her.

Diritas sighed and shook his head. "Son, I never took you for an idiot. I raised you to be headstrong, willful, smart, cunning, and invincible. And you threw everything I taught you out the window and fell for a fucking goddess. You're screwed. You know that, right? There's no way this is going to end good."

Every word out of his dad's mouth felt like a nail in Cal's chest. Every breath hurt like being shot with shards of glass.

"No." He started to shake his head and then he couldn't stop. "No, I don't believe that. There's got to be something we can do. Something I missed."

Cal stared at his father... and realized he was waiting for Diritas to come up with something Cal hadn't thought of. He realized he was counting on it. Counting on his dad to come through for him.

"Hell, don't look at me like that." Diritas rolled his eyes and scrubbed a hand through his hair, looking nervous for the first time ever. "Like I kicked your damn puppy. Damn it. We'll figure something out, kid. Just... give me a few minutes, will you? I can't be brilliant on demand. I gotta work at these things."

LISTENING to the drone of voices from the next room, Tessa lay on the bed where Cal had slept for the first five years of his life before moving to the barracks.

The mattress was not uncomfortable, surprisingly. She'd almost expected to find he'd slept on the floor without a pillow or blankets. She hadn't expected the house to be as inviting as it was.

Probably due to Serena's influence.

The *aguane* had the attitude to go with the name, but she must also have a steel backbone to have lived with Diritas for the past century without being completely subsumed by him.

Cal's father commanded attention. He filled a room with strength and power and practically sucked all of the air from the atmosphere. He had Presence, with a capital P.

No wonder Cal idolized the man. Not that Cal would ever admit it. Fathers and sons. Always such complicated relationships.

Cal and Diritas had been talking since they'd arrived. They'd talked for hours, hashing out her problem.

And she'd grown weaker with every second. Until she hadn't been able to hide it anymore. She hadn't wanted to make a big deal out of it. Had almost been able to pass it off as normal fatigue and slip out of the room before Cal could notice.

But then he'd narrowed his eyes and really looked at her. And his expression had turned to stone.

Which, of course, made his father notice. And demand to know what was happening.

Which was how she'd wound up here, banished to the bedroom to rest like a child.

Yes, she was tired. Okay, maybe she was too tired to hold her head up. But she couldn't fall asleep. Fear refused to allow her.

So she closed her eyes, willing their encounters to play through her mind. Every breath-stealing, heart-stopping, thigh-clenching moment.

She remembered the look on his face the first time she'd felt his touch in his home in the woods. Remembered the feel of his hands on her skin, the strength of his kiss.

She saw him above her on the altar and below him as she rode him. The slide of his cock in her sheath, his hands as they held her hips. The pinch of every single one of his fingers on her skin, the width of his cock as he spread her wide, the pleasure setting her nerve endings on fire.

Her hand slid beneath her pants and between the thighs, her index finger tunneling through the tight curls on her mound to find her clit, already engorged and sensitive to the touch. A sharp sizzle shot through her sex and clenched her stomach as she ran her fingertip in tight circles over the jutting nub.

She closed her eyes tighter and imagined Cal's finger on her clit, Cal's hand on her breast, squeezing and kneading the flesh, pinching the nipple and rolling it between his fingers until she panted in frustration.

Her body needed the release, her sheath contracting around nothing in its fight to climax. She needed Cal.

"Hey, babe. Go ahead. Let go. I'm right here with you."

Oh, blessed Uni. He'd come back to her.

Her eyes flew open, and with a glad cry, she wrapped her arms around those broad shoulders, clinging and not caring. His body crowded against hers in the small bed, plastered together from hip to thigh. Strength, confidence, and dominance poured from him.

His mouth covered hers, his lips hard and demanding. His tongue pushed into her mouth, demanding she give him what he wanted. His hand burrowing between her legs, and his fingers took over from hers, stroking her, flicking at her clit then dipping into her sex.

He touched her with reverence mixed with pure lust, a heady combination that made her gasp as her body shot into an orgasm that made all others seem tame in comparison. When she could open her eyes, she saw that Cal had stripped and was between her legs.

Wait, she didn't remember him undressing. But she didn't think any more about it when he fitted his cock to her slit and thrust into her.

She heard herself cry out as if from a great distance, heard her voice begging him to fuck her.

"I will, baby. I will."

And he did, with an almost brutal force that made her arms tighten around him as her body welcomed the pounding. His hips slung back and forth in a rhythmic onslaught. His arms crushed her against his body, almost as if she was the one moving and he was just along for the ride. Which didn't make any sense.

And his skin was cold. Not cool, like normal, but cold.

While her skin burned with the strength of the sun. She felt its heat, felt it rise from her like steam. It'd been so long since she'd led that burning orb around the earth that she'd almost forgotten what being so close to it felt like. It felt like heaven.

She soaked in the warmth, basked in the glow, and let it flow out of her and around until it encompassed her.

Cal's scream shot her out of the bliss. He writhed next to her on the bed, his face a mask of pain—Wait, when had he moved? She didn't remember him falling to the side—

"Oh, God, help me." His voice cracked with agony. "Make it stop. It burns."

Terror at his pain consumed her. She had to get help, had to get out of here and find someone to help her. Cal was suffering. All her fault. Had to make it stop.

She ran for the door, tore it open, and ran down the hall, headed for the door at the end. Help was waiting there for her.

COOL, misty air hit her skin, a slap against her senses, and Tessa realized her mistake as her eyes flew open.

"Oh, shit."

She froze, blinking rapidly to accustom her eyes to the gray mist surrounding her.

Son of a bitch. She was so screwed.

"Yeah, that about sums it up, don't it, Thesan. Charun definitely knew which button to push, didn't he? But that's what you get when you fall for a mortal. You get stupid."

The voice of the Tukhulkha demon that had tried to take her before floated in the mist around her.

Gasping, Tessa spun in a circle, trying to spot the demon. She saw only the faint outline of massive tree trunks. No demon. No village. Nothing.

So... maybe the demon couldn't see her either. Maybe it only knew her general location and needed to hear her voice to track her down.

"Are you scared yet, Lady? You really should be."

Fighting to keep any sound to a minimum, Tessa forced herself to calm her breathing and think. If she ran, she'd make a racket and be easy to find. Still, she couldn't sit here like a terrified rabbit, hoping the predator wouldn't spot her.

"I'm going to find you. It's just a matter of time."

There. Tessa thought for sure the voice was coming from her left. So she needed to go to her right.

Go ahead, keep taunting, you bitchy blue SOB. And I'll be long gone before you realize I've slipped away from you.

Creeping along, she made her way in the direction she believed the demon was not. The mist was so thick, she had to hold her hands out in front of her so she didn't collide with a tree. Fortunately for her, there didn't seem to be a lot of brush on the ground and that, combined with the sound-dampening properties of the mist, meant she could move relatively quietly.

"Relative" was the operative word, however. Every move she made sounded like a colony of angry monkeys attacking a herd of elephants.

"Running won't help, though you can probably go a little faster if you feel like it. It won't matter in the end."

Damn, was the demon closer? She just couldn't tell, not through the mist.

Which way do I go? Damn it, Cal. I'm so sorry.

There! Was that a break in the mist? Could that be the village?

Does it really matter at this point?

She took off at a run, barely managing to avoid trees trunks and limbs before they smacked her in the face.

With her heart pounding in her ears and fear making that beat insanely loud, she couldn't hear anything else. And as the mist parted in front of her, she nearly tripped over the damn demon.

It lounged against a tree directly in front of her. Its blue skin and red-tipped, raven-black hair gleamed despite the lack of sunlight, while yellow sparks glinted in its black eyes.

Oh shit. Stupid. How could I have been so stupid?

She'd let her guard down and now she would pay the price.

I'm so sorry, Cal.

"Go ahead." The demon shrugged. "Make another run for it. Won't get far."

So true. Even though her muscles flexed and twitched with the need to run.

"Besides," the demon continued, its gaze darting around, "I kinda like it here. It's cool."

Unfortunately, the cool air was doing nothing to bring down her body temperature. Her skin felt as if she'd touched the sun itself.

There was no way she'd let the demon know that, though. She was still a goddess. And this creature didn't have the right to frighten her. She should remember that.

Tessa drew herself up to her full height and stuck her nose in the air. "I'm not running now. I prefer yoga to running anyway. Running's hard on the knees."

The demon smiled, showing off a mouthful of sharp, pointed teeth. "Good run gets your blood pumping."

"I don't have any trouble getting my blood pumping."

The demon's eyes narrowed. "He must be good in bed."

Oh, no, you don't even get to go there. "You know Charun will never be able to accomplish his insane plan. Why are you helping him? What do you think you'll get out of it?"

Laughing, the demon shook its head, the coils of its hair moving as sinuously as a snake. "Oh, please. Like I'm stupid enough to answer that. I've read the Evil Overlord List on the web. Good advice there."

The demon pushed off the tree and started toward her. "Don't make this difficult on yourself, Thesan. Just come along.

I don't want to damage you. You wouldn't be much of a challenge anyway."

Oh, now that was just cruel. Tessa narrowed her eyes and planted her hands on her hips. "Listen, you blue bitch-demon, don't underestimate me. I'm more powerful than you can know."

The demon snorted. "So disappear already." It paused, eyebrows lifted. "What? No powers here? Not enough sunlight, huh? Then I guess you're coming with me, considering your male left you unprotected."

Her back stiffened. This was in no way Cal's fault. What she wouldn't give to claw out the demon's eyes for even suggesting that. "Before you serve me up to Charun, could you at least tell me your name?"

"Ah, yeah, really not that stupid." One blue hand wrapped around her upper arm, the fingers long and skinny, nails filed to points. "Let's go, Blondie."

Eyes downcast, Tessa followed for a few steps before twisting in the demon's grip. She'd hoped to catch it off guard and twist out of its hold. When that didn't work, she kicked and scratched and yanked at her arm.

The demon sighed and shook its head. "You know, I was trying to avoid this. But suit yourself." Then it lowered its mouth to bite Tessa on the shoulder.

Tessa screamed as the cold poison seeped into her blood.

Cold. So bloody cold.

She screamed until the poison robbed her of her voice and her movement. That only took seconds, and then the demon threw her over its shoulder and began to run.

"YOU BROUGHT an Etruscan goddess here and plan to go up against the Etruscan God of the Underworld to save her? Have all those years in the sun robbed you of what little sense you were born with?"

Cal bit his tongue as Cuspis, leader of the Council of Elders, continued to question not only Cal's sanity but his manhood. The old guy was almost three hundred years old and, as far as Cal knew, hadn't left Cimer in more than one hundred fifty years.

"This council will not let you drag us into..."

As Cuspis raged on, Cal looked around the table and realized that probably most of the seven-member council shared their leader's opinion.

They'd become complacent. Content to rule their tiny corner of the world as tyrants, conveniently forgetting how they'd once been a force to be feared. How they had fought those who were weaker.

Now, they hid in the shadows and pretended that they still were those men.

Hell, Cuspis didn't even hide the fact that he probably couldn't lift a sword anymore, not with the amount of weight he was carrying. They'd gotten fat and lazy and arrogant.

At least, most of them.

Cal let his gaze fall directly on Pavor. Juliana's father had not aged well. Good.

He hoped the bastard relived Juliana's death every night. That was the only thing that had stopped Cal from killing Pavor after she'd stepped in front of an assassin's knife meant for Cal.

He'd wanted Pavor to suffer. And, from the looks of him, he had.

He'd had lost his hair and most of his eyesight, if that blank stare was anything to go by. His flesh hung on his big frame after massive weight loss in the eighty or so years since Cal had left.

Every breath Pavor took appeared painful, and every movement looked like agony.

Sometimes the fates were good. That bastard deserved to rot in whatever hell he landed in.

Juliana had never wanted Cal, though he'd thought he was in love with her. She'd been merely an obedient daughter, a pawn in Pavor's games. And she'd let herself be killed rather than mate with Cal.

He'd failed Juliana. He wouldn't fail Tessa.

"A war with Charun would condemn us all to death."

Cuspis finally shut his mouth and leaned back in his chair to stare at Cal. Cuspis didn't bother to check the mood of the other Elders, secure in his control. He fully expected Cal to bow and scrape as well.

But, as Cuspis had said earlier, Cal had been away for too many years.

Cal stood, and every single man in the room followed his actions. He let his lips pull into a smile and watched Cuspis's expression slowly fade into wary watchfulness.

Yeah, you just keep watching, you bastard.

"I don't think you understand why I'm here, gentlemen." Cal used that word deliberately, rather than address them as Elders. "I'm not asking your permission. I've accepted the task of protecting Thesan, and I'm not going to go back on my word. There was a time when the Cimmerians wouldn't have backed down from a fight, especially one like this. But you've gotten old. And fat."

A collective gasp rose from the men, who sounded more like a coffee klatch of old women than once-powerful men. But none of them stood to challenge Cal. Because they knew they couldn't. He'd cut them down in seconds.

"Thesan requested my aid, and I will not allow a rabid god to take her."

"But you're fighting a losing battle, Caligo." Aestus shook his head. He was the only one who'd spoken against Pavor when he'd attempted to assassinate Cal. "You can't go up against a god and win."

Cal opened his mouth but his father beat him to it. "Not alone, no. I believe if we can hit at Charun's front line hard enough, maybe he'll back the fuck off and leave Thesan alone."

His father's quietly spoken words threw the council into an uproar, and Cal watched them bicker amongst themselves.

His dad had actually come up with a plan, and he'd been the one to suggest they approach the council for help. Not that Diritas thought the Elders would agree but he'd said they needed to be paid lip service.

Cal had been more than a little stunned that his father had agreed to back him. Diritas was in line for a council position when one of these geezers dropped over, and Cal had never expected his father to commit what amounted to career suicide.

Yet here Diritas stood, arguing on Cal's behalf. He wondered if his father would still be fighting for him if Cal had told him about Tessa's effect on him.

Would he consider Cal flawed? A failure?

Cal considered it a gift. One he'd fight to the death to keep. Even if that meant being banished from Cimer forever.

"Cal! She's gone! Tessa's gone."

Cal spun toward X's voice and saw his brother running toward him through the meeting hall.

The bottom dropped out of his stomach as his brain processed X's words.

"No—"

"Mom went to check on her after I came over from Frentani's, and she was gone. I looked for her but I couldn't find—"

Cal was already halfway to the exit. He knew exactly where

to go.

The gate to Aitás.

Behind him, he heard his brother and his father, their footsteps pounding in rhythm as they tried to keep up with him. They couldn't. Cal left them behind in a minute. His heart raced as adrenaline flooded his system.

He couldn't lose her. He wouldn't.

Yet, he knew sometimes there just wasn't anything anyone could do to affect the outcome of a shit storm.

TESSA DIDN'T KNOW how long the demon ran, but it didn't seem far before they stopped.

Which didn't seem quite fair. In the movies, the trip to the heroine's doom took forever and the hero always got there to save her before anything really bad happened to her.

But here she was, hanging over a blue demon's shoulder and paralyzed because she'd been stupid enough to fall asleep and let Charun invade her dreams.

Cal probably had no idea she was gone. However she'd left the house, it hadn't seemed to raise any alarms. By the time Cal discovered she was missing, she'd probably be wasting away to nothing in Aitás, her powers consumed and Charun one goddess closer to getting free.

She frowned... Well, she tried to frown but she was still paralyzed. Leave it to Charun to know that the only poison that would work on a goddess would come from a Tukhulkha demon.

She wondered if Cal would mourn her.

She already mourned him. She'd actually hoped to spend a few hundred years with Cal. Hell, she wanted to spend an eternity with him. But no. She'd lived up to her blonde, bubble-headed image and been scooped up like a white rabbit on green grass.

The demon stopped abruptly and dropped Tessa on the ground in front of a large rock that stuck out of the earth like the jagged tooth of some long-dead monster. Good thing she couldn't feel anything because that probably would have hurt.

The boulder stood at least eight feet tall and held faint markings. Etruscan runes, she realized. They formed a spell entreating the god of Aitás to welcome those who sought entrance to the Afterworld.

"Last stop, Thesan." The demon looked over its shoulder. The mist behind them seemed to be growing darker. The sun must be setting in the outside world. At least Tessa couldn't feel the drain on her powers any more.

"Sun'll be down soon," the demon affirmed. "Better get a move on."

The demon leaned forward to place its hands on the rock, muttering a spell in the long-dead Etruscan language. The demon's guttural voice hid the beauty of the ancient words but none of the power.

The earth rumbled and shook as the demon chanted. As Tessa watched, the rock began to quiver and shake until finally it disappeared.

In its place stood a jagged hole. Beyond it, Tessa saw only darkness. She'd never been to Aitás. Not once in her very long life. She'd never had any desire.

And now she had no choice.

Tessa flinched and realized she could move her fingers and toes.

Too little, too late. And isn't that a sad commentary on my life.

Closing her eyes, she thought of her sister goddess Lusna.

If you can hear me, Lucy, take care. Warn the others. Charun will be coming for one of you now.

Tears leaked from her eyes. No way out now. End of the road.

Cal. I love you.

The demon turned back to look at her. "Sorry, Goddess. Seems like a waste to trash such a pretty face." Then it bent and tossed Tessa over its shoulder again. "Better if you don't struggle much. Just takes longer. And believe me, you don't want this to take long."

CAL HEARD distant thunder and forced himself to run faster.

The demon was opening the gate into Aitás, and if Cal didn't get to it before the demon took Tessa through, he wouldn't be able to save her.

A trip into Aitás was one way unless you were Charun or one of his demons.

Lungs burning from his sprint, Cal pushed even harder, the misty dark of Cimer hiding his approach from the blue demon as it stooped to pick up Tessa and throw her over its shoulder.

No. I won't fail.

Never slowing, he ran at the demon full force, catching it off guard and taking it to the ground before it had a chance to avoid him. The demon couldn't hold on to Tessa as it fell. She hit the ground with a thud but didn't cry out. And didn't move.

The thought that she was already dead made his blood run cold. He couldn't stop to help her, though, because the demon bounced to its feet and came at Cal with its claws exposed. It raked at his face and he veered away, feeling the brush of air as its hands passed within centimeters of his skin. He countered with a right hook that caught the demon on the chin but didn't slow it down.

Neither had the advantage in the fast-falling dark, their eyes equally adjusted. They battered each other with fists to the face and body, both enduring a fierce beating. Out of the corner of his eye, Cal saw his father approach and try to get to Tessa, but Diritas was unable to get past the knot Cal and the demon made.

Cal had to put this demon down, to beat it into submission. The knowledge put more force, more power into his punches. He felt his knuckles connect with and shatter a cheekbone, felt a rib give way under his fist. Rage made him strong, but he wouldn't last forever.

He needed to get the demon away from Tessa so Diritas could get her out of there.

The demon swung out with an open hand, aiming for Cal's chest. Seeing an opportunity, Cal let its razor-sharp nails rake across his chest.

He sagged as if the demon had hurt him, and with a hard grin, it came after him. He took a step back and then another, stumbling a little, and the demon took the bait. It leaped, baring its teeth and going for Cal's throat. Cal fell on his back, put his hands up as if to hold off the demon, then caught it and flipped it over his head, away from Tessa.

Scrambling to get to Tessa, Cal got within two feet of touching her before the demon landed on his back, wrapped one wiry arm around Cal's throat, and tightened it. Cal's esophagus began to close, and he ripped at the demon's arm and scratched at the flesh. A blast of foul breath blew by his cheek.

Shit, its teeth. He had to get away from its teeth. Poison.

He twisted as hard as he could and got his hand under the demon's arm before he felt it yank back. The demon hissed and spit and turned on Diritas, who'd grabbed its shoulders and yanked it away from Cal.

"That's right, you blue-skinned fiend," Diritas taunted.

"Come dance with a master of the craft."

As if unable to stop, the demon launched itself at Diritas like a missile, hitting him hard and taking them both to the ground.

Cal turned and scrambled on his knees to Tessa, who hadn't moved yet.

Please, let her be okay. Please, please, please...

Behind him, he heard fists on flesh but he couldn't take his eyes off Tessa. She lay so still in the dark, and when his hands reached for her, he moaned at the ice-cold feel of her skin.

"Oh, fuck. Tessa, love..."

Her eyes opened, tears welling before spilling down her cheeks. Her lips parted but no sound emerged.

Then his eyes landed on the wound at her neck. Oh hell, the demon had bit her. She was paralyzed. Not dead.

He gathered her close and—

The demon hit him in the back of the head, making stars burst before Cal's eyes. Falling forward, he caught himself before he crushed Tessa, but he took the combined weight of the demon, Diritas, and X, who'd joined the fight, for several seconds before they rolled off him again.

Cal didn't have a single qualm about leaving his father and brother to deal with the demon. He had to get Tessa out of there. That was the only thing that mattered.

Still... He glanced over his shoulder.

Diritas was taking a beating. His face bled from several cuts and he actually winced when the demon's next blow caught him in the side. X's left arm hung limp and the back of his head was covered in blood. If Cal, X, and their father fought together, they could kill the damn thing.

He looked back at Tessa, still lying frozen in his arms, and he swore he saw her nod.

"Do it," she said, her voice barely above a whisper. "Kill it.

One less Tukhulkha demon to worry about. The neck. Sever the spinal cord."

Torn, Cal forced himself to lay Tessa back on the ground, bracing her against the thick trunk of a tree. Bending, he pressed his lips to hers for a brief second before he turned to help his father and brother defeat the demon.

Diritas took another hit to the solar plexus before Cal tackled them both and took them to the ground.

The demon screeched like a pissed-off cat just before it reared back and bared its teeth. X had stepped into range as he tried to get to their father. Cal knew the demon would go for X's jugular.

Grabbing the demon's head before it could strike, Cal yanked it away. Diritas and X immediately grabbed for the thing as well, holding its legs as Cal found the strength necessary to twist hard.

Though the demon fought them, Cal found greater strength because he had more to lose.

The crack as the demon's neck broke reverberated through the forest. Cal tossed the demon to the side and a tremor shook the ground, hard enough to make him stumble. With a crash, the gate to Aitás closed.

After a quick glance to make sure his father still breathed, Cal forced himself to his feet and back to Tessa.

Her skin looked pale; her eyes were closed; and he could barely see her chest move as she breathed. He gathered her in his arms and stood. And then he had no idea what to do.

Above. He needed to get her into the sun. He needed to open a gate into—

"Cal. Love you."

Tessa's weak voice sent a bolt of pain straight into his chest. His gaze connected with her beautiful blue eyes, now dull and listless.

And his heart stuttered.

She'd just given up. "Gods damn it. No, Tessa. Don't you dare give up on me. I'll take you up. We'll find the sun and you will be fine."

Her smile flickered for a brief second. "Not gonna be fine. You know that. And we can't let Charun have me. Take me to Invol."

No. Absolutely not. "That's *not* gonna happen." He glared into her eyes, willing her to fight. "We're going back to the sun. I won't lose you. I don't want to live without your heat in my life. You gave me back a part of myself I thought I'd lost forever. I'm never cold with you."

Her smile flickered again but she couldn't hold it. Her eyes closed and Cal panicked. He closed his eyes to summon a gate... but couldn't gather the necessary power.

Shit. Concentrate, you idiot.

"Cal." Tessa's weak voice forced his gaze down to hers. In the twilight, he saw the light leave her eyes.

Agonizing pain, unlike anything he'd ever felt before, encased his body in a fierce grip, squeezing his lungs, tearing at his heart, and ripping at his stomach. He screamed until he couldn't any longer, until his bruised esophagus gave out.

The warmth of Tessa's body was fading fast.

No. He couldn't accept this.

Turning, he saw his father push himself to his feet and head for Cal, his expression darker than usual.

"Damn it, Cal. I'm sorry."

"No, she's not gone." He shook his head, unwilling to believe. Even though he could no longer feel her warmth. "I can't... I have to take her back to the..."

No, she'd been right. "I have to take her to Invol."

The light there would heal her. He knew it would.

It had to.

THIRTEEN

"Caligo, you can't go in there. You're not strong enough, You'll die. Let me take her."

Cal shook his head, as he stood by the oak tree that marked the gate to Invol. "Open the gate, Dad."

Diritas got that look on his face, an expression Cal knew damn well. Stubborn intractability. His father wasn't moving.

"Son, there's nothing more you can do for her. She wouldn't want you to sacrifice yourself like this."

"I'm not. I just have to see this through."

He had to know for sure that she was gone. Someone over there had to tell him. And if she was...

"I'll be back, Dad."

The lie sounded like truth. At least it did to Cal's ears.

His father wasn't buying it. He crossed his arms over his thick chest and widened his stance. "You will break your mother's heart if you don't. And mine."

His father had never once said he loved Cal. Cimmerian men didn't express feelings they didn't have. Or at least pretended not to have.

For years, Cal had thought he was an aberration because of

his half-blood status. That he had emotions because he was flawed in some fundamental way.

He knew now that wasn't true.

His father had feelings. He just worked hard to keep them concealed.

"You've been gone for years, son. I know that's mostly my fault. That mess with—"

"Doesn't matter. And I never blamed you for that."

"I should have said something, spoken up." Cal heard the remorse in his father's voice, the anger. "But I thought it'd be best if you got away for a while. I never wanted you to leave for good."

"That was my fault. Not yours."

And if he hadn't left, he might never have met Tessa. He wouldn't have traded that for anything, not even for the respect of the Cimmerians.

"Cal—"

"Dad. I love you and Mom and X. But I have to do this."

Diritas stood his ground for another few seconds before he closed his eyes and took a deep breath.

Laying his hand on the trunk, Diritas spoke the spell to open the gate. There was no crashing, no lightning flashing, no quakes. Just the rush of air displacing and then the smell of ozone.

Cal had already donned the cloak hanging from the tree. He didn't intend to walk into Invol, hand over Tessa, and then let himself burn to a crisp.

He planned to return. He just didn't think he'd be in any shape to actually live when he did.

Cal stepped through.

Once more into the light.

He didn't go far though. Knew he didn't have to. He'd

figured that no matter where he was in Invol, its residents would know he was there.

So he waited.

After a minute, he realized he was holding his breath, praying for Tessa to move, to twitch, to gasp for air. Something, anything that would let him know she was still with him.

Nothing.

"You are upset. I am sorry."

The voice came from above him, and he realized he'd fallen to the ground cradling Tessa on his lap.

He looked up for a brief second before he realized what he'd done, and the sound he heard was his skin blistering.

"I couldn't save her."

"No, you couldn't."

Rage boiled in his gut, almost as painful as his anguish. "You let her die."

"No. But neither could we interfere. You are not capable of understanding the situation."

"I understand enough. And it doesn't matter now. She's gone."

"And we thank you for returning her to us."

It was a dismissal, and Cal almost expected to feel a foot on his ass pushing him back through the gate. His arms tightened around Tessa's lifeless body as he thought about leaving her here.

He didn't know if he could do it. But he'd told his dad he'd be back.

He had to let go of Tessa.

Staring down at her too-still face, he felt his heart contract into a tight, painful ball. He bent forward, pressed his lips against hers and tried to imagine a response, tried to imagine that her mouth moved against his as she kissed him back.

But he felt nothing. No warmth at all.

She really was gone.

"You must leave, or you will be damaged beyond repair. Go now, Caligo."

He wanted to snarl, to curse, to cry. He couldn't. There was nothing left inside.

Barely conscious of his actions, he laid Tessa on the ground, stood, and walked through the gate his father held open for him.

"I REALLY WISH you would reconsider, Cal. It's just too soon. You're not healed yet."

Cal glanced at his mom, who paced from one side of his room to the other, distress in every jerky motion. Serena had been hovering over him for the past four days, ever since his father had carried him back to their house and laid him in the bed that still smelled of Tessa.

His mom had taken one look at Cal and burst into tears. His dad had run out the door for a healer before Cal passed out. The burns had been bad. So bad that they hadn't been sure he was going to make it for the first twenty-four hours.

He couldn't have cared less. Not that he wanted to cause his parents grief, but they could live without him. They had for years.

Unfair? Yeah.

He didn't care. He didn't really care about anything at the moment. Wasn't sure he ever would.

"Mom, I'm fine. I just need to get back to my own place. I promise I'll take it easy."

Mostly, he planned to drink himself into a coma for the next month. Then he'd see how he felt.

"Maybe I should come with you."

Cal set his pack on the bed and turned to face her. Cal

could count on one hand the number of times Serena had left Cimer for the outer plane. For her to offer now... "Mom, I'm not gonna do anything stupid. I just need a little time."

"Leave the boy alone." Diritas leaned against the door jamb of Cal's room. His father had been quiet until now, watching every move Cal made. "He'll be fine."

He wondered if his father actually believed that or if he was saying it to appease his mother. When he looked at Diritas, Cal saw understanding in his dad's eyes.

He nodded, knowing what his father was saying without words. He was trusting Cal not to break his mother's heart by doing something stupid in his grief.

He wouldn't. He just needed... solitude.

With his mother still literally wringing her hands, Cal hiked his pack over his shoulder, kissed his mom good-bye then walked out the door.

Diritas walked with him to the oak Cal used to travel to and from his home on the earth plane. They bypassed the sprawling town, but as they approached the tree, Cal realized someone stood there.

Apparently waiting for him.

"Caligo."

He didn't recognize the man at first but there was something about him...

Diritas stepped in front of Cal, as if to defend him from attack. "Not now."

Then it clicked. And he couldn't even muster enough anger at old slights to care. "Furor. I see you've moved up in the ranks."

Cal noted the cord around the other man's neck, the color of the cord and the stone hanging from it signifying his rank as Excubitor. Head of the Sentinels and Watchmen. Technically, since Cal had never lost his rank, Furor was Cal's boss.

Which didn't mean a damn thing. Cal would never return to his post.

"Cal, we need to talk."

"Yeah, well, I'm in no mood for it today, so don't bother. I'm leaving."

In his current mood, he might kill the guy. He wouldn't actually care but if he did kill Furor, Cal would inherit the guy's job. And there was no way in hell he wanted that position.

Furor nodded, his dark hair and light gray eyes a near match for Cal's, though he was shorter and stockier. And fifty years older. "I'm not here to keep you. Or start a fight. I don't hold you responsible for Frigus's death, Cal. I never did."

Yeah, he knew that. And Cal held no grudge against Furor, even though Furor's brother had murdered Juliana and forced Cal's self-imposed banishment from Cimer. "Then I don't need a going-away party either."

"Understood. I only wanted to assure you that if you ever desired to return home, your old position would be waiting for you."

Cal's eyes narrowed. "What the hell are you talking about?"

"Let's just say I had an extremely unusual conversation with a certain... party who's grateful for your recent assistance."

The Involuti. Furor was talking about the Involuti.

"You served your office as Watchman with honor, Cal. And should you want to return, know that you'll have no problem with me."

Cal honestly didn't know what to say to that one. He actually felt a tug somewhere in his chest, some distant remnant of his past life. At one time, he might have jumped at the chance to return.

Now...

Fuck, he didn't have a clue. He just wanted to get the hell away from here.

The walls he'd built around his emotions had fissures. If left unattended, those fissures would become cracks. Those cracks, major breaks.

He couldn't afford to break down here. If he did, he'd never be able to live with himself.

Nodding in Furor's general direction, Cal moved to the tree to open the gate.

And willed himself away.

FOURTEEN

Someone was trying to break into his house.

At least, it sounded like they were trying to break down the front door.

Why the fuck anyone would want to was beyond Cal. People usually went out of their way to avoid his place. If they even managed to find it in the woods.

The last person who had...

No, not going there.

It'd been almost two weeks since he'd returned from Cimer, and he'd made good on his promise to drink himself into a drug-fueled haze where he didn't know right from left, up from down.

Today, he'd made an insignificant attempt at personal hygiene by brushing his teeth, so they didn't feel coated in fur, and taking a shower.

Bully for him.

His hair hung wet and too long around his face. He hadn't gotten around to shaving it off yet. He'd thought about it after his shower. Then he'd remembered Tessa running her fingers through it.

And he'd reached for the last bottle of tequila on the counter of the kitchen. That had been... He checked the clock on the stove. An hour ago.

Good, he was still drunk.

He really fucking hoped whoever was pounding on his door would go the fuck away soon because if they didn't, they might find themselves on the receiving end of his emotional torment.

And he didn't think they'd enjoy it.

Damn it, his chest still felt like it was going to crack open at any moment. He might not feel physical pain but he still had to deal with the emotional shit storm. And that fucking hurt. Like someone had slammed a wooden pole into his heart and left it there to rot.

Jesus Christ, that pounding was getting on his nerves. Why didn't they just break a window instead of trying to break down the door?

Oh, yeah. No windows.

Shit.

Maybe a good fight would make him feel better. But even if whoever was out there broke down the door, no one could get through the wards. Well, no one but...

He took a deep breath.

Eventually, they'd have to give up and go away.

"Cal."

He froze. Damn it, that sounded like Tessa.

He thought he'd stopped hearing her voice. The first few days back, he'd heard her everywhere. Her voice had awakened him every morning and put him to sleep at night. When he dreamed, he'd heard and seen her.

Even though he knew she was gone.

Thump, thump, thump.

Damn it, when the hell was that idiot gonna stop pounding on his door?

As if he'd willed it, the noise stopped.

Then he could have sworn he heard the door open. Only one other person had a key to his door.

"X, go the fuck away."

Silence. And then, "Cal? Where are you? Why didn't you answer the door?"

Shit. That *was* X's voice.

"I told you to stay the fuck away," he grumbled. "Why the hell don't you listen to me?"

"Because you don't really mean it."

With his back to the door, Cal couldn't see X but he felt his presence. The sun must've set if his brother had shown up at his door.

He really wasn't up to dealing with his well-intentioned but pain-in-the-ass brother. Although, he guessed he should be happy X had left him alone this long.

"Cal, you're really gonna want to turn around, dude."

"Is he still injured?"

His heart tripped over then began to pound like a bass drum. Tessa's voice again. And this time closer and more distinct than it had been.

He was finally losing it.

He turned his head, ready to blast X for disturbing him. But his lungs seized up on him.

He was hallucinating. He had to be.

Tessa stood behind his chair, her eyes so blue they sparkled, her hair the same bright, sunny red-tinged gold. Dressed in a pretty little pink sundress that tied behind her neck, she practically glowed.

Fuck. He must be asleep because she only came to him in his dreams now. Which really sucked because when he woke, he'd be so fucking depressed he'd need to make a run to the liquor store.

With a sigh, he turned away from her and slumped back into his chair.

"I didn't answer because I know you're not real."

He heard footsteps, and out of the corner of his eye, he saw her walk around his chair until she stood in front of him.

With her hands on her hips and her head cocked to the side, she frowned down at him. But her frown looked more than a little amused. "How do you figure?"

He just shook his head. "Because no one returns from Invol."

And he really had to get that through his thick fucking head.

When she didn't disappear into thin air, he resigned himself to having a conversation with a dead woman. And since he figured he was still asleep, it wouldn't matter if his brother witnessed him talking because X wasn't really here, either.

"I'm sorry I couldn't save you, babe. I'm so sorry."

Tears welled and began to slip down his cheeks. He blinked, knowing he was completely embarrassing himself. This was getting to be a constant refrain in his dreams. He'd apologize and beg her to come back to him, and she'd just shake her head and disappear. Then he'd wake up.

"But of course you saved me, Cal. Here I am."

That was new for the dream but he just shook his head.

Tessa's perfect teeth bit into her upper lip, so hard that the skin turned white. Then she glanced over his shoulder, presumably at X.

"Has he been like this the entire two weeks?"

"I don't know," X said. "This is the first time I've seen him. I'm thinking I should've gotten here a little sooner. But Dad was adamant. He said Cal needed the time alone."

"And dear old dad was right. I'm still hallucinating, X, but she's so damn beautiful that I just don't care."

She smiled then but she looked kind of sad. Definitely not how he wanted to remember her.

"X, I think I can take it from here," she said. "Thanks so much for bringing me. I'll make sure he calls you later."

Cal looked over his shoulder at his brother, who just shook his head. "You sure?"

"Absolutely," Tessa said. "We'll be fine."

X looked torn but since none of this was real, Cal let himself brush off his younger brother's concern. "Fine. Just... make sure you call, okay? We're all damn worried about him."

"I'm not a goddamn child," Cal grumbled, narrowing his gaze at her, afraid that if he closed his eyes, she'd disappear. And he wasn't ready to lose her again.

"I know that, Cal. But you've scared your family. And frankly, you're scaring me, too. You need to snap out of this."

Tessa stepped closer and reached out to lay her hand over his on the chair's arm. Warmth shot up his arm at the contact, making him draw in an unsteady breath.

Wait, this wasn't how this dream normally ran.

He flipped his hand and let their palms meet, her fingers threading through his, the delicate bones of her hand so tiny against his, her skin soft.

Damn, maybe he'd finally fallen completely off the sanity train. But if he could stay here with her for just a little while longer, he'd die happy.

He stared up into those blue eyes, thinking how warm they looked. "I miss you, Tess. I miss your heat."

Her smile was so sad. "I missed you, Cal. But I'm here now and everything will be okay."

"Are you here to take me over?"

She frowned again, making such an adorable expression that he had to smile at her. "Take you over where?"

"Well, I figure since I'm dying, and you're already gone, you must be here to help me cross the barrier into death."

She shook her head, her expression rueful. "You're not dying. And even if you were, I wouldn't let you."

Her hand tightened on his, and she came closer until her knees bumped against his. She lifted her left knee and squeezed it between his right thigh and the side of the chair then squeezed her right one on the other side. Looping her arms around his shoulders, she sat on his lap and brought her face so close they were practically nose to nose.

"Does this feel like you're dying?"

She closed the remaining distance between them and laid her lips on his, sucking on his mouth with gentle persuasion until he gave up the fight and kissed her.

Hell, might as well enjoy the illusion while he could. He'd be dead soon.

Except... his body didn't feel like it was dying.

He had a hard-on so stiff it hurt, a pain he gratefully accepted because he hadn't felt anything but a huge aching hole in his chest since she'd been gone.

He groaned and opened his mouth to her tongue flicking against his lips. He'd never deny her anything and she wanted into his mouth. Her tongue slicked against his, her taste exploding in his mouth with the force of a bomb.

He wrapped his arms around her waist and held on, never wanting to let go. Fuck sanity. Overrated, if you asked him.

Especially when he felt the heat between her legs as she settled her mound over his cock, even through the layers of his worn jeans and the thin cotton underwear she had on under the floaty little skirt.

His hands spread against her back, left bare by the dress, then worked at the knot holding the dress around her neck. Fucking hell, her skin. So fucking soft, like silk beneath his hands. He stroked her like a cat, her body moving beneath this hands, so damn responsive.

And so damn warm. He soaked himself in that warmth, let it surround him.

He'd been so fucking cold these past two weeks. So... dead.

He kissed her harder, his mouth pressed against hers as desperation started to creep in. His hands slid from under her shirt and down to her smooth, rounded hips. He curved his hands around her smoothly muscled thighs, kneading her flesh before allowing his fingertips to graze the edges of her silk panties.

They were wet. With a shudder, he tunneled his fingers beneath them to feel the moisture coating her sex and breathed in her soft moan as his fingers dipped into her body.

Arching against him, she lifted up onto her knees so he could delve deeper and stroke her where he knew she liked it.

She felt like sleek, wet silk, tight and hot.

Her lips slid off his and across his cheek to his ear, where she nipped the lobe before whispering, "Oh, Cal, I missed you so much."

He wanted to respond but couldn't; he was too intent on soaking in her response to his every move. Her sex contracted around the two fingers he slid into her. So tight. His thumb hit the jut of her clit, and she moaned and clenched tighter.

His eyes shot open wide and he stared at her beautiful face, her expression a mask of pure pleasure. His breath caught in his throat as his body shuddered.

"Tessa. Oh, fuck, Tessa, it really is you. What... How..."

Her eyes opened slowly, and her smile made his heart pound so hard it hurt.

"Shh. It's me, love. I'm right here with you." She undulated, shifting her body up and down on his fingers as he remained frozen. "You feel so good, Cal. Don't stop. Questions later. I need you now."

No, he wouldn't stop. Not ever.

Need built like a raging inferno, until he swore he was shaking. "I need to be inside you, Tess. Right now."

"Then have me."

With a groan, he pulled his fingers free to fumble with the waistband of his boxers. Tessa helped him shove them down over his hips and down his legs, his cock springing free so she could wrap her hand around him.

His groan rumbled in his chest as she pumped him with her warm hand. Ah, Christ, he could so easily go over just by her touch. He wanted her so much. Needed her so damn badly.

"Tess, come on," he breathed against her lips. "Inside. I gotta get inside you. Please, baby."

He didn't have to ask twice. With a few graceful movements, she positioned herself over the tip of his erection then sank down, covering him in wet, hot ecstasy. His head kicked back against the cushion as his hips arched, seeking to go deeper. Eyes closed, he reveled in sensation.

He felt the smooth skin of her ass hit his thighs then leave again as she pulled up, working herself on his shaft. Long, slow drags up and down, the grip of her sex decadently tight.

Hands on her hips, he held her but let her control the motion. She knew just how to move to drive him insane with desire. To heat him from the inside out and make his blood boil lava hot.

He had to see her. Forcing his heavy eyes to open, he let his gaze take in her expression of longing, the teeth caught in her lip, and the soft exhalations of breath with each movement.

His gaze slid down to her slim neck, where her pulse beat wildly. Leaning forward, he let his mouth settle over that pulse, feeling her life's blood pulsing under her skin. So strong.

She gasped as he bit her, unable to help himself. She smelled too damn good; he just had to taste her.

Skin. He needed more skin.

Pulling back, he gripped the waist of the dress and drew the whole thing over her head. When he tossed it away, he had unfettered access to her breasts, full, plump, and beautiful.

He bent his head and fastened his lips to her breast. Such beautiful, tight nipples that he nipped and bit and suckled as her hands dug into his shoulders. He focused on loving her breasts while she rode him, trying not to fall over the edge too soon.

Which became increasingly difficult when she picked up her pace, slamming down on him in jerky, fevered motions.

Too much, way too much sensation, too much feeling. Too good.

When she gasped and froze, he sucked her nipple hard and used his free hand to flick at her clit. Her head fell back, her shout of completion the most wonderful sound he'd ever heard.

So fucking wonderful. He groaned as he jerked and released in her warmth. And the whole damn house shook as a blast of pure power rolled from them in a wave.

As his cock continued to pulse inside her, he tightened his arms around her warm, limp body as he tried to catch his breath.

She sighed against him, her warm breath brushing against his neck as she shifted. His arms went rigid around her, crushing her against him, terrified she would disappear.

"Oh, Cal. It's okay." Her arms slid around his neck, her skin soft on his, like silk. "I'm not going anywhere. Not ever."

His heart started to race and his lungs couldn't get enough air. Christ, he shouldn't be having a panic attack now.

But what if he was still dreaming? What if he'd finally lost it, even though he could feel her sheath snug around his cock and her breasts pressed against his chest?

"How? Tessa... oh fuck, can't breathe..."

"Shh," she whispered against his ear. "I'm right here. Cal, sweetheart, take a deep breath. You're going to pass out."

Yeah, that was a distinct possibility and wouldn't that be a totally wimp-ass thing to do.

Tessa eased back from him but kept her hands on his shoulders. Her gaze shot from his chest to his eyes and held there.

Tessa. Thank the Gods, it was her. He framed her face in his hands and pulled her close to lay his lips on hers. "What happened?"

"The Involuti healed me and sent me back."

"Just like that?"

He felt a smile curve her lips against his. "No, of course not. There's always a price, but I would gladly pay it again."

He pulled back so he could see her face. "What was it?"

She stared straight into his eyes, her fingers kneading the tight muscles of his shoulders. "To take me out of Charun's grasp, they had to remove that part of me that he wanted."

He drew in a shocked breath. "They removed your powers. Tessa, Christ—"

She shook her head, laying her fingers over his lips. "Not all of them, no. I retain my midwifery duties. That power was never as strong, and Charun didn't covet the ability to bring healthy children into the world. He only wanted my ability to control the sun's path."

And she'd given that up, her control of the sun. For him.

"I love you. I didn't want to live without your heat. I've been so damn cold."

Her smile widened. "But I thought Cimmerians didn't feel heat or cold or pain."

"You make me feel, Tessa. Only you, and I don't want to live without it again."

"You won't have to. I'm not leaving you again."

Then his eyes narrowed. "What about Charun? Are they going to do anything to stop him from going after the other goddesses?"

"I honestly don't know. My time in Invol was like a dream and I don't remember much of it. I don't even remember seeing the Involuti. It was like... they didn't have true form. Like they were ghosts, spirits. There but not really. It's just so hard to explain."

"Then it doesn't matter. It only matters that you came back to me. And if Charun decides to take another shot at you, we'll be ready."

Her smile brightened her expression. "I don't think he will. You were able to defeat one of his demons. You're strong and he knows that. I don't think he'll risk another demon. Especially now that I'm of no use to him."

He brought her lips down to his again, worshipping his goddess. "Tessa, I promise to love you so much more than you've ever been loved you won't miss the sun."

Her smile would always be warmer than the sun to him. "I love you, Cal," she said. "I won't miss the sun as long as I have you."

ACKNOWLEDGMENTS

Although I may write in a vacuum, I couldn't exist in one.

To my parents and brother for their unfailing love.

To Judi for sharing her mostly full glass.

To Deb for commiserating with my half-empty glass.

To April for more than I can repay.

To Adele and Marilyn for much more than lunch.

To Daria and my Valley Forge Romance Writers sisters for chocolate and hugs and smiles.

In memory of Sheila Conway, taken before she could realize her dream or say, "See, I told you so."

ALSO BY STEPHANIE JULIAN

DIVINE DESIRES
Dark Desires at Dawn

Rough Caress of Midnight

Double Fantasies at Twilight

Enchanting Temptations in Shadow

MOONLIGHT LOVERS
Kiss of Moonlight

Visions in Moonlight

Edge of Moonlight

Temptation in Moonlight

Grace in Moonlight

Shades of Moonlight

MAGICAL SEDUCTION
Seduced by Magic

Seduced in Shadow

Seduced & Ensnared

Seduced & Enchanted

Seduced by Chaos

Seduced by Danger

Moonlight Seduction

DARKLY ENCHANTED
Spell Bound

Moon Bound

REDTAILS HOCKEY
The Brick Wall

The Grinder

The Enforcer

The Instigator

The Playboy

The D-Man

The Machine

The Comeback Kid

FAST ICE
Bylines & Blue Lines

Hard Lines & Goal Lines

Deadlines & Red Lines

INDECENT
An Indecent Proposition

An Indecent Affair

An Indecent Arrangement

An Indecent Longing

An Indecent Desire

SALON GAMES
Invite Me In

Reserve My Nights

Expose My Desire

Keep My Secrets

Rock My Heart

LOVERS UNDERCOVER

Lovers & Lies

Sinners & Secrets

Beauty & Brains

Thieves & Thrills

ABOUT THE AUTHOR

Stephanie Julian is a USA Today and New York Times bestselling author of contemporary and paranormal romance. Make sure you sign up to receive all of her news at www.stephaniejulian.com

Copyright © 2011 by Stephanie Julian

All rights reserved. No part of this book may be reproduced in any form or by any electronic or mechanical means including information storage and retrieval systems—except in the case of brief quotations embodied in critical articles or reviews—without permission in writing from its publisher, Moonlit Night Books.

The characters and events portrayed in this book are fictitious or are used fictitiously. Any similarity to real persons, living or dead, is purely coincidental and not intended by the author.

Formerly titled HOW TO WORSHIP A GODDESS

Printed in Great Britain
by Amazon